HCaptiveEART

OTHER BOOKS AND AUDIO BOOKS
BY MICHELE PAIGE HOLMES:

Counting Stars

All the Stars in Heaven

Captive HEART

A NOVEL BY

MICHELE PAIGE HOLMES

Covenant Communications, Inc.

Cover images: *Female Portrait* by McKenzie Deakins, For photographer information please visit www.photographybymckenzie.com. *Old Paper* © Marcin Pasko, iStockphoto.com. *Old Retro Steam Train* © remik44992, iStockphoto.com. *Luxury Floral Pattern #3* © Tatarnikova, iStockphoto.com.

Cover design copyright © 2011 by Covenant Communications, Inc.

Published by Covenant Communications, Inc.
American Fork, Utah

Copyright © 2011 by Michele Paige Holmes

This is a work of fiction. The characters, names, incidents, places, and dialogue are either products of the author's imagination, and are not to be construed as real, or are used fictitiously.

Printed in the United States of America
First Printing: April 2011

17 16 15 14 13 12 11   10 9 8 7 6 5 4 3 2 1

ISBN: 978-1-60861-0662

This one is for the grandmas—

One with the kindest heart and most generous spirit. Grandma Howard, you were the first one who believed in me. Thank you for the hours you spent listening patiently while I told you the stories in my head.

One with red hair and a temper to match. Grandma Cramer, you never succeeded in teaching me to crochet, but you taught me to laugh during those magical summer weeks. Oh, the memories I have!

One who became a grandmother while still raising her own children. Grandma Ruth, thank you for never being too tired to play another game or do another project or give a lot more of your love. You taught me the most about love as you cared for Grandpa the last months of his life.

One I never knew very well but who I think of often when I face hardships in my life and wonder over those you endured. Grandma Marjorie, I look forward to getting to know you better someday.

ACKNOWLEDGMENTS

Once again, I would not have a book in print without the help of generous, talented friends. Annette Lyon, Heather Moore, Lu Ann Staheli, Lynda Keith, and Jeff Savage went the extra mile with this manuscript, reading and responding via e-mail during the very stressful week I wrote over half the story (to meet a contest deadline—not recommended!).

I am grateful to my editor at Covenant, who went to bat for this book when she knew very little of me or my writing. Samantha, it was a pleasure to work with you, and I look forward to many more projects together.

My family gets much extra credit for this story as well for their willingness (most of the time, anyway) to drive all the way to South Dakota so I could experience the Black Hills in person. Dixon, thank you for driving all those miles and for traipsing around the forest with me, ignoring the No Trespassing signs and sharing my excitement at finding old, abandoned buildings and mines. I will always cherish the memories of that trip. I continue to appreciate all of your support and love.

I always had a way of just going ahead
at whatever I had a mind to do.

—*Davy Crockett*

CHAPTER 1

Aboard the Central Pacific Railroad, August 1878

"OUTLAWS—PLEASE, GOD. DON'T LET them choose me." Emmalyne Prudence Madsen whispered the prayer to herself as she looked down at her white knuckles gripping the handles of the valise on her lap. A drop of perspiration trickled down the side of her face, but she resisted the urge to lift her hand even enough to wipe it away. The heat was stifling—especially now that the train had stopped—but she didn't dare move at all for fear one of the brigands would notice her.

She kept her gaze downward, eyes shifting only enough to look out the window for any sign of the law or a nearby town. She saw nothing but the flattened prairie grasses of Nebraska, and she remembered the conductor saying it would be nearly nightfall before they reached their next stop.

Nightfall. She shuddered with fear then stiffened her back, holding her breath as another pair of dusty cowboy boots strode past her seat. Thank heavens she wasn't sitting by the aisle. The thought of one of those terrible men touching her—even unintentionally as they walked by—was horrifying. She felt a pang of guilt for the sweet old lady next to her who had offered the window seat. But, Emmalyne consoled herself, at least her companion was of an age to be safe from the men's lecherous pursuits.

Emmalyne hoped she too looked of an age to be safe from these men. For once, she felt grateful for the distasteful brown wool suit she wore. Aside from being itchy and hot, she knew it was long out of fashion, and it modestly covered her from neck to wrist to ankle. Surely the men would be more interested in the other women on this train. She'd noticed many of them when they boarded two days ago. Their becoming hairstyles, pretty hats, and colorful gowns indicated they were headed west as brides or possibly even . . . She wouldn't think it.

Emmalyne swallowed the lump that had formed in her dry throat. It was terrible of her to imagine such things of those women simply because they were attractive. It was as much their lot in life to be pretty as it was hers to be plain. And right now, it seemed *she* was the fortunate one.

"I'm wantin' you, darlin'," a deep voice rumbled somewhere behind her, followed by squeals from the next chosen victim.

Emmalyne's grip on the carpetbag tightened until the dear lady next to her reached over and placed her hand over Emmalyne's.

"It'll be all right. They'll go soon," the old woman reassured her. "They've taken near a dozen."

"A dozen?" Emmalyne whispered, appalled. "Those poor girls."

Her companion nodded solemnly and squeezed Emmalyne's hand. "But you've noticed," the old lady continued, disapprovingly, "not all of them are protesting."

Emmalyne's eyes widened at her implication. "You can't mean they *want*—" Her whispering ceased as another pair of boots slowly walked past.

"Hurry it up, Thayne," a man's voice called from the back of the car. "We been stopped too long already. Get yourself a pretty, grab the gold, and get off this train."

"I'll be along in a minute. And I don't want no pretty." The man directly behind her muttered the last bit under his breath. Just past their seat, he stopped. The old woman's fingers squeezed hers.

"You. Look at me."

Emmalyne kept her chin tucked but sensed movement from the seat beside her.

"Not you, old woman. The one next to ya. You, brownie."

"No." The refusal was out of Emmalyne's mouth before she'd had a chance to think. A second later, she heard the unmistakable sound of a pistol being cocked.

"Don't think I heard you right, lass."

Emmalyne raised her head and turned to face the man. Blue eyes pierced hers, and she sensed his scowl behind the faded bandana covering most of his face. Blond hair sprang out at wild angles from his head, and muscles strained beneath his worn, dirty shirt. She felt her nose wrinkle in distaste as she viewed the patches of sweat beneath his arms.

Along with the sheer terror threatening to overwhelm her, she felt a surprising spark of anger ignite somewhere deep inside. Her face grew warm as he sized her up.

"You a schoolteacher?"

"Yes. They are expecting me in Sterling. School begins Monday morning. Twenty-two students—"

"That's enough," he cut her off. "You'll do. Come on." He waved his gun toward the aisle.

Emmalyne thought her heart would leap from her chest. "No. I can't. I-I'm—" She glanced at the elderly woman. "I'm traveling with my grandmother. She needs my help . . ." *It's only a little lie, Lord. And for my safety, since You didn't answer that last prayer a few minutes ago.*

"My apologies, ma'am."

To Emmalyne's surprise, the man removed his hat and nodded to her companion.

"But I believe I've a greater need for your granddaughter right now. I wish you the best with your journey." He placed the dusty hat back on his head and looked expectantly at Emmalyne. His surly tone returned. "Let's go. I don't have all day."

She shrank toward the window, a whimper rolling from her lips. "Please don't do this. I'm not that kind of woman. I—"

A rough hand reached over, jerking her from the seat.

"Oh my," the old woman exclaimed as the man dragged Emmalyne across her lap.

"Pardon us," her abductor said, all politeness and manners as his grip tightened.

Emmalyne winced as his fingers dug into her arm. He hauled her into the aisle just as the train lurched forward. His arm wrapped around her middle, the gun wavering in front of them, warning off anyone who might try to help. No one looked inclined to anyway.

Apparently God had no intention of saving her. Emmalyne decided it was now or never. Bending her head, she sank her teeth into her captor's hand.

He cried out, jerking his hand away. The gun clattered to the floor at their feet, and she kicked it as hard as she could, sending it spinning down the aisle toward the back of the car. The outlaw unleashed a string of obscenities in her ear, reinforcing Emmalyne's belief that, at all costs, she *had* to get away.

Lifting her foot, she brought her heel down sharply on his toe, then worked to twist free of his grasp. Her other arm flailed in the air as he tried to capture it too. She squirmed and screamed, trying to reach his face so she could use her nails.

"Help me," she cried. "Someone, please help me."

Their car, Emmalyne realized, was strangely devoid of men—and nearly women, too, now that the outlaws had taken so many. Her only hope was her previous seat companion, who was rifling through Emmalyne's abandoned valise.

"Get the dictionary," Emmalyne shouted. "Hit him on the head with it." She continued fighting, kicking ineffectively as he towed her to the door. Beneath her feet she felt the train picking up speed.

He finally succeeded in capturing her other arm and pinned it behind her back as he bent to retrieve his pistol and then shoved the door open with his shoulder. Emmalyne looked down at the rails sliding past. Did the madman intend to push her to her death? A swell of anger surged through her. She hadn't come this far and fought so hard for her freedom for a stranger to take it away. He *wouldn't* take it away, she vowed and threw her head back full force into his chest.

He let out a grunt of pain, loosening his grip on her wrist just enough that she freed her hand. Swinging around, she jabbed her finger in his left eye, hard enough that this time he released her to favor the injury.

"Dang woman! Ya didn't have to go and blind me." With one hand still covering his eye, he lunged to grab her again.

Emmalyne ducked and charged forward, using all the strength in her five-foot-three-inch frame to plow into him. Caught off guard, he stumbled backward, out through the open door of the train. Emmalyne screamed, scrunching her eyes closed, expecting to feel the jerk of the train as it ran him over.

Instead, she heard nothing but the steady clicking of the wheels against the rail. Holding her breath, she darted to the nearest window and was half relieved to see her would-be abductor on his feet, running alongside the train.

She hadn't actually killed the man, then. Good. And she had saved her virtue. So much for her father's dire prediction that she wouldn't last a week in the untamed West. Feeling extraordinarily pleased with herself, Emmalyne left the window to close and bolt the door, lest the man should catch them and board again.

The elderly woman came up beside her.

"He's gone." It was Emmalyne's turn to be the reassuring one.

The woman stepped closer, a peculiar look on her face.

"It's all right," Emmalyne said, turning away as she reached for the handle. "I'll secure the door and—"

A shove from behind sent her sprawling forward, out the back of the car. Hands flying in front of her, she could do nothing but close her eyes as the track, gravel, and prairie rushed to meet her.

CHAPTER 2

THAYNE'S HAND CLOSED OVER THE woman's arm, jerking her forward, away from the train. She landed face down on him, her head striking his chin hard as they fell back in the dirt.

Stunned and breathless, neither moved, aside from the murmur of pain that escaped her lips. Beside them, the train rolled by, the sounds gradually fading as it left them behind. A moment ago, he'd caught the train again and been safe and sound on the step, about to go through the car door to try to reason with that teacher again. Now it seemed she'd changed her mind all on her own, literally jumping off the train after him—a slight problem since his horse was long gone and they were in the middle of nowhere.

"So much for your claim of modesty," he breathed into her ear.

The woman's eyes flew open, and she lifted her head, staring at him with those immense brown eyes.

Her only good feature, thank goodness.

"*You,*" she started. "This is all your fault."

Beneath the bandana he chuckled. "I don't see how, as you're the one who jumped out and landed on top of me."

"*What?*" she cried and then realized he spoke the truth. Hastily, she tried to push herself off him, but as she rolled to the side, her ankle tangled with his pant leg, and she shouted.

"Quiet," he ordered, bringing a calloused finger to her lips.

"I will not be quiet. I—"

"Shh." His whole hand covered her mouth. "Keep quiet—unless you *want* to work in a brothel."

Her eyes widened, and Thayne saw the fear return. *Good,* he thought. A woman with a little fear might just show a bit of common sense.

"Get up," he ordered as he stood and looked around. The Martins were just a speck in the distance. If he was fortunate, the others hadn't seen them or heard all the commotion she'd made, and when he didn't show, they'd think he had met ill luck on the train. Then again, when was the last time anything fortunate *had* happened to him?

Two years back when you found that gold vein. He pushed the thought aside. The success of his mine no longer qualified as good fortune but rather the beginning of several disasters that had sent his life spiraling downhill.

Thayne tugged the bandana from his face and reached for his canteen. At least he'd had sense enough to keep that with him. And the way he saw it, that was about all he had to get him and the woman back to the Lakota camp. Yep. A couple of hard weeks lay before them, for sure.

He unscrewed the cap and lifted the canteen to his lips for a brief drink before looking at the woman, who was still sitting in the dirt.

"Thirsty?" he asked, holding the canteen out to her.

She shook her head.

"Suit yourself. Let me know if you change your mind." He twisted the lid back on. "We'd best get going. I'd like to have some better cover if they come looking for us."

"If *who* comes looking for us?" She held a hand to her forehead and squinted as she looked up at him.

Thayne nodded to the east. "Martin's gang, of course."

"Of course," she said tartly, folding her arms across her chest. "I've no intention of going anywhere with you."

He gave her an exasperated look. "Listen, missy. It's come with me or die out here, so get off your high horse and let's go." In what he thought was a measure of extraordinary gallantry, he leaned forward, extending his hand to help her up.

She struck quickly, her booted foot kicking his inner thigh almost before he'd realized what hit him. A second later, she was up and running—in the right direction, at least.

Doubled over, Thayne swore under his breath as he watched her lopsided run. Had he picked a female who was *lame*? His forehead creased with concern. That'd be just his luck. Straightening, he spied a dark piece of wood nestled among the grasses. He reached over, picked it up, and felt relief when he realized he held the heel of a lady's boot. For the first time all week, he smiled.

She wasn't lame. He looked eastward and saw that the horses had disappeared.

"Thank you, Lord," he said. He'd got himself a teacher who wasn't pretty and who could walk, and that was about all he could ask for.

* * *

"When we reach that outcropping, we're going to angle north." Thayne looked behind them for the hundredth time in the past couple of hours. He felt uneasy, though there wasn't any sign of Russell Martin or his brothers.

The woman gave no indication that she'd heard him but kept up her same resolute pace several feet ahead. Her limp had somewhat lessened since he'd broken off the heel of her other boot a couple of hours ago. She hadn't spoken but maybe a dozen words all day, and that suited him fine. Though just now, he needed her to listen.

"North, I said." He spoke firmly, hoping he wouldn't have to get his gun out again.

"Feel free to go where you'd like." Her voice was filled with disdain. "However, *I* am going to stay near the tracks until I reach the next town."

"Be a long, cold night out here alone—especially with nothing to keep the coyotes away."

She threw a glance over her shoulder. "I'll take my chances."

It was the first time he'd looked at her face since she'd run off from him this morning. And her cheeks, flush with color, worried him.

"Stop a minute," he ordered. "You need to drink some water."

She shook her head and kept trudging forward.

"Stubborn woman," Thayne muttered under his breath as he lengthened his strides to catch her. He reached for her arm just as she spun around to face him.

"*Don't* touch me. Or—I'll scratch both your eyes out." She held her hands up in front of her chin, fingernails threatening.

"I've no doubt," he said dryly. His eye was still sore from her earlier handiwork. He pulled the strap from his shoulder and held the canteen out to her. "Here."

She looked at it a moment, and Thayne could see her stubborness battling with her need for a drink. Finally, she took it from him. He watched, exasperated, as she bent over, using her skirt to wipe the rim of the canteen—as if she couldn't stand her mouth touching something his had.

"Not too much," he warned as she gulped down the water. "That's all we have."

"Until when?" Her tongue licked the last of the moisture from her lips.

Irritated that he'd noticed, he looked away. "Until we find a creek or river to replenish it."

She frowned at him. "Didn't plan this too well, did you?"

"I didn't plan on such a mouthy woman." An image of Christina popped into his mind. *Should have, though. Seems to be the only sort I can ever find.*

"Pardon if I failed to thank you for abducting me," she said as she screwed the lid back on the canteen and slung the strap over her shoulder. "I'll just keep this."

He scowled but decided it wasn't worth fighting over. The water was almost gone anyway. But he did set the record straight. "I *didn't* abduct you. I saved your hide when you jumped outta that train. If it weren't for me, you'd have been crushed."

"I did *not* jump. I was pushed." With a flounce of skirts, she turned away and began walking.

"Hmmpf. And just who woulda done that?" He grunted his disbelief as he followed, keeping well enough away that she couldn't strike him if her temper suddenly flared again—which he had no doubt it would. "Russell and his brothers were long gone by then."

She continued her unbalanced walk, though her pace slowed a little. "I think it was the old woman sitting next to me."

"Not dear sweet granny?" he asked, feigning surprise.

"I—" Her mouth closed as quickly as it had opened.

"You lied," he accused, his lips twitching.

"Perfectly acceptable under the circumstances." She glared at him, daring him to say otherwise.

"And here I thought I was getting a respectable schoolmarm."

She said nothing to that but turned her face away, continuing her forlorn limp.

"Still hard to believe you were pushed, though. What did you have in your bag besides a dictionary? Cash—gold?"

She shook her head miserably. "No gold. Just a bit of family silver. But who would have thought that sweet old lady . . ."

Her voice trailed off, but not before Thayne heard a catch of sadness.

"Can't trust nobody," he said, shaking his head. "People aren't always what they appear to be."

She glanced at him. "Lesson learned. Though you appear *exactly* as you are—a low-down, conniving desperado, taking advantage of the innocent. A despoiler of women."

"That's where you're wrong," he said, stopping her tirade. "I'll give you low-down, thieving, and whatever else it was you called me, but I'm not that last bit. I've never taken advantage of a woman, and I never will."

"And I'm supposed to believe that? After you forced me off—"

He shook his head at her.

"You *tried* to abduct me."

"It was just a show till the Martins were all off the train. I was planning to stay on board until Sidney—hopefully having persuaded you to join me by then."

"As if I'd believe you were searching for a teacher," she said.

"Believe what you want. But if all I'd wanted you for was a roll in the hay—or prairie—" Thayne made a point of looking around at the vast emptiness surrounding them, "I could've done that hours ago."

"Well then, Mr. . . ."

"Kendrich," he answered brusquely without removing his hat or bothering with niceties. Their conversation was getting a little long as far as he was concerned.

"Mr. Kendrich," she continued. "Where are we going, and what is it you intend to do with me?"

He touched her elbow, pointing her northward. "We're going to Dakota territory, to a Sioux camp in the Black Hills.

Her feet stopped, and she pulled away from him. "*Indians?*"

He heard the alarm in her voice but didn't feel inclined to ease her fears just yet. He had enough worries of his own at the moment. Someone was following them. He could feel it.

"Yes, Indians," he said impatiently. "They've got something valuable of mine, but now that I have you, I can get it back." He peered over his shoulder again.

Her eyes widened in alarm. "What do you mean, now that you have me? What—"

"Listen, Miss—"

"Madsen," she said with as little formality as he'd used.

"Miss Madsen, neither of us is going to reach that camp alive unless we quit talking and get outta here. I've got a bad feeling the Martin gang isn't too far away, and I've seen personally that Russell Martin doesn't like deserters." He took her elbow, firmly this time, and steered her north.

"But—"

"*Later,*" he insisted.

She pursed her lips into a thin line and stopped once more. "I'm not going one step farther until you explain what you intend to do at that Indian camp. Because if you think for one minute—"

Thayne pulled his pistol from its holster. Holding the gun, he leveled it at her. "Move."

She shook her head and put her hands on her hips. "If you've never taken advantage of a woman, then I imagine it's safe to assume you won't shoot one."

Thayne's eyes narrowed. "Wrong again," he said in complete seriousness. "I *have* shot a woman before, and I won't hesitate to do so again."

CHAPTER 3

SHE SLEPT LIKE THE DEAD. Thayne had briefly considered tying her up in case she got some hair-brained idea to scratch his eyeballs out or walk off in the middle of the night, but less than five minutes after he'd finally announced they could call it a day, she'd slumped over and fallen fast asleep. Somehow it didn't seem right to bind the hands of a sleeping woman.

But you felt all right kidnapping her?

Watching her now, he felt a strong wave of guilt. Curled up on her side, with her hair in disarray and her lips slightly parted, she looked innocent and young—a whole lot younger than he'd first thought her to be. At this time yesterday, she'd probably been full of dreams for an adventure out west. And if she had come from a family with silver to spare, he wagered she hadn't come to be a schoolteacher out of necessity but rather because she wanted to.

And he'd snatched those dreams right away from her.

But I had no choice, he argued with his conscience. *She's the one who jumped off that train. And now that I have her . . .* It was her dreams or Joshua, and Thayne knew he'd board that train again if he had to. He'd do anything for Joshua. And that was what he needed to concentrate on now—keeping himself and the teacher alive as they crossed the next three hundred miles.

They'd made surprisingly good time today—he estimated they'd walked near twenty miles. Not too bad, considering they'd had to go it without a horse. If they kept going at the same pace, another two weeks ought to get them to the Lakota camp. *Two weeks too long,* he thought. It had been plenty foolish of him to lose his supplies and his horse. But worse than that was the feeling he couldn't shake that the Martins were bent on returning them to him. He'd have a hard time explaining why he'd taken the woman and run off instead of bringing her back to work with the rest of the women as they'd agreed upon.

This was the part where his plan grew fuzzy. It had seemed pretty simple and straightforward beforehand. Join up with a gang of outlaws. Pretend to rob a train with them and find a teacher in the process. Then get the teacher and yourself away from the outlaws. Get Joshua. Get home.

With a grimace, Thayne realized how much Miss Madsen had spoken the truth today when she'd accused him of not planning well. He hoped his flaw wouldn't prove fatal to them both.

She sighed as she rolled onto her back. Thayne wished he had something to cover her with—not just so she'd stay warm through the night but, more importantly, so he wouldn't have to look at her. Already, he was irritated with himself for the dozen little things he'd noticed about her today. He hadn't wanted to notice anything but instead found himself thinking of her big brown eyes when she first looked at him on the train. He'd called her *brownie* because of the gosh-awful getup she wore, but once he saw those eyes, he could hardly think of her any other way.

A wry grin curved his lips as he remembered her determination to fight him off tooth—literally—and nail. She had a surprising amount of strength for such a little slip of a thing. *All good qualities*, he reasoned, as he caught himself again glancing at the rise and fall of her chest. Would she fight like that for Joshua? If so, what more could he ask for?

Sleep. That's what. Watching her sleep brought a longing for him to do the same, and after another look around, he pulled off his hat and lay a few feet away from Miss Madsen. The unease that had been with him all day lingered a few minutes more, until, at last, even that was overcome and he drifted off to a restless sleep.

* * *

Emmalyne hardly dared to breathe as she looked at the sleeping outlaw and tried to decide whether to take his gun. She decided it wasn't worth the risk of waking him when—even if she had gotten the weapon—she doubted she could use it on him, probably not even on an animal. She'd never held a gun before and had no idea how to work one.

Her decision made, she eased away, carefully turning her body just enough that she could get on her hands and knees. She moved first her right hand and then foot, stopping to see if he'd heard the rustling of her skirts. After several seconds, all remained quiet, and Emmalyne reached down, gathering as much of her petticoats as she could. Stuffing the edge of the layers beneath her tucked chin, she began a slow, painstaking crawl through the tall grass, putting distance between herself and the outlaw. She was pretty sure she could find the railroad track again, and if she walked hard like yesterday, it ought to bring her to a town by tomorrow.

Another whole day. She wanted to die. Her feet were overrun with blisters, and her face felt tight and hot with sunburn. The miracle of train travel was brought sharply into focus as her body protested even her slow, quiet movements. What would happen when she tried to stand and use her legs? Muscles she hadn't even known existed were already crying out in pain. She forced herself to keep going. A little farther and she'd feel it safe to stand and move faster.

As she crawled, she looked down at her hands. The last thing she needed was to come across an unsuspecting snake. *Left. Right. Left. Ri—* Something clamped around her ankle and pulled. A scream tore from her throat as she fought for her balance and lost, landing facedown, spread-eagle on the ground.

"So beat you can't even walk? Gonna make for a long day."

Emmalyne clenched her teeth as she rolled over onto her back and looked up at the outlaw.

"Mornin'," he said cheerfully. He let go of her ankle and straightened. "Glad to see you're an early riser. Let's get going and enjoy the cool while we can."

She rose up on her elbows but made no move to go any farther. Thayne pulled the gun on her again.

"I'd act the gentleman and offer you a hand, but last time that didn't go so well."

Emmalyne hesitated another second, wondering if he'd actually shoot her. After all, didn't he need her for something? What good would she do him if he shot her now?

His eyes narrowed. "I could shoot you in the arm and you'd still be able to walk fine," he said as if in answer to her question. Gone was his cheerful disposition.

Did he read my mind? Filled with alarm, Emmalyne scrambled to her feet, her aches momentarily forgotten at the possibility of the outlaw putting a bullet in her arm.

"Give me the canteen." He held his free hand out.

This time she hurried to comply. Though she knew it was foolish, she couldn't seem to help herself from speaking smugly as she handed it to him. "It's empty. I drank the last of the water this morning."

She watched warily as he removed the cap and tilted the canteen up to his lips. She couldn't tell if anything came out but knew it couldn't have been more than a drop or two. A knot of worry formed in her empty stomach. Just watching him reminded her of her own unquenched thirst.

Yesterday, sheer terror and the hope that following the tracks would bring her to safety had kept her walking. But now they were away from the rail line, and she was already hungry, thirsty, and sore. She knew she'd never make it all day as she had yesterday. Would he shoot her if she collapsed?

"Don't fret," he said as he replaced the lid and pulled the strap over his shoulder. "We'll be to water within an hour or two."

She wrapped her arms around herself, further unnerved that he seemed to have read her mind again.

"And then *I'll* have the *first* drink." He waved her in front of him with the gun, and they were off.

CHAPTER 4

THAYNE'S BROW DREW TOGETHER WITH concern as he watched the woman misstep once again and nearly tumble to the ground.

"Careful," he admonished, closing the gap between them to grasp her elbow. When she didn't protest, he knew her condition was getting serious. He'd been wrong about finding water in the first hour or two. Both creeks he'd counted on had come up as dry beds, and according to the sun, it was nearing midday. They were going to be in real trouble if something didn't go their way soon.

The thought of Joshua kept him going, but Miss Madsen had no similar motivation. Whereas earlier he'd been irritated by her sharp tongue, he was now alarmed by her lack of fight. He knew misery when he saw it, and she was there—from the tips of her pointed-toe boots to the top of her head and the disheveled hair hanging limply down her back. He didn't dare pull his pistol on her again for fear she'd invite him to use it.

He let go of her arm a minute, pulling out his bandana so he could mop the sweat from his face. As he raised the cloth to his forehead, he saw her go down, crumpling in a small heap at his feet. Cursing himself for his carelessness, he crouched beside her, unfolding her limbs to lay her out straight.

Her face was beet red—how much from sunburn and how much from her current temperature he couldn't tell. Placing two fingers on her neck, he was relieved to feel a thready pulse.

He hadn't killed her, then. Good. It'd be a pain to start this whole process over, finding another teacher for Joshua—though Thayne knew if he wasn't careful, that's exactly what he'd be doing. He took the battered hat from his head and began fanning it in front of Miss Madsen's face. It wasn't much in the way of a breeze, and he knew what she really needed was water, but for now, it was the best he could do.

"Miss Madsen." With his free hand, he patted her face lightly. "I'm sure we're just a little ways off now." He looked around at the open prairie, hoping he was right. "And you *really* don't want to die out here. Think of what the coyotes would do to your body . . ." He stopped fanning and looked at that body, clad from neck to toe in brown wool.

"Fool," he muttered, meaning himself as much as the woman. She must be suffocating in that getup; he should have thought of that hours ago. Placing the hat back on his head, his calloused fingers began unbuttoning the thick, scratchy fabric. He reasoned that even a few buttons opened at the neck ought to give her some relief from the heat surely trapped inside. But when he had the top few buttons undone, a white cotton shirtwaist revealed itself beneath. Thayne couldn't believe it when he saw it. Why on earth had she not removed the jacket hours ago—a day ago?

"Women." His care gone, he yanked the last three buttons free from their holes. None too gently, he lifted her and pulled the sleeves from her arms, tossing the jacket aside. As he went to lay her down again, his hands felt the unmistakable strings of a corset beneath her blouse.

Oh no. He nearly dropped her. *I won't,* he argued with himself. *I won't touch it. I won't touch her. I—need her to make it to Joshua.* He hung his head in defeat.

He needed her—alive.

That she'd survived the heat this far, wearing a wool suit, a cotton shirtwaist, *and* a corset was nothing short of a miracle. Thayne frowned, knowing that for her own good, the restrictive corset should come off.

Reluctantly, he rolled Miss Madsen to her side. Tugging her blouse from the waist of her skirt, he forced his hand to touch the offensive corset, his eyes consciously averted to the prairie.

He tried, to no avail, to avoid thinking of the last time he'd untied a corset. Christina's image was burned in his mind.

Thayne squeezed his eyes shut against the vision of her beauty. *Why must everything relate to a memory of her—even a plain schoolteacher in an ugly brown dress?*

He forced himself to look down at Miss Madsen as he struggled to untie the bow. "Ridiculous contraption." His frown deepened when, after a couple of seconds, the knot remained firm. Pulling out his knife, he bunched the blouse up higher and sliced through the strings. A sudden popping sounded, and the whalebone stays shifted beneath his fingers. Working quickly, he pulled the remaining strings loose and then gave one side of the corset a good tug. It budged a little.

Frustrated, Thayne studied her face for any sign of awakening. It'd be just his luck she'd choose that moment to return to consciousness, and she'd think him—what was it she'd said—*a despoiler of women.*

Better despoiled than dead, his common sense told him. He reached for the corset again, this time successfully wresting it from her body. He flung the intimate article away, but not before he'd noted it was as fancy as Christina's had been. Surprising for someone who dressed in brown wool.

Thayne pulled the hat from his head and began fanning Miss Madsen once more.

A minute or so later, he was rewarded for his efforts when she began to stir.

"No, Papa. I can't. I won't . . ." Her protests trailed off, as her head moved side to side.

Obstinate—even when she's half asleep. "Good to know I'm not the first man who's had to suffer your tongue." Thayne stood, picked up her brown jacket, and then lifted her into his arms. Tired as he felt, she seemed light, and he realized just how petite she was. His worry intensified. Someone so little would die a lot faster out here. Dehydration was no idle threat. With determined steps, he continued walking, carrying her in his arms as he headed north.

* * *

Thayne cranked the windlass, his parched lips anticipating fresh, sweet water as the bucket drew nearer to the top of the well. He could hardly believe their good fortune, and not for the first time, he wondered if the abandoned homestead were some kind of mirage. Having gone three quarters of the day without water and having gone two days now without food, hallucinating seemed a very real possibility. But the wood handle was smooth beneath his palm, and the rope taut as he drew up the bucket. Strange, he thought, that whoever had left this place hadn't taken the bucket with them. Thayne decided he'd be sure to take it when they left. He'd be only too willing to carry it and the extra water along.

At last the bucket reached the top, and Thayne pulled it from the well. Brackish water floated on the top of mud. Disappointment surged through him as he angrily tossed the mixture to the ground. Thayne leaned forward on the platform, peering down into the depths of the well. He glanced over at Miss Madsen, lying on the grass. Her eyes were closed and her breathing shallow. They *had* to have water. He would have to go down.

Thayne removed his hat and checked the knot on the windlass as well as the entire length of rope. It seemed to be in satisfactory condition. Satisfactory enough—with a little luck—that it would hold him. Glancing into the well again, Thayne's wish, next to water, was for a candle. Who knew how long it was since the well had been used—or what noxious gas might be lurking below the surface? Shoring up his courage, Thayne lowered the rope and bucket and swung his legs into the hole. He perched on the edge, looking down. Hopefully a dozen or so bucketfuls and the water would flow clear again. It wouldn't be easy without a spade, but he had no choice.

Grasping the rope, Thayne took a deep breath and began lowering himself hand over hand down into the black hole. He told himself it was no different than working his mine. If he'd been able to find gold in the Black Hills, surely he could reach a little water now.

Gradually, the light above him grew dim until it was just a far-off sliver. Thayne felt his feet hit the bucket, and he stepped down into several inches of muddy water. Working fast, he tipped the bucket on its side, both hands reaching beneath the surface to scoop as much of the mixture in as possible. As soon as the pail was full, Thayne righted it, grasped the rope, and began pulling himself up once more.

By the time he reached the surface, he was spent and nauseous. There was definitely something bad down there. He'd have to hold his breath longer next time. Collapsing on the grass beside Miss Madsen, he decided he had to rest a few minutes before going down again. He closed his eyes, giving in to the drowsiness, sleep claiming him in an instant.

CHAPTER 5

A CRACK OF THUNDER SHOOK Emmalyne to full consciousness. Her eyes flew open as lightning flashed once again, silhouetting the outlaw standing in a doorway.

"It's difficult—to believe I could feel worse." Though she hadn't meant them to, the words came out sounding angry. Her voice was hoarse and her lips parched.

He gave her a wry smile. "It would seem your tongue is no worse for the wear."

Emmalyne glared at him then turned her head, taking in her surroundings. The only light came from a misshapen mound of wax encircling a piece of twine. Its feeble flame sputtered on the floor near a fireplace. They were inside a rather crude cabin, with walls, floor, and ceiling of rough wood and earth. A steady dripping trickled from the roof in several places, making miniature pools of mud on the floor. There was no furniture save one stool and the bed she lay on—a lumpy, scratchy tick to be sure—nevertheless far better accommodations than the previous evening. And it *was* evening. Behind the outlaw, she saw the black of night. Where had the day gone? She remembered walking, feeling ill, and . . .

Lightning lit the sky again, making her flinch. A few seconds later, thunder sounded directly overhead. Instinctively, she cringed, wishing away the storm. But outside it raged on, and through the open door, she saw a steady rain falling.

She raised a hand to her forehead—an exhaustive effort—and touched a moist, cool cloth. Pulling it away, she saw it was the outlaw's bandana.

He came to her side. "Best leave that a while longer. Between sunburn and that fever, you've been plenty hot." He took the cloth from her and placed it across her brow.

A shiver ran through Emmalyne as his calloused fingers brushed her skin.

"Here." He removed his canteen and unscrewed the lid. "Remember, drink slowly."

She nodded and didn't argue when he helped her sit up and bring the canteen to her lips. The water was pure heaven. She drank slow and long, not caring the least when a bit dribbled down her chin onto the front of her shirtwaist—*her shirtwaist?*

Emmalyne's head snapped up, and she looked at Mr. Kendrich accusingly. "Where are the rest of my clothes?" She crossed her arms in front of her, realizing as she did that her jacket was not the only thing missing.

He had the audacity to look sheepish. "It was you or that corset. But both weren't gonna make it in this heat." He shrugged. "I figured you'd see things my way—choose practicality over fashion."

"Fashion has nothing to do with it, whereas modesty—"

"And that wool," he continued, nodding toward the foot of the bed where her jacket lay in a crumpled heap. "Winter don't come for a few more months. There's no need for a heat trap like that in August." He held the canteen out to her once more.

She snatched it away, nearly losing her balance and falling backward as she did. "So much for your noble promise." Fortified by the water and her anger, she spoke boldly.

His eyes narrowed. "Believe me, Miss Madsen, there was no pleasure taken in the task. Did I not require your assistance, I'd have been most happy to leave you to bake out on the prairie. As it is, you owe me your life. I carried you over five miles today, and I risked my own neck getting water."

"Did you conjure the rainstorm then, you and your Indian friends?" She didn't wait for him to reply but looked away as she took another drink, replaced the lid, and then rolled onto her side, away from him.

Her body protested the move, and Emmalyne bit her lip to keep from groaning. Another shiver ran through her as gooseflesh sprang up along her arms. He wasn't joking; she did have a fever. Though her head felt on fire, the rest of her was freezing. She tucked her feet—her *bare* feet she realized, further mortified—up under her skirt. At least she was still wearing *that*.

She heard the outlaw rise and walk toward the doorway again. The rain continued steadily, though the thunder seemed to be passing them by. Emmalyne was grateful. She hated storms and didn't feel up to dealing with the usual terrors they evoked.

The cabin grew silent, and she looked over her shoulder to see if he had left. He stood in the doorway, his back to her. Perhaps she'd made him angry, referring to the Indians like that. She'd just wanted to provoke him into telling her something—*anything* about his plans. She rolled onto her back and, gathering her courage, dared to start their conversation again.

"Will you tell me about them?"

"Who?" His voice was wary.

"The Indians, of course." *Who did he think I meant?* Emmalyne wished she could see his face, but he continued staring out into the darkness.

"The Lakota are friendly enough. They'll not harm you."

"Friendly?" she asked, disbelieving. "Surely you know what they did to General Custer and his entire army last year."

"Yup." The outlaw nodded. "Custer deserved it."

"How can you say such a thing?" Feeling it too difficult to argue while lying down, Emmalyne struggled to sit up. The bandana fell to her lap. She watched as the outlaw grabbed the lone stool from the center of the room and placed it by the door. He sat down, tipping the stool and leaning against the wall.

"The U.S. Army promised the Sioux that land, said we'd leave 'em alone. Then Custer's expedition goes in a few years back—finds a pittance of gold—rumors spread . . . Next thing, white folks are settling all over the place, repeating history." His face was grim.

"What do you mean?" Emmalyne asked. The chill permeated the room. She pulled her skirt tighter around her legs and reached for her jacket.

"Indians have lived on this land for years. The land thrived, they thrived. Then we came along, destroying everything in our path. Trees are cut down, buffalo killed, mountains dug up in search of gold . . ."

Emmalyne was confused at the regret she heard in his voice. Across the room, he caught her eye as he continued. "Did you know that Custer boasted—said he and the Seventh Calvary could whip all the Indians in the Northwest?"

"Well—" She wasn't certain what to say. He had presented a valid point of view she'd never before considered. But it did nothing to lessen her fear. "Regardless of your opinion, regardless of who was in the right or wrong of things, the Indians have proven themselves dangerous. *Friendly* hardly seems the word to describe their actions toward white men."

"The chiefs who fought Custer have all gone north into Canada or been killed. There's no one left to cause you any concern."

"But why must you take me there? Am I to be traded? I've heard stories of tribes taking whites to replace their own lost. Is that—"

"No."

His tone told her the discussion was over. Still, she could not let it go. Anxiety over what was to be her fate overcame even her fatigue and fever. She persisted. "Is it so terrible you cannot tell me what is to become of me?"

He ignored her question. "Why don't you tell me first why you were headed out west?"

"I already have. I was contracted to teach school in Sterling, Colorado."

"How 'bout the real reason?" Leaning forward, elbows on his knees, he turned all his attention to her. "What're you running from, Miss Madsen? What did you and your father argue about?"

"How do you—" Emmalyne could not mask the surprise on her face. "That is none of your business."

He shrugged. "I suspect you're right. And I'd say the Lakota are none of yours."

Emmalyne pursed her lips together to keep from lashing out at him. How dare he ask her such things. How dare he suggest he knew anything about her father or the argument that had led to her present dilemma. Folding her arms across her chest, she scooted back on the bed, pouting like a child.

He paid her no heed but rose from the stool and stepped outside. "I suggest you get some sleep. I have a feeling we'll be entertaining visitors before too long."

* * *

Miss Madsen eagerly accepted the piece of charred meat Thayne held out to her.

"What is—no, never mind." She held her hand up to stop him from speaking. "It's probably best I don't know. I'm hungry enough, I'll just eat it."

"Good idea." Thayne dug into his own piece, watching from the corner of his eye as she did the same. He waited, expecting more complaints and was surprised when she said nothing. He watched as she took one bite, then another, her eyes closed in unmistakable bliss.

"Mmm," she murmured, her lips turning up ever so slightly.

In that moment, she looked almost pretty, and Thayne shifted uncomfortably on the stool. If she was that appreciative of a little piece of burnt meat, what would she be like if . . .

He turned away, not allowing himself to finish the thought. Suddenly, too aware of the woman beside him, Thayne forced himself to concentrate on his own breakfast—none too tasty by any standard except starvation.

"That was good," she said a few minutes later. "Is there any more?"

"Nope." He shook his head and willed himself not to watch her licking her fingers. "It was a small critter."

"Oh." Her face fell. "I don't want to know—"

"Then don't ask."

Anger flashed in her eyes. "I didn't."

Thayne breathed an inward sigh of relief. It was better when she was this way—spunky and indignant. He didn't want to like her, and much to his surprise, he was having a hard time not doing just that.

"If you need to take care of any business outside, now would be the time. I want you well hidden before the Martin gang arrives."

"Why are you so certain they're coming?" Emmalyne reached under the bed, retrieving her boots and stockings.

"I come from a long line of intuitive Scotsmen. When we sense something is going to happen, it does."

"What a useful talent. Pity I don't possess it, or I'd never have boarded that train." Facing away from him, she wriggled her sore feet into the stockings, then picked up one of her boots, tugging at the laces to loosen them. She looked regretfully at her feet, covered with multiple blisters.

Thayne took the boot from her and pulled out his knife.

"What are you doing?" she cried, trying to reclaim the boot.

He held it out of her reach. "Making it easier for you to wear these."

"No, thank you." She rose from the bed, lunging forward until her fingers closed around the leather.

He looked at her sternly. "You need to trust me."

"If you were the last man—"

"Might as well be, seeing how I'm all that stands between you and a dozen heinous deaths." He tugged the boot away from her and proceeded to slice open the toe. "This still isn't great, but it'll let up on those blisters a bit." He swiveled on the stool to face her, his hand held out expectantly. "Give me your foot."

"Are you intending to cut that off as well?"

He rolled his eyes and grabbed her ankle. She opened her mouth to protest, but Thayne shot her a warning look.

"We don't have time for theatrics, Miss Madsen. Not if you value your life." He loosened his grip, carefully slid her foot into the boot, then used his knife to slice the sides a bit as well. *What kind of idiot designed women's shoes?* he wondered. Her boots were about the most impractical things for walking he'd ever seen. She'd do better just going barefoot, but he knew Miss Prim and Proper—with her wool already rebuttoned to the neck—would balk at that idea, so he kept his mouth shut.

Thayne made adjustments to her other boot, and she held her foot out to him. He slipped it into the boot, tied up the laces as loose as he dared, and leaned back. "There. That'll be . . ." His voice trailed off as he took in her face, a brighter shade of crimson than even the sunburn had produced. He watched as she tucked her feet beneath the bed, demurely crossing her slender ankles.

"In the future, I would prefer . . . to . . . put on my own shoes," she said in a halting voice. She looked down at her hands, clasping and unclasping them in her lap.

He puzzled at her behavior for a second, half expecting her to deck him if she was that angry. When she didn't and refused to look up, it became clear she wasn't mad at all—or at least not as much as she was embarrassed. Belatedly, he realized she'd probably never had a man touch her ankles before. *She's not Christina. Thanks be for that.*

Thayne stood and walked toward the door, thinking it was a darn good thing Miss Madsen had been unconscious when he'd taken her corset off. If a simple thing like him putting her shoes on had thrown her off balance, she'd have probably died if she'd felt his hands on her back.

Instead, he was the one left bothered by the memory.

He tried but couldn't entirely shake the image away—her parted lips, the sudden intake of breath as her lungs had filled, unrestricted.

He clenched his fists as he recalled balling her jacket beneath her head and brushing the wisps of hair from her delicate face.

Cursing silently, Thayne stepped outside into the sunshine. He picked up the bucket, cupped his hand, and splashed cool rain water onto his stubbly face. He didn't like where his thoughts were heading and recognized the need to change their direction quickly. Best to keep things safe by getting her all riled up again. He didn't suspect it would be too hard to do.

Apparently she had the same idea.

"I suppose it'd be too much to hope you're civilized enough to have some sort of privy around here." Her voice was firm again—and annoyed.

"How should I know what's—" Understanding dawned. Thayne turned to her, irritation written plainly on his face. "You think I *live* here?"

"Don't you?" She stepped outside, her hand to her forehead, shielding her eyes from the sun.

"No." He looked around at the deserted yard and poorly built soddie, offended that she'd thought it was his home. Then again, he reasoned, what else should she think when he hadn't been able to provide even the basic necessities of food and water for the past two days?

What did he care what she thought, anyway?

"This isn't my place. My circumstances are somewhat—different."

"Oh. Of course." She folded her arms across her chest and seemed to look down at him, though she had to be close to a foot shorter. "You're an outlaw. You don't *have* a home." She turned on her heel and, with a swish of her ugly skirt, walked around the corner of the cabin.

Thayne pulled the dusty hat from his head and wiped perspiration from his brow. The storm had only added to the humidity, and his attempts to help Miss Madsen had only upset her more. It seemed today was going to be more miserable than the previous.

CHAPTER 6

THAYNE EMPTIED THE BULLETS FROM the chamber into his palm, then closed the gun and handed it to Miss Madsen. "It'd be better if you could shoot at some targets, but we haven't got bullets to spare."

She looked up at him. "Just how many do you have?"

"Three." He took her shoulder and turned her away. "Hold your hand like this. Index finger on the trigger."

"*Three?* How many Martins are there?" She tilted her head back to see his face.

"Six. Don't worry about it. You're gonna want to wait till he's close, then aim dead center. As long as you hit somewhere on his torso you'll do some damage—hopefully enough you can get away. But if you go too high, your target just got smaller. There'll be a kick, so—"

"Are you planning to stack them up and hope one bullet will go through two at a time?" Emmalyne asked sarcastically. She knew her question was absurd but couldn't imagine what else he had in mind.

"Would you pay attention? This might save your life."

At the unmistakable irritation in his voice, she lowered her head accordingly, trying to listen as he explained how to shoot a man. As if she could do such a thing. *Could I?*

"You may have to."

Emmalyne jumped at the words whispered in her ear. It was more than unnerving that Mr. Kendrich seemed to hear her thoughts. She felt her cheeks heat once more. Had he known what she was thinking a few minutes ago as he put on her shoes?

Heaven help her if he had. *Heaven help me anyway,* she thought, scandalized again by the improper feelings that came over her every time he got too close. When he'd held her foot, she'd felt so dizzy and light-headed she thought she might faint. Now, as he stood close behind to show her how to hold the gun, she felt the same agitation start in her stomach. It was not wholly unpleasant, and *that* was what worried her most. Some part of her wondered if this was why she'd been so insistent on going against her father's wishes. *Was this why I couldn't marry Wilford?* Whenever *he* had tried to hold her close, all she'd ever felt was repulsion.

"Got it?" The outlaw loosened his grip on her hand and stepped back. "Now turn around and pretend to shoot me."

Emmalyne's eyes widened. "I can't. What if there's a bullet you missed? What if—"

"Do it," he ordered tersely. "Think of all the trouble I've caused you and get mad and shoot me."

"All right." Her eyes narrowed as she took aim.

"Arms straight. Feet planted," he ordered. "It'll send you back when you really shoot."

She grimaced and pulled the trigger, squeezing her eyes shut as she did.

"No. All wrong." He came toward her, grabbing her hand and yanking her to him. "If you don't shoot me, I'm going to take my knife to your throat. I'm going to throw you down on the dirt and—"

"All right, I understand." Emmalyne jerked away from him.

"I don't think you do." He looked down on her. "The Martins are ruthless killers. They'll use you any way they want, and then—if you're lucky—they'll shoot you."

"Then why did you rob that train with them? If they're so awful and you're not, then why am I here? Why did you take up with those men anyway?"

"Because I was desperate," he said. "We don't have time to discuss this again."

"Why don't *you* keep the gun?" She shoved the offensive weapon back into his hands. "I don't understand why you expect me to do the shooting."

"I don't. Hopefully it won't come to that, but if it does, I want to know you can handle it."

"Well, I can't."

"You'll have to." He looked past her, out across the prairie.

Emmalyne followed his gaze but saw nothing.

"Get inside." He took her arm again, guiding her into the cabin. "We're real lucky I found this place. It's got two root cellars, and we're gonna pray like mad the Martins don't notice the second one." He went to the bed, lifted, and tugged it a couple of feet away from the wall.

She looked down at the dirt floor, not seeing anything at first. He stepped behind the bed and began brushing the dirt away, revealing wooden boards beneath. After a minute he removed his knife and pried one of the wide planks from the floor. She crept closer, peering into the dark below.

"We're hiding down *there*?" It didn't look big enough for the two of them.

"You are." He took her hand, guiding her toward the hole.

She balked.

"Tell me you're not afraid of the dark," he grumbled.

Emmalyne shook her head. "No, but where are you going to hide?"

"I'm not."

Her eyes met his, and she became truly frightened when she saw his own worry. "I don't understand."

"I'll explain later. Come on." He pulled her closer, and Emmalyne complied. He took her arms. "I'm going to lower you down slowly."

She nodded, holding her breath as he lifted her and then lowered her through the hole. A few seconds later, her feet hit the ground below, and he released her arms.

"All right?" he called down.

She nodded, though she felt anything but all right. The cellar wasn't very deep. Her head was only an inch or two below the floor. But the space was wider than she'd first thought. She suppressed a shudder as her imagination ran wild. "What if there are other things down here—spiders or mice?"

"Then you might have some supper." His words were teasing, but his tone was not. He left her, returning a minute later with the gun and his canteen. He handed her the latter first, then, butt down, gave her the gun. "It's loaded now. Be careful."

She shifted from one foot to the other uneasily. "Am I supposed to sit on the floor?"

He frowned but left the opening, returning with the stool a minute later.

"Thank you," she said after he'd lowered it through the hole. "What if—"

His finger to his lips cut her off. "From now on, you're quiet. And no matter what you hear, stay put until I come get you."

"And if you don't?" She clutched the gun to her chest as she looked up at him.

"Then wait until you don't hear nothin' for a good *long* time." He paused, as if he were deciding what else he should tell her. "Due west, about a day's walk, you'll hit Sidney. If I don't come for you, get yourself there as fast as possible." He shifted the board back into place, and Emmalyne was left alone in the dark.

* * *

Though Thayne itched to go to the window to check things just one more time, he forced himself to stay put, resting—or so it appeared—on the bed. Slouched against the headboard, his eyes took in the cabin, sweeping carefully over the floor, checking again for any trace, any footprint, a single thread, a track of dust that might reveal Miss Madsen's presence. He saw nothing, but that didn't ease his worries for her, for himself . . . for Joshua.

Thayne was furious that he'd gotten them into this situation, and more than that, he was furious with Christina because it all circled back to her. He didn't much care what happened to his own sorry life anymore, except that others were depending on him—Joshua and now Miss Madsen. Thayne was pretty sure that so long as the Martins didn't find her, she'd make it okay. He smiled faintly. She was one tough nut. Whether she realized it or not, he was pretty certain she could use that gun if she had to.

Joshua was another matter entirely. There'd be no one for him if his dad didn't make it. Once again, the weight—and joy—of being a father descended. Thayne closed his eyes, picturing Joshua, his sweet smell, his chubby hands clinging to him. Guilt and sorrow bubbled to the surface, and Thayne swore another oath to be a better father, to return and take care of his son.

Several more minutes passed, and Thayne felt his eyelids growing droopy. How long had it been since he'd had a decent night's sleep? He couldn't remember, and dozing for even a few minutes became a delicious temptation. A foolish idea—one he couldn't afford to indulge.

At last, he heard horses approaching. They weren't galloping but cantered into the yard at a slow, steady pace. From behind half-closed eyelids, Thayne peered at the open doorway, willing the tension to leave his face as he heard men dismount and walk toward the soddie.

"Well, well. If it ain't the deserter." Adam Martin tipped his hat in Thayne's direction. "Looks like we found him, boys. But where's the lady?"

"She's gone." Thayne opened his eyes all the way and feigned surprise as he took in Adam and his two brothers. *Just three. Where are the rest?* "And *deserter* seems a bit strong, considering you all took my horse and supplies and left *me* behind." Thayne shook his head as he made sitting up on the bed appear to take great effort. "Pot calling the kettle black, if you ask me."

"Don't recall asking. Do you, boys?" Adam glanced at his brothers. They shook their heads in unison. "Didn't think so. But I am asking—for the last time—where's the woman—and *the gold*?" Adam pulled his pistol from its holster and pointed it at Thayne.

He held his hands up. "Whoa. I don't have any gold, don't even have my gun, and I'm too sick to try anything else, so there's no point in waving that around. If you'll listen a minute, I'll explain."

"Go ahead." Adam made no move to put the weapon away.

Stick as close to the truth as possible, Thayne reminded himself. He licked his lips and began. "I took my time on that train, looking for a woman Russell would really like—one that hadn't been used before. And I'd just found her when the train started up again."

Next to Adam, Michael pulled his gun out as well. "Hurry it up. I don't have no patience for long stories."

"She fought like a mad cat," Thayne said emphatically. He held out his arm. "See here where she bit me." He pushed back his sleeve, revealing the bruised oval Miss Madsen's teeth had left. "I knew for sure then I'd chose well. Russell was gonna be pleased as punch when he saw her."

"He's none too pleased right now," Adam said.

"Well, neither am I." Thayne sat up straighter, warming to his topic. "You took my horse, water, food, rope—near every last thing I had, and I was left alone with a more resourceful woman than you can imagine."

"I'm having a devil of a time believing your tale," Michael said. He looked at Adam. "Can't we just fill him full of lead and get back?"

Thayne didn't wait for Adam's answer. "Where is Russell, anyway?"

"Back at camp," Adam said. "Enjoying himself with the whiskey and women, while we traipse after the likes of you."

Thayne cursed himself silently for not keeping his gun. He was a good marksman and could have picked off at least two of the three—evening the odds quite a bit. But, believing he'd face all six, he'd thought the only way to protect Miss Madsen—to convince the Martins she truly was gone— was for them to think he was ill and she'd taken his gun and escaped.

Adam walked to the center of the room and knelt on the muddy floor. It took him only a few seconds to find the hole and pull the board loose, revealing the empty root cellar below.

Thayne leaned his head against the wall and looked bored. "I told you, ain't nothin' or no one here. Last I saw, Mark had his paws all over that sack of gold. And I *did* have a woman, but she escaped—passed out on me first, though. I carried her here, found this well, and thought we'd been saved. But the water wasn't clear, so I went down to see if I could dig past the murk. I near died from the fumes—barely crawled outta there before passing out myself. When I came to last night, the woman and my gun were gone."

"Nice story," Clay, the youngest Martin, said as he stepped forward. "Except you left out one part . . ." From behind his back, he withdrew Miss Madsen's discarded corset.

Thayne shrugged. "Michael didn't want a long story, so I left out the details—like how I cut that off her so she could breathe or how I been puking my guts out since last night. If you don't believe me, go outside, walk around and see."

"I believe you," Adam said, rising from the floor and slipping his gun back into the holster. "Mark's the one told us you had the money—right before he took off himself. Dirty double-crosser. We'll find him next." Adam glanced at his brothers then back at Thayne. "I told Russell— first time we met you—that you didn't have the brains to be an outlaw. Problem is, what are we gonna do with you now?"

"Just shoot him and be done with it," Michael suggested.

Adam shook his head. "Too easy. We've got to do something to appease Russell. He's so mad now, thinking you took his loot and his woman . . . I know what we'll do."

Thayne didn't much care for the evil glint that came to Adam's eye. *Stay calm. Think of Joshua. Keep your wits, and you can get out of this.* Thayne forced his hands to stay relaxed. Adam was watching him closely.

"Take a real good look around, boys. See if you can't find the gal, and then . . ." Adam's lip curled. "Thayne here's gonna have a little swim."

CHAPTER 7

Behind his back, Thayne rotated his tied hands, trying to keep the circulation flowing. He was going to need all the feeling he could get in them if he was going to be able to untie the rope once they lowered him down into the well.

Across the room, Adam Martin sat on the floor and chewed a piece of jerky as he watched Thayne. "Failed at farming, failed at mining, even failed at being an outlaw. You should thank me for putting you out of your misery."

Thayne's reply was merely a grunt. For the past hour, he'd mostly listened as Adam had carried on a one-sided conversation. After searching the well, cabin, and surrounding area, Michael and Clay had ridden out in opposite directions to see if they could find Miss Madsen.

Left behind with Adam, Thayne had been forced to listen to the coarse details of Adam's time with the captured women—one of whom had already died. Thayne was repulsed and more than a little guilt stricken for his part in the abductions. Miss Madsen's accusations rang true, and after listening to Adam, Thayne couldn't even rationalize Joshua's care as a good excuse for joining up with outlaws. A woman had died; several others were being terrorized, and he was at least partially responsible. He vowed that if he got out of this alive, he'd get the necessary information to the law so the Martins could be captured.

The sound of a horse galloping into the yard brought Adam to his feet. Gun drawn, he walked to the window. When he saw it was his brother, he moved to the door.

"No sign of her anywhere," Michael said as he dismounted.

Clay rode up behind him. "Nothing my way, either. She mighta made it to Sidney if she left last night."

Adam turned to Thayne. "Too bad. Time's up." He waved Thayne outside with his gun.

Thayne leaned forward, again exaggerating weakness as he struggled to rise from the bed.

They'd left his feet untied, so he walked slowly toward the door. *Stay put, Miss Madsen. Just stay quiet and stay put a while longer.*

Once outside, he squinted against the sun. Adam's pistol at his back prodded him toward the well. Thayne thought of the little stub of candle he'd made from bits of wax melted on the mantel. He wished he'd had the foresight to send it down this morning to see if it burned. Then again, if he'd known he was only going to face three Martin brothers, he'd have kept his gun and wouldn't be facing a trip down the well.

Looking up, Thayne watched as Clay knocked the remaining piece of wood from the platform. The splintered windlass fell to the ground, the fraying rope coiled beside it. Thayne thought it a miracle it had held his weight the previous day. He was in need of another miracle now—a few of them—if he was going to survive this.

"Up," Adam ordered Thayne. He and Michael each grabbed one of Thayne's arms and lifted him the couple of feet onto the stone side of the well. Adam leaned over, looking down. "It'll be the gasses or drowning—either one ought to assure Russell you're no longer a nuisance."

Thayne didn't say anything but looked down, judging his chances for surviving the fall without breaking a leg or bashing his head open. He had no hope they would lower him down gently.

"You gonna jump, or do I push you?" Ever impatient, Michael put his hand on Thayne's back.

Thayne shrugged it off and barely managed to contain his anger, reminding himself it was his fault he was in this situation.

Without a word, he put his foot out and stepped into the hole, eyes closed, back straight as he plunged down the narrow shaft.

* * *

Emmalyne huddled on the stool, arms wrapped around her, eyes squeezed shut as she listened to the gunshots.

One. Two. Three.

She bit down on her cracked lip and drew blood. The taste was bitter in her mouth and brought forth an image of Mr. Kendrich, sprawled on the ground, blood gushing from his chest. Terror enveloped her. They'd killed him, and now it was only a matter of time before they found her.

Body trembling, she began rocking back and forth on the stool, willing her heart to stop racing and her mind to clear. She needed to think, to formulate a plan. What to do? Wait. Mr. Kendrich had told her to wait a good long time. Had he known they'd kill him? He must have. Tears pricked the back of her eyes, and an unexpected sense of loss washed over her. Rational thought told her she ought to be relieved. He was an outlaw too, for heaven's sake. He'd threatened her with his gun, he'd removed her corset . . . he'd saved her.

Hearing voices overhead, Emmalyne ceased her rocking and sat perfectly still, save for her hand, which crept to the pistol in her lap. Furniture scraped across the floor above, and she held her breath, pointing the gun upward, waiting for the moment the board was pulled loose and her hiding place revealed.

She no longer had any doubts about her ability to pull the trigger. After listening to the Martins talk of what they'd done to the other women from the train, Emmalyne knew she'd fight with everything she had. Mr. Kendrich had left her three bullets, and she intended to use every one of them. Carefully, she backed the stool against a solid wall of earth, lending her the support she needed.

Her hands wavered under the weight of the pistol, and she fought to steady them. Above, she heard a final shout, then the sound of feet running toward the door. A few seconds later, a deafening explosion threw her to the ground. Her head slammed against the wall as dirt and debris crumbled down on her. The gun flew from her hands, and blindly she crawled around the floor, groping for the weapon. Keeping it now seemed the only thing that mattered.

At last, her fingers closed over the barrel, and she picked it up, positioning it in her hands as Mr. Kendrich had shown her.

She stood several minutes, anxiety building as she waited for them to find her. But she heard no voices. *Maybe they've left. But Mr. Kendrich said to wait a good* long *time.* Her fingers trembled, the pistol quavering in her hands. Beads of perspiration dotted her forehead, and she raised her arms, trying to wipe it away. She realized suddenly that the cellar had gone from cool to warm. Emmalyne felt her eyes watering again, not from tears—they were burning from the dust . . . no, smoke.

Fire. The cabin is on fire.

She bit back a scream as she looked up, imagining the wood planks burning, crashing down on her. Sharp cracks sounded overhead as she felt for the stool, then righted it and climbed on top. She could face the enemy outside, or she could die in this furnace.

It didn't take long to decide. Tucking the gun in her skirt, she reached her hands up, feeling the floorboards above. They were hot, but she continued to touch each until she felt one shift a little. With both hands she pushed again and again until the board popped loose, sending a blaze of heat her way.

Emmalyne cringed back down into the hole, then forced herself to look up once more. Thick smoke filled the soddie, obscuring everything but the bright orange flames burning the bed in the center of the room. She could still make it outside. Reaching her arms up, Emmalyne struggled to lift herself out. Smoke filled her lungs, and her eyes burned, watering so badly she could barely see. As she lifted her knee to crawl out, a calloused hand closed around her arm.

Emmalyne screamed as she pulled away and fell back into the hole beneath the floor.

CHAPTER 8

"Miss Madsen," Thayne yelled over the blaze roaring behind him and the screams from below. Wincing, he leaned over the root cellar, his hand groping blindly in the dark. A second later, her slender fingers grasped his arm. Relief, followed by caustic pain in his shoulder, washed over him as he leaned back to pull her out.

Her eyes were tearing, and she coughed as her waist came level with the floor. He let go, and she crawled out on her own.

"Keep low," he shouted over the roar of the flames. Smoke filled his lungs as he waved his good hand toward what used to be the door, and she followed him on hands and knees from the cabin. Once outside, he staggered to his feet, glanced to see that she was still behind him, then made a path away from the soddie, walking as far as he could before finally collapsing on the grass.

"Mr. Kendrich, are you dead?" she cried, dropping beside him, her hand held over him tentatively.

Thayne opened one pain-filled eye. "Not yet. But working on it."

"Please don't," she begged. Her eyes grew large as she looked him over, taking in the gash on his forehead and the blood seeping through his shirt. "You're shot."

"Reckon so," Thayne grumbled. "A blind man coulda hit me. Hard to miss when you're shooting down a three-foot-wide shaft." He reached his good hand up and began unbuttoning his shirt.

"They shot you in the *well?*" Emmalyne looked over her shoulder toward the burning cabin.

"Yeah." Thayne grimaced as he moved his arm, his fingers still fumbling with the first button.

She turned back to him. "But however did you get out? I heard the shots. Then they started the fire. I thought you were . . ." Her voice trailed off. After several seconds, his shaking fingers had managed to free only one button, and he looked to Miss Madsen for help. "I've got to stop the bleeding, or I *will* die."

She nodded and swallowed in one motion but made no move to assist.

"Miss Madsen," he said gently. "I could really use your help about now."

She looked past him and remained sitting perfectly still, hands clasped in her lap to the point of white knuckles. Thayne wondered how she made even her eyeballs freeze like that. He recognized the signs of shock setting in and knew they'd both be in real trouble if she went there. Perhaps he could get her riled up again.

"Miss Madsen? If it's your intent for me to die, then do me the favor of using that pistol." He nodded toward the gun in the grass beside her. "You seem like a merciful sort, and there's no sense in dragging things out."

She didn't respond.

"Miss Madsen," he said sharply, reaching for the canteen strapped around her neck. "Will you—"

"Emmalyne," she whispered.

"*What?*" Thayne's brow wrinkled as he tried to decipher what she'd said.

"My name is Emmalyne." Her voice quavered. "You've saved me twice now. I suppose you can know my name."

He scowled. "That's *four* times if you count the corset and train."

She shook her head. "I don't."

"Be that as it may, you owe me one." Thayne let his hand drop as he looked into her eyes. "So you gonna shoot me or save me?"

She hesitated, biting her lip in indecision. "I'm not so good at saving people."

Thayne saw her eyes glazing over again. "I'll tell you exactly what to do." He reached for her hand and placed it on his chest. "Get this shirt off, and we'll see how bad things are. If we're lucky, the bullets went clean through."

"And if they didn't?"

"One problem at a time." He didn't want to explore that possibility yet. "Just take off the shirt."

She pursed her lips and bent her head to the task. Thayne noticed her hands trembled more than his had as she began with the buttons where he'd left off. He closed his eyes, knowing he didn't dare sleep, knowing he couldn't with his shoulder throbbing as it was. If only he had some whiskey.

"Now what?"

He opened his eyes and looked up into her face, pale behind smudges of dirt and ash.

"Pull the cloth back. Real slow now on my left here." He braced himself for the torture, but her fingertips were gentle against his skin, taking great care as she peeled the fabric from his chest and shoulder.

Her sudden intake of breath startled him.

"That bad, huh?" He lifted his head, trying to get a better look at himself.

"You were hit twice—in nearly the same place. And the skin is . . . is practically peeled off your shoulders—and back."

"That'd be from scooting myself up out of the well. Are the holes clean?" Thayne lowered his head back to the ground, cursing the nausea and light-headedness assaulting him. He'd seen and dressed worse wounds before, so what was the problem?

"Clean as in . . ."

"Did the bullets go through?"

"I don't know. How do I tell?" she asked anxiously.

"If you can't see it, you'll have to feel inside with your finger." Thayne reached for her hand, feeling the nail at the tip of her index finger. "Take care. That's pretty sharp."

Emmalyne pulled her hand back. "Oh no. I couldn't do that. I—"

"You *have* to," Thayne insisted. "If you don't . . . If infection sets in, I'm a goner, and then you're left alone out here, alone to deal with men like the Martin gang."

A look of horror crossed her face, and Thayne wasn't certain if it was the thought of touching him or the thought of facing the Martins that upset her more. Finally, she gave a little nod and her hand reached toward him.

"All right, Mr. Kendrich." Her finger found the first hole.

"Thayne," he gasped. "Name's Thayne in case ya need it for my tombstone." He felt her fingers reach muscle. His eyes rolled back in his head, and he was gone.

* * *

Emmalyne poured water over the last strip of her petticoat, then wrung it out over the grass beside Mr. Kendrich—Thayne—she reminded herself. Not that she thought she'd need his name for a tombstone. He was still unconscious, but his breathing remained deep and even, and she was nearly finished dressing both wounds. He'd been fortunate. One bullet had passed clean through. The other had lingered near the surface and was easily removed. She'd been able to discover that in one long, horrifying minute as she'd pushed her finger through his flesh. Sometimes slow and gentle wasn't the best.

Applying the cloth to his second wound, she leaned back on her heels and watched a minute to see if blood would seep through. It didn't, and she sighed in relief. Her entire petticoat was used up, and she wasn't certain which article of clothing she'd have had to sacrifice next. As it was, she was already eyeing her jacket, thinking the wool would make a nice strong sling as soon as Mr. Kendrich was ready to travel again.

And when will that be? she wondered. Looking back at the charred remains of the soddie, she longed for shelter of some sort against the approaching night. There would be none. No food, either, though water was ample, thanks to his bravery in the well. She'd hardly dared believe his tale when she'd heard him talking to the Martin outlaws, but when she'd dipped the bucket an hour past, it had brought up clean, clear water. Thinking of it now and hearing her stomach grumble, she picked up the canteen and took a long drink. The water soothed her raw throat but did little to ease her hunger. Was it only this morning Mr. Kendrich had fed her that delicious wild game? So much had happened in the hours since that it seemed as if days had passed.

Emmalyne fervently hoped days wouldn't pass before Mr. Kendrich returned to his usual bossy self. Even the prospect of being traded to Indians seemed better than indefinite days of starvation out on the prairie. Placing her palm across his brow, she checked for fever and felt reassured that he had none. She sat beside him and drew her knees up to her chest, watching as the sun sank lower on the horizon.

A coyote howled somewhere in the distance, and Emmalyne shuddered. Dark was coming on strong now. Scooting closer to Mr. Kendrich, she curled herself in a ball on her side and fell into an uneasy sleep with one hand on the gun.

CHAPTER 9

THE MORNING SUN WAS ALREADY beating down on them when Emmalyne finally opened her eyes. She struggled to sit up, her arm numb from acting as a pillow much of the night. Shifting her weight, she turned to Mr. Kendrich, who was lying completely still—in the exact same position she'd left him last night. Her own pulse quickened as she placed her hand to his chest. She was relieved to feel the slow, steady beat of his heart.

Keeping her hand on his skin a moment longer than necessary, she took comfort in his presence. Before yesterday, she'd never seen a man without his shirt on. Now, curiosity held her riveted. A variety of scars—large and small—spread over his muscled arms and chest, indications of a hard life. *He is an outlaw,* she reminded herself. *Though nothing like those men who were here yesterday.* She studied Thayne's face and was surprised to see worry and pain etched there, even as he slept. *Who are you? Not a cold, heartless man as I first believed.* A shudder of fear rippled through her as she realized how easy it would have been for him to simply hand her over to the Martin brothers. Instead, he'd handed her his only gun and faced them unarmed, risking his own life. *What kind of an outlaw does that?* She didn't know and was not inclined to find out. *He's still dangerous,* she reminded herself. *He's the reason I'm stuck out here.*

Gently touching the rust-colored strips of fabric covering his wounds, Emmalyne was pleased to find the blood dry. She was not pleased a moment later when her stomach grumbled and she felt the gnawing ache of hunger. With a groan, she stood and stretched her sore muscles. *Now what?*

Yesterday's "rest" hadn't really been a day of rest at all—what with the Martin gang, the fire, and Mr. Kendrich's gunshot wounds. As Emmalyne carried the empty bucket to the well, she realized she felt more physically and emotionally drained than she'd felt in her entire life.

In a strange sort of way, neither feeling was wholly unwelcome. Wasn't this what she'd wanted? To have an adventure? To do something with her life? To have purpose—other than being a banker's sweet, docile bride?

Water sloshed down the front of Emmalyne's skirt as she hauled the pail up from the well and lugged it back. The past few days definitely qualified as adventurous. But purpose? Certainly it wasn't her purpose in life to be traded to an Indian tribe. And now was her chance to do something about that.

She stopped beside Mr. Kendrich, stooping to take the strip of petticoat from his forehead. The cloth felt dry—warm even. Emmalyne touched his brow. Hot. Enough for concern? She didn't know.

Lines of worry creased her face as she brought her fingers to her lips, thinking. Fever or not, Mr. Kendrich needed care beyond that which she could give. Perhaps she could leave him and go for help. He'd said she could make it to Sidney in one day.

She rose slowly and stood, looking down on him. Leaving was the smart thing to do. Alone like this, she was no good to him. They had no shelter, food, or medicine. Stark reality dictated she should definitely go. *So why do I feel so guilty?* She bit her nail in indecision.

Because I'm leaving as much for myself as to help him. "And just what is wrong with that?" Emmalyne said aloud. "The man kidnapped me. Why shouldn't I try to get away?" With those words, she turned resolutely from the sorry sight of Mr. Kendrich sprawled helplessly in the dirt.

She would go. She would find the railroad line, and she would find Sidney. Once there, she could send someone back to help Mr. Kendrich while she stayed in town and sent a telegraph to Sterling. Surely her teaching position hadn't already been filled. She'd ask the school board to wire her money for another ticket, and she could pay them back from her salary. Most likely, her trunk had already made it safely there. The lines of worry eased as she thought of such a happy possibility.

Dipping the cloth in the water, Emmalyne wrung it out and placed it across Mr. Kendrich's brow. He didn't move—didn't even stir. Guilt tore at her. How could she leave him? How could she not? He'd saved her twice. She owed him one more. She would pay her debt by getting help.

Turning her back to the sun, she looked west over the prairie. Could she find Sidney on her own? Doubts crept into her mind. But if someone had asked her last week if she could dig a bullet out of a man's shoulder, she would certainly have said no.

And somehow she'd done that.

Somehow she would make it to Sidney—and get them both out of this mess.

Emmalyne filled the canteen, picked up the pistol, and looked longingly at her jacket, balled up beneath Mr. Kendrich's head. She supposed she'd better leave it to provide what comfort it could, though the thought of walking into town without it, in her dirty shirtwaist—with no corset beneath—was appalling. She tried not to think of the embarrassment, reasoning instead that it would likely be dark by the time she arrived.

Looking around one last time, she made certain the bucket of water was within his reach.

She took a step backward, nearly crushing his worn hat. She picked it up, holding it thoughtfully. It was filthy to be sure, but . . . With a grimace she plunked it on her head. The hat might save her from further sunburn and maybe keep her going a little longer. She glanced down one more time.

"Good-bye, Mr. Kendri—" Her voice caught. "Good-bye, Thayne."

* * *

Using his good arm, Thayne lifted the pail, purposely dumping half the water down the front of his shirt. It brought immediate, though short-lived, relief, and he savored the moment before starting out after Emmalyne Madsen.

"Fool woman," he muttered under his breath as he felt for his hat and remembered it was gone. What he didn't remember was when he'd lost it—before he jumped into the well or when he'd rescued her in the fire—but he knew without its protection he was in for a long, hot walk. He already felt unnaturally warm, and letting the sun beat down on his head all day was going to do nothing to improve his situation. He eyed Emmalyne's crumpled wool jacket, still lying on the ground. She must have put it under his head last night after he'd passed out.

Thayne frowned, disgusted with himself for such unmanly behavior over a couple of little gunshot wounds. As if to prove he was stronger than that, he rotated his injured shoulder, gritting his teeth through the pain then cursing when he saw the bright red stain of fresh blood appear. Maybe it *was* worse than he'd realized. He only hoped Miss Madsen had been successful in getting the bullets out.

Doing his best to ignore his shoulder, he bent and picked up the jacket, dipping it in the bucket. When it was good and wet, he tossed it over his head, arranging it so the sleeves hung down on either side of his face, over his ears. The wet wool smelled awful, and he didn't want to think about the humiliation he'd feel walking into town looking like this. He'd be sure to lose the makeshift hat before then. But for now, while following a foolish woman across the hot Nebraska prairie, it would have to do.

Thayne walked to the well, filled the bucket once more, dumped half of it again, then sliced some of the rope from the broken windlass. He was grateful he still had his knife, though he felt close to naked with his holster hanging empty around his waist. Looping the rope around the handle and over his good shoulder, he rigged a way to make carrying the pail a bit easier. Apparently, Miss Madsen had seen fit to take not only his pistol but the canteen as well. He told himself it was good she had. Those two things might just keep her alive. He'd be considerably upset if he found her any other way. She'd been far too much trouble to go off and die on him now. He just hoped he could get to her before anything or anyone else did.

With great strides, he started off in the direction she'd gone—made evident by the prints of her sorry boots in the dirt between the prairie grasses. Flat as the land was, he didn't think it would take him too long to catch up with her. He might be injured, but he'd bet he could still move twice as fast as she could. Thayne glanced at the sky, guessing it to be around ten in the morning. If he hurried, he might make Sidney before nightfall. He decided going into town was probably best. He'd get some money from the bank there, and they could get a good meal, a decent night's sleep, and some supplies. Then—somehow—he'd have to convince her to continue with him to the Hills tomorrow.

Only problem was, while he was convincing her and arranging everything, how would he get Miss Madsen to keep her mouth shut? No one in Sidney really knew him. If she cried outlaw and pointed a finger his way, there was no one who could vouch for his character. Thayne began walking faster, counting his steps into seconds, adding up the minutes, watching the sun as it caught up with him and came to rest directly overhead.

Noon. He stopped for another drink, careful this time not to break open the wound on his shoulder when he lifted the pail. His thirst satisfied, he started walking again. The rail line ought to be close now, and he'd bet his gun—if he had it—she was following the track west.

An hour later, his hunch proved right when he spotted a lone figure pathetically bobbing up and down beside the rail. At first he didn't think it was her but some half-drunk cowboy slogging along. After all, he didn't know too many women who wore a hat like that—like *his*. He blinked rapidly and pushed the jacket sleeve out of his line of vision as he looked again. The straggler wore a dark brown *skirt*.

"She stole my hat," Thayne said, his temper rising. Here he was, a fool wearing wet wool on his head. Thayne yanked the jacket from his head, slapping it against his thigh.

She'd taken his gun, his hat, and his canteen. He'd saved her twice, and she'd not only left him for dead but robbed him as well. He'd prove to her right now that he wasn't dead. In fact, he suddenly felt better than he had all day. The sun could take it out of you, but it could also do a lot toward healing a man—as could the knowledge that he'd soon be in possession of his hat and pistol again. Lengthening his strides, Thayne marched toward the figure, closing the distance between them.

Less than a hundred yards off, he heard her bloodcurdling scream, and she dropped from sight, disappearing in the tall grass growing beside the track.

CHAPTER 10

THE SOUND OF A RATTLE stopped Thayne cold. He looked down just in time to see a three-foot prairie rattler slither alongside Emmalyne. Thayne searched for a rock, but seeing none, he slowly crouched down, enough to reach for his pistol lying in the grass a few feet away. He lifted the gun, took aim, and pulled the trigger. The sound reverberated across the prairie, leaving silence behind. Emmalyne hadn't even flinched.

Thayne picked up the headless remnant of the snake and flung it across the track to the other side. Holstering his gun, he dropped to the ground beside Emmalyne. *Had she been bitten? Or just scared?* He hoped fervently for the latter as he checked her arms, then lifted the hem of her skirt, revealing a distinctive, angry welt just above her left ankle.

All this and a snake— Thayne took out his knife and cut a strip of fabric from the hem of her skirt. He tied the cloth just below her knee then lifted his blade again, slicing an *X* across the bite. Lowering his mouth to her leg, he began the arduous and uncertain task of removing the venom from her bloodstream.

* * *

"Upstairs, second door on the left," Mrs. Beckett instructed as she clasped and unclasped her hands. "Doctor's not in, you know."

"Yes. I'd heard that," Thayne said dryly. It was the third time in about three minutes the distraught woman had mentioned her husband wasn't at home. "I'm sure—where you've been his assistant—you must know of something to help the lady." He started up the steep, narrow stairs, Emmalyne limp in his arms.

Behind him, Mrs. Beckett looked out at the street, considering. "Well, yes. Yes." Her voice rose with sudden certainty. "There *is* something." She closed the front door and turned to go into the dining room. "I'll be right there," she called up the stairs.

Thayne entered the bedroom and gently laid Emmalyne across the bed. Her eyes remained closed and her breathing shallow. He took her hand and felt for her pulse. It seemed unnaturally quick. *The venom doing its job?*

Behind him he heard Mrs. Beckett's heavy footsteps.

"Bought this just last month. Mr. Beckett was none too pleased, but he didn't see the demonstration like I did." Mrs. Beckett bustled into the room, brown bottle in one hand, a spoon in the other. "Miraculous. That's what it was. Cured Miranda Bigbee, and that woman ain't been right for years."

Thayne looked doubtful. "When did you say the doctor might return?"

"Oh, not for a long while." Mrs. Beckett seemed almost cheerful. "He's out to the Nielson farm for a birthing. And Mary's so big, she's likely having twins."

Not good news. Thayne rubbed the stubble on his chin as he watched the woman pour a spoonful of greenish syrup. "What exactly is that?"

"Humphrey's Homeopathic Number 28." Mrs. Beckett held up the bottle, peering at the fine print on the label. "A sure cure for nervous debility, vital weakness or depression, a weak exhausted feeling, no energy or courage, the result of mental overwork, indiscretion, or excess."

"It doesn't say anything about snake bites?" Thayne walked around to the other side of the bed.

"Sure it does." As if sensing his intention to stop her, Mrs. Beckett leaned over, pinched Emmalyne's mouth open, and shoved the spoon inside. Emmalyne began to gag, the greenish liquid spilling from the sides of her mouth.

"Now hold it in there, girl," Mrs. Beckett said firmly. She turned to Thayne, who was standing beside her, an angry look on his face. "She *is* weak and exhausted, and if venom doesn't qualify as excess, then I don't know what does." Mrs. Beckett took a cloth from her apron pocket and returned her attention to Emmalyne. "Leave the doctoring to me, and we'll have her good as new in no time."

* * *

Thayne's head tilted to the side as a snore escaped his open mouth. Mrs. Beckett clucked her disapproval as she marched into the room, an armful of clean linens held tight to her ample chest.

"Mr. Kendrich," she said loudly. Thayne responded with another, deeper snore. Her eyes narrowed as she advanced and gave a swift kick to the raised front leg of the chair he rested in, already propped at a precarious angle against the wall.

The chair wobbled, and Thayne's head snapped up, his eyes opening wide as one hand flailed in the air and his other went automatically to the holster at his hip.

It was empty. The chair spilled him to the floor, and he struck his head on the wall. Looking up, he remembered belatedly where he was and that the stout woman standing over him had demanded he leave his gun with her before entering the house.

"I told you earlier, there'll be *no* sleeping in here. I'm not running a boardinghouse, you know."

"Yes, ma'am." Thayne reached a hand up to tip his hat in apology before remembering the woman had taken that too. *No gentleman wears a hat in my house,* she'd insisted. *Am I correct in assuming you* are *a gentleman, Mr. Kendrich?* What could he say then or now? He needed her to think him as gentlemanly as they came.

He rose slowly to his feet, wincing at the pain in his shoulder. "I'll get me a room just as soon as my Emmalyne wakes and I know she's all right."

"She's right as rain," Mrs. Beckett insisted, striding toward the bed. She deposited the linens at the foot, then leaned toward the headboard, reaching out to feel Emmalyne's forehead. "No fever." She picked up Emmalyne's limp arm, clamping a hand around her wrist, feeling for her pulse. "Steady as can be," Mrs. Beckett announced less than ten seconds later—not long enough to really tell, Thayne thought.

She dropped Emmalyne's arm unceremoniously to the bed and turned to him. "Your lady is fine. Off with you now. You can come back tomorrow."

Thayne racked his brain for an excuse to stay. "But—"

"Nope." She cut him off, her palm flashing in his face. "Having a strange man in our house don't sit right with Mr. Beckett *or* me."

She was not going to be persuaded. He looked past her to Emmalyne, sleeping peacefully on a comfortable bed, while he was ordered out like a stray dog.

Mrs. Beckett held her arm out, indicating he was to precede her out of the room. Thayne took one step then turned to her. "She's like to be in a panic if I'm not here when she wakes."

Mrs. Beckett shook her head. "Nonsense. A woman always feels better in the company of another woman."

Thayne was afraid she was right, especially considering all Emmalyne had been through the past few days. Waking up in a bed—in a *house*—with a woman nearby instead of him would probably seem like heaven after being dragged across the prairie, starved, dehydrated, nearly burned, and bitten by a snake. If he was any sort of decent man, he'd just walk away and leave her here in peace.

Too bad it'd been so long since he'd been decent. His needs—or rather, Joshua's—trumped Miss Madsen's just now, and that was all there was to it.

Thayne stepped out into the hallway, and Mrs. Beckett closed the door behind them. He had no choice but to walk down the stairs and wait in the parlor while she retrieved his things.

"My gun?" he asked, irritated when she returned with his hat and nothing else.

"Collateral. It will be returned after we're paid, of course." She gave him a forced smile.

"Of course," he grumbled. He could pay her now with his remaining money, but he decided to wait. If he wasn't able to get the bank in Deadwood to wire him a note for a wagon and supplies, he might need that cash to get them home. What he needed right now was a tale that would keep Emmalyne safely here until he *could* get her home.

"Take care of her," he said, glancing toward the door at the top of the stairs. "We haven't known each other all that long. Mail-order bride, you know."

Mrs. Beckett's eyebrows rose. "I see. How . . . interesting."

Clearly, she wanted to know more. Thayne grinned inwardly as he stood there, watching as she struggled against asking him. No doubt she was imagining what a juicy piece of gossip she'd have to share with her friends. He turned his hat in his hand, a thoughtful look on his face as he constructed his tale. "She's a city girl. We wrote a couple of letters. I took the train and met her in Chicago, and we were married. Next day we boarded the train heading back to Colorado, then three days ago, in the middle of Nebraska, that train was waylaid by outlaws."

"Oh my," Mrs. Beckett exclaimed, one hand covering her heart. "I suppose it was dreadful."

He nodded emphatically.

"Were there many of them—outlaws, I mean? Do you know what they were after? Was there some special cargo on the train?" Mrs. Beckett's tongue practically tripped over itself as she struggled to get all her questions out.

"I'm not certain what they were after," Thayne said. "But they threw all us men off the train, myself included. But Emmalyne, my little Emma—"A half smile touched his lips as he remembered the way she'd fought *him* on the train. "She launched herself at the nearest outlaw, somehow threw him off balance, then she jumped right outta that train after me. We both nearly died."

"I'd wondered at her bruises," Mrs. Beckett said.

Have you now? Good thing I thought to explain these few things, then. "Once we'd recovered enough to walk, we started out along the track. Trouble was, we didn't have much in the way of food or water. After a bit, we ventured away from the rail line, searching for a spring to get us by." Thayne shrugged. "That's about the whole of it—oh, *except* for the holes." He touched his shoulder gingerly. "Outlaws shot me twice. I lost a fair amount of blood. Emmalyne took care of me." He looked up the stairs again with what he hoped was a tender expression.

"Only thing I did was carry her here after she stepped in that snake's path. But you see, she's had a time of it—hardly slept at all except with me to comfort her. She's had terrible nightmares about them outlaws." Thayne shook his head. "Heck of a way to start a marriage."

"Well she's sleeping beautifully now. Must be the tonic." Mrs. Beckett studied him for a long minute. "Unbutton your shirt, Mr. Kendrich." She folded her arms across her chest, waiting expectantly.

He stared at her. "Excuse me?"

"That's quite a tale you've just told, and I wish to see if it's true. Beyond that, you may be in need of some doctoring yourself."

"I'm well enough," Thayne grumbled. But he began unbuttoning his shirt, only too eager to have such proof to offer the doctor's wife. When he'd undone the last button, he pulled the shirt back as much as he could. Carrying Emmalyne had hurt, but rotating his shoulder brought a fair amount of pain as well.

Mrs. Beckett stepped forward, lips pursed as she inspected his wounds.

Thayne grimaced, then swore under his breath as her fingers tugged at the makeshift bandages stuck to his skin with a mixture of dried blood and sweat.

"Hush now," Mrs. Beckett scolded. "From the looks of this, it appears that maybe you are in need of a bed." A genuine smile touched her lips. "A bed and a spoonful of Humphrey's Homeopathic Number 28." She stepped aside and directed her newest patient up the stairs. "Arthur will be singing a different tune when he discovers I've cured not one but *two* patients in his absence."

CHAPTER 11

THAYNE WHISTLED CHEERFULLY AS HE left the bank and headed toward the livery. The promissory note from Deadwood had arrived that morning, and he was out to purchase a team of horses, a wagon, and supplies for the remainder of their trip and the winter ahead. Had Emmalyne recovered faster, he'd have simply bought a couple of horses for them to ride, but she'd slept most of the past two days, waking only for short periods of time.

He was worried about her slow recovery—more worried that her already tiny frame was shrinking further without proper nourishment—but he hoped that would soon be amended. After being forced himself to take Mrs. Beckett's nasty tonic, then sleeping like the dead for the next twelve hours, he was pretty certain he knew what was causing Emmalyne's continued drowsiness. Fortunately, today *Doctor* Beckett was around to keep his wife out of the sickroom. Thayne fervently hoped they'd see vast improvement in their patient by evening.

Thinking about Emmalyne and what the two of them would need to get to the Lakota camp and then home, Thayne paused in front of one of Sidney's two general stores. He watched through the window as two women talked over a bolt of fabric, their heads bent in conversation. He thought of Emmalyne's torn brown wool, her discarded corset, her ruined shoes. He hadn't done right by her at all, and it was time he changed that—time he showed the woman he expected such great help from that he could provide all she needed. And even a little more.

* * *

"I need to send a telegraph," Emmalyne insisted as she tried—with only partial success—to sit up in bed. Her head felt twice its normal weight, and the room spun dizzily, the man and woman standing over her moving in and out of focus. Emmalyne concentrated all her efforts on the woman. "I'm supposed to be in Sterling, but outlaws boarded our train. One abducted me and—"

"I *told* you. She still needs that tonic." Hands on hips, the woman looked from Emmalyne to the man beside her.

He wagged a finger. "It's the gosh-darned tonic caused her to hallucinate in the first place."

"You're wrong, Arthur. For once, just please admit that you—are—wrong. Her husband told me she's had nightmares ever since they were waylaid by those outlaws."

"I don't have a husband!" Emmalyne's voice was shrill, and she gripped the covers, pulling herself up straighter. "I'm a schoolteacher. I answered an advertisement to go to Colorado."

"There, there, dear." The woman sent one more glare the doctor's way then sat on the edge of the bed and took Emmalyne's hand in her own. "I'm Mrs. Beckett, and this is my husband, *Doc* Beckett. I know it's difficult, but let's try to help you remember where you are. You were on your way to Colorado, just after you were *married*."

"No—I . . ."

"It's only natural you'd forget," Mrs. Beckett interrupted. "You were barely wed when those bandits stopped that train. You remember being on the train now, don't you?"

"Yes. But I'm not—"

"Do you remember getting bitten by a snake?" she prodded.

Emmalyne shuddered. She'd likely never forget. She had walked that day until she was certain her feet were going to fall off, and then out of nowhere, the snake had struck. "I'd almost made it. I was almost safe, and that horrid snake bit me." Her temper flared again. She brought a hand to her head, massaging her temple as she looked up at the couple imploringly. "I was trying to get away, and I was even going to get help for Mr. Kendrich."

"Of course you were." Mrs. Beckett reached for the bottle on the night table. "It must have been terrible."

"You have no idea," Emmalyne said. "I nearly died in a fire. They shot him twice."

"Yes, yes. We saw his wounds. You were a good wife to treat him so carefully." Mrs. Beckett arched an eyebrow and looked knowingly at her husband. He shook his head, but she turned her back on him, hand touching the tonic as she spoke soothingly to Emmalyne. "We'll have you feeling better in no time."

"She's already better." Dr. Beckett towered over his wife. "Give me the bottle, Agatha, and go down and fix this poor woman something to eat." He placed one hand on his wife's shoulder while the other tried to pry the bottle from her fingers.

"Arthur, I—"

"*Now,* Agatha." His tone was stern, leaving no room for argument.

Emmalyne shrank back onto the pillows, watching the peculiar exchange between her caretakers. With a huff, the woman stood, lips scowling, eyebrows drawn together. Her husband held his hand out, clearly expecting her to give him the medicine. With a pained expression, she surrendered it, then stomped out of the room. He followed quietly, turning in the doorway to address Emmalyne.

"We'll bring supper shortly, and don't worry about any more of Mrs. Beckett's cures. She means well, but I'll watch her close tonight." Half closing the door, he stepped into the hall.

Emmalyne shut her eyes, head hung in defeat as she thought of what to do now. Clearly, Mrs. Beckett was not going to believe or help her, but the doctor might possibly. And Mr. Kendrich? Where was he? When had they seen his wounds and heard his twisted version of her abduction?

Married, indeed.

She felt the same spark of anger as when he had first demanded she get out of her seat on the train. Thinking of all she'd faced since then, Emmalyne knew she could still figure a way out of this mess. She just needed to get to the telegraph office. Wondering if the house had a back stairway and an exit other than the front door, she leaned forward, pushing the blankets away, her intent to walk to the window and survey the street below.

"You'll need some new clothes before you leave."

Emmalyne's hands froze on the quilt, and she slowly raised her head, looking at Thayne Kendrich, standing—hale and hearty—in the doorway. She met his eyes, crystal clear and blue, looking at her almost as if he were concerned.

"You're alive." It was a ridiculous thing to say, but all she could think of was the last time she'd seen him and the guilt she'd felt at leaving him alone and injured.

"No thanks to you." He stepped into the room and closed the door behind him.

Emmalyne drew the quilt back up to her chest. "You wouldn't wake up. I didn't know what to do. I left to get help." She didn't know why she cared, but it suddenly mattered that he believed she hadn't left him to die.

"I'm sure that was your plan," he said sarcastically. "Help would have been a little late, seeing how you left me with no gun, canteen, or hat."

"I left you a pail of water," Emmalyne said. "And what could you do with a gun when you couldn't even move your arm?"

"And my *hat*?" Thayne walked closer, tossing a package on the bed.

"It was hot," Emmalyne said, defending herself. "I thought it might help me get to Sidney without fainting again."

"Nice try, and I might have believed it, except Mrs. Beckett just told me how you said you were almost safe when that snake bit you."

"I was!" Emmalyne cried, leaning forward, her hands balled into fists at her side. "Was I so wrong to want to get away from you, to get to Sterling where I'm supposed to be?"

Several seconds passed before Thayne answered. At last he shook his head. "Not wrong at all, Brownie. I can't blame you for wanting to leave. Trouble is, I still need you."

"You don't." Emmalyne shook her head. "What could you possibly need me for? You've gotten out of more predicaments in the past few days than most people see in a lifetime. Surely you can get whatever you need from the Indians—without my help." Her fingers clenched the blanket, and she looked at him, pleading.

Thayne pulled the chair away from the wall and turned it around. Straddling it, he sat, leaning closer to her. "You feeling all right?"

"Marvelous," Emmalyne grumbled, realizing he wasn't about to be swayed. "How long does snake poison stay with you? My head feels like it's full of cobwebs."

Thayne nodded, understanding. "That's not the venom—took care of that myself. And for the record, that's five times I've saved your hide now."

Emmalyne glared at him.

"Mrs. Beckett's tonic is what's muddling your mind. I had a dose myself, and it knocked me for a loop."

"I don't think she'll rest until she's given me more," Emmalyne complained.

"It's not likely I can convince her to leave you be, but how about something to take your medicine with?" Thayne reached into his empty holster and pulled out a shiny silver spoon. He held it out to Emmalyne.

Her brow furrowed a moment before her mouth opened in surprise, and she snatched the spoon from him. "My silver? Wherever did you find it?"

Thayne grinned. "Seems your dear old granny is staying at the Sidney Imperial for a few days."

"My gran—" Emmalyne stopped abruptly, realizing he'd caught her in her lie again.

"I said I'd bring her here so you two could catch up, but she declined the offer."

Emmalyne lifted her chin. "As I told you before, considering the circumstances, my falsehood was perfectly justified."

"Whatever you say." Thayne's grin broadened. "Anyhow, I persuaded Granny to return your bag."

"You've my entire valise?" Emmalyne asked, unable to conceal her delight.

In answer, Thayne reached down and retrieved it from below the foot of the bed. "Seems to be yours. Still got that heavy dictionary. I'll let you keep it if you'll promise not to hit me."

Emmalyne ignored his barbs and reached for the carpet bag. Cheered, she held it on her lap, quickly opening it and looking inside. A wistful smile touched her lips as she sorted through the familiar treasures, laying them out across the coverlet.

"She looks just like you," Thayne said a moment later as Emmalyne lifted a miniature portrait.

Her head snapped up. "You went through my belongings?"

"Only to see that your silver was still there. I wasn't about to pay good money for some old books."

"Money?" Emmalyne scoffed. "What'd you do, convince the old woman you'll work with her again on the next train robbery?"

Thayne shook his head. "Nope. Just got some money the good old-fashioned way. I went to the bank here in Sidney."

Emmalyne's eyes widened, and she opened her mouth, horrified. The portrait slipped from her fingers, landing softly on the quilt. "You *robbed* a bank? Did you hurt anyone? Are they looking for you? Oh my." She began shoving the books and silverware back into the valise.

Thayne rolled his eyes. "I didn't rob it. I wired my bank, and they sent a note. The only people looking for me are the Doc and Mrs. Beckett, waiting on me to join them for supper downstairs."

"Supper?" Emmalyne said indignantly. "Why should they invite a common outlaw to their table?"

Thayne shrugged. "Could be on account of how I've paid a pretty penny for your care. And Mrs. Beckett is particularly taken with me. I drank her tonic and survived to tell the tale. She's downright beholden to me for showing up her husband, not to mention she thought it particularly heroic how I carried my bride here while I had two bullet holes in me."

Emmalyne's eyes narrowed. "You're despicable. You—you—"

"Could charm the skin off a snake?" Thayne asked with a disarming grin.

She nodded vigorously, arms folded across her chest. "Thank heavens I'm no viper."

"My thoughts precisely," he concurred, rising from the chair.

"And we're *not* married." Her tone was sharp, but she couldn't help looking up, questions in her eyes.

Thayne laughed disdainfully. "'Course not. Tried that once before, and believe me, I won't be making that mistake *ever* again."

CHAPTER 12

EMMALYNE PILED HER WET HAIR on top of her head, leaned back, and sank down into the tub until the warm water lapped at her chin. Her eyes closed in bliss. *Heaven. This is absolute heaven.* For the first time in nearly a week, her stomach was full and she was clean. Such luxury seemed positively decadent.

She relaxed for several minutes, thinking of her father and all else she'd left behind. A smile parted her lips. Back home, if someone had told her that a bowl of soup would seem a delicacy and a hot bath an indulgence, she would have laughed aloud. But then, who knew a few weeks ago that she would be thrown from a train, marched across the scorching prairie, trapped in a fire, chased by outlaws, and bitten by a rattlesnake? Not to mention being slowly poisoned by a country doctor's wife.

With a sigh, Emmalyne opened her eyes and sat up in the tub. Recalling the list of horrors ended her peaceful respite. Luxury couldn't last forever. The water was already growing cold and the night dark. She'd best finish her toilette, get dressed, and be gone as soon as possible.

For good measure—who knew when she'd have the chance to bathe again—she ran the lavender-scented soap over her shoulders and down her arms once more. Raising her leg to do the same, she spied the neat *X* a few inches above her left ankle. The red raised scab did not make her feel faint, nor did the thought of the snake any longer make her shudder, but the image of Thayne Kendrich, lips pressed to her skin, did cause her to blush profusely and sink back into the tub.

Her eyes slid closed again as mortification washed over her. It had been bad enough when he'd held her foot and put her boots on. It was appalling that he'd sliced through the strings of her corset so she could breathe. But the thought of him lifting her skirt—even slightly—and pressing his *lips* to her leg was enough to make her want to sink to the bottom of the tub in shame.

What would her father say about such behavior? That she was a ruined woman—fallen—and no respectable man would ever have her now. She thought of Wilford, as respectable as they came, and was relieved she felt no regrets on that account. Still, Emmalyne did not want her father to be displeased with her. She wanted him to believe, as she did, that she'd made the right decision in turning her back on Boston, marriage, and society. She'd given all of that up to do something with her life, to make a difference—a contribution much more than her attendance at the latest soiree.

Emmalyne pulled herself out of the bath and wrapped a towel tightly around her. Gooseflesh sprang up along her arms as she hurriedly dried off and ran the towel over her wet curls that tumbled from the top of her head, dripping trails of cold water down her back.

As she rubbed her legs briskly, her thoughts became determined once more. Her father never need know any of what had passed in the last week. She could still continue on to Sterling, where she could have her year alone. The townspeople would come to know and respect her. She would be a marvelous teacher; the children would adore her and she them, and maybe, just maybe, some kind, intelligent gentleman would sweep her off her feet.

Just as Mr. Kendrich swept you off that train? No. Absolutely not. Thayne Kendrich is neither kind nor intelligent, and he is certainly not a gentleman.

Emmalyne shook her head to dry her curls and clear her mind. She wanted nothing more to do with Thayne Kendrich. Tonight she would leave, and a week from now she would scarcely remember he existed. *You won't forget him so quickly.* Her thoughts continued to taunt her. In truth, she knew it would be some time before the deep blue of his eyes left her memory or recalling the feel of his hand on her arm ceased to make her skin tingle.

Well, she would try hard to forget him anyway.

She reached for the package next to the basin and untied the string. Peeling back the paper, she saw a gown of soft blue calico. Her fingers traced the sprigs of white flowers dotting the fabric, stiff and new. *You cannot accept such a gift—especially from* him.

"I know," she whispered, as if to appease her conscience, though she knew she really had no choice but to accept the clothing. She had no idea what had become of her shirtwaist and brown skirt, and she could not remain in Mrs. Beckett's borrowed night rail forever. It was only right, Emmalyne reasoned, that Thayne had replaced her clothing. After all, it was entirely his fault that her garments were ruined in the first place.

Lifting the dress by the shoulders, she could not keep the smile from her face as her eyes took in the tiny buttons and lace edging at the neck and wrists. Though plain by the standards of Boston society, the dress seemed perfect to her. The lightweight cotton would suit the climate so much better than the wool of her traveling suit.

Setting the dress aside, Emmalyne removed a white bonnet, petticoat, bloomers, and corset—minus the whalebone stays. She felt her face warm again as she imagined Mr. Kendrich holding the corset and removing the stays. *Did he think he was doing me a favor?* She didn't know what to think but continued to blush as she wondered if he had selected each of the articles himself. Another impropriety to be certain. She didn't even know of any of her married friends' husbands who saw to such intimate details of their wives' wardrobes.

She tried not to imagine Thayne touching each of the fabrics as she pulled on the bloomers and wiggled herself into the corset, doing her best to tie the strings. Once the dress was on and she'd finished with the buttons, she chanced a look in the glass above the bureau. The reflection staring back so shocked her that she took a step away, her hand coming to her mouth in horror. Unable to resist, she leaned close once again, this time bringing her finger to the tip of her nose to examine the cause of her distress.

Bright pink and peeling, her nose practically glowed. The only thing saving it from being the entire center of attention was the peppering of freckles sprinkled across her cheeks. *Where did those come from?* Pulling her gaze away from the appalling state of her skin, Emmalyne lifted her eyes, looking at her hair in the mirror. The soggy, tangled mass that hung limply over her shoulders did nothing to improve the picture. With a sigh that was part frustration and part despair, Emmalyne dug through her valise until she located a brush. With violent strokes, she began pulling it through her curls, wincing at each snarl.

"I *am* ruined," she whispered, furious. "What will the good citizens of Sterling think when I arrive looking like this?"

She worked at the tangles several minutes until her hair hung smooth and flat down her back, then looked around on the bureau and night table for hairpins but found none. Searching through her bag yielded only four, plus her two tortoiseshell combs, usually reserved for special occasions. With no choice but to use them to secure her hair, she wove the wet strands into a tight bun at the nape of her neck—not enough pins for anything higher or more stylish. But her hair was soon forgotten as she retrieved the last item from the brown wrapping.

As she picked up the pair of white silky stockings, she realized she had no shoes. The parcel was empty, and her old ill-used boots were nowhere to be seen. Just to be sure, Emmalyne checked under the bed and in each of the bureau drawers.

Nothing.

With a groan of discouragement, she sat on the bed, the new stockings still clutched tightly in her hands. He'd done it on purpose. Of that she was positive. Thayne had likely guessed she'd try to leave before he came for her tomorrow morning, and to ensure she'd go nowhere, he'd left her without shoes.

"The gall of that man." Emmalyne folded an arm across her middle and brought a hand to her chin as she contemplated what to do next. The Becketts were still downstairs. Perhaps she could sneak into their bedroom and see if Mrs. Beckett had an extra pair of shoes.

I can't do that. It's stealing. Emmalyne's hand moved to her forehead as she hung her head in shame. How could she even think such a thing? She supposed that's what came of associating with a common criminal. She wondered how long it would take her to repent and get back to her strait and narrow ways.

She couldn't steal a pair of shoes. *But perhaps I could borrow some,* she thought, with the intent to send them back once she had safely arrived in Sterling. But she knew at once that that idea was no good either. A thief was a thief, and that was exactly what she would be if she went poking around Mrs. Beckett's bedroom.

If only she might ask to borrow a pair, but after eavesdropping on the earlier dining room conversation, Emmalyne knew Mrs. Beckett would not be accommodating. She was much too enamored with Thayne to believe anything Emmalyne said. There would be no assistance from that quarter.

Forlorn, Emmalyne looked down at the stockings in her hand. Realizing she had no choice, she rose from the bed and placed them inside her valise along with her brush and the bonnet. She snapped the bag shut and held it to her. Slowly, she turned around and looked toward the bedroom door. It was simply scandalous to imagine walking through town barefoot, yet that's what she would have to do.

She had to get away from Mr. Kendrich. She had to get to Sterling.

And it had to be tonight.

Tiptoeing to the door, Emmalyne opened it slowly and looked down the hall and stairs. Voices came from below. She debated whether it was better to go now or wait until later when the Becketts had gone to bed. After a moment's hesitation, she decided not to wait, in the hope she might still find someone at the telegraph or sheriff's office.

With utmost caution, she descended the stairs, stepping near the edge lest she encounter a squeaky board. Once on the main floor, she paused to listen again. The voices came from the parlor on the other side of the wall. Could she make it past the doorway without being seen?

Taking a deep, silent breath, Emmalyne gathered her skirts, knelt down, and crawled toward the kitchen, hugging the wall as she went. Mrs. Beckett was a fastidious housekeeper, and Emmalyne's knees, in her new bloomers, practically skimmed across the waxed floor. When she was safely away from the parlor, she stood again, heart pounding as she headed toward the back door, eyes focused on the brass knob, her portal to freedom.

Reaching the door, Emmalyne stood to the side, peeking through the lacy curtain to ensure no one was outside on the stoop. The alley appeared dark and deserted—exactly as she wished it to be. Still clutching her bag, she turned the knob, opened the door, and stepped outside, free at last.

CHAPTER 13

EMMALYNE WINCED AS HER BARE feet touched the cold, sharp gravel. She did her best to ignore the discomfort, walking as quickly as possible toward what she hoped was the town center.

"Bit cool to be without shoes tonight, don't you think?"

She took another step before her mind registered Thayne's voice. Snapping her head up, she saw him leaning casually against a clothesline post in the next yard. With a gasp, she turned and fled in the direction she'd just come, her panicked thoughts tumbling over one another as her feet did their best to keep her body upright on the uneven ground.

Racing up the steps, she flung open the Becketts' back door, then slammed it shut, wishing she had the key for the lock. She hurried through the kitchen, slowing momentarily as she passed in front of the parlor on her way to the front door. Bobbing in a half curtsey, Emmalyne nodded to Dr. and Mrs. Beckett, half risen from their chairs.

"Thank you for your kindness. 'Tis most appreciated." Emmalyne didn't wait for a response but rushed to the front door, pulled it open, and ran down the walk—straight into Thayne Kendrich.

"Whoa there, Emma." He held her arms firmly. "I was just coming to get you. We're not quite ready to go yet."

"You—" Emmalyne looked up at him, confused.

"Jumped the fence," Thayne said, nodding toward the side of the Becketts' house. He turned Emmalyne toward the street and the waiting team and wagon. "I guessed you'd try to leave tonight."

"Is everything all right?" Mrs. Beckett called from the doorway. The doctor came up behind her, concern etching his brow.

"Told you she was eager to get to her cousin's," Thayne called, looking back at them. He released one of Emmalyne's arms and pried the carpetbag from her grip. She pulled her other arm free, but Thayne grabbed her hand before she could escape again.

"Let go," Emmalyne sputtered.

"We'll go in a minute, darling," Thayne drawled, his tone solicitous. "Why, Emma," he exclaimed, grinning as he shook his head. "You couldn't even wait for me to fetch your new shoes." He glanced down at her bare toes, peeking out from beneath the dress.

Mrs. Beckett clucked her disapproval and called out to him. "I think you'd best take some tonic with you, Mr. Kendrich. I'm worried she's still a little touched from that bite."

"No!" Emmalyne and the doctor both spoke at once.

"Come inside, Agatha," Dr. Beckett ordered, taking her arm just as Thayne had taken Emmalyne's. "Good eve to you folks. Have a safe journey." He pulled his wife inside with him and began to close the door.

"Wait," Emmalyne called. "I—" Thayne's gun in her back silenced her.

"We both thank you," Thayne called as he steered Emmalyne toward the street.

Behind them, the door shut soundly. Ignoring the gun, she began fighting for all she was worth, kicking and scratching. But in the dark and without boots, she was not nearly as effective as she'd been on the train. Thayne lifted her easily onto the wagon seat and, without letting go of her arm, climbed up behind her before she could jump off the other side. He tossed her bag in the back of the wagon.

"We can do this the easy way, or I can tie you up and feed you Mrs. Beckett's brew." He withdrew a familiar brown bottle from his pocket.

Emmalyne wrapped the fingers of her free hand around the far edge of the wagon seat and pulled, trying to free herself from Thayne's grasp.

"Still stubborn," he muttered, pocketing the bottle. He reached behind the seat to retrieve a coil of rope.

A flash of light at the front window of the Becketts' home caught Emmalyne's attention. "Go ahead and tie me up," she said, suddenly smug. She let go of the wagon seat and held her hand out. "You're being watched."

Thayne glanced at the window, gave a friendly wave to Mrs. Beckett, then dropped the rope on the seat beside him. He turned to Emmalyne, a sly smile on his face. "Let's give Mrs. Beckett something to talk about." He took Emmalyne's hand and pulled her into his arms.

Emmalyne opened her mouth in a shocked *O* then instantly realized her mistake as Thayne's lips descended on hers. She tried to purse her lips, tried to bite him, tried to do *anything* other than participate in the kiss, but somehow he made that impossible.

His lips were surprisingly soft and warm. They moved against hers patiently as his arms wrapped around her. One hand pressed into her back, pulling her closer. The other crept beneath her bun, caressing the nape of her neck, playing with the hairs that had already escaped their pins.

Emmalyne's eyelids fluttered shut, and for a moment she allowed herself to indulge in the entirely unexpected feeling of being held and touched.

Against her will, she felt her body leaning toward his, yielding to his demands. Her balled fists slackened, fingers sliding down his arms. A strange sense of desire stirred within her. Ever so slightly, she parted her lips again.

As surprised as she, Thayne pulled back and looked deep into her eyes.

"Well now." The words rolled softly off the lips that had just been kissing her, shocking Emmalyne right back to the present. She brought a hand to her mouth, shamed with the reality of what she'd just done.

Thayne looked away, grabbed the reins, and snapped them hard. "Giddyap."

The wagon lurched forward down the dark street. Thrown off balance, Emmalyne slammed into his side. He didn't reach out to steady her, didn't offer a word of assistance or even a threat to sit tight. Instead, he leaned forward, snapping the reins again.

Their pace increased, the wagon careening recklessly down the road and out of town, leaving Emmalyne no choice but to hold on for dear life.

At the window, Agatha Beckett let the parted curtains fall back into place. She stepped aside, one hand to her brow as she walked across the room and sank into her rocker.

"Well?" Dr. Beckett asked. "Will your patient survive? Are you satisfied?"

Agatha nodded absentmindedly as she picked up her embroidery and used it to fan her face. Somehow, *satisfied* wasn't the word that came to mind just now after the shameful display she had just witnessed.

She crossed her legs, foot pushing off the floor as she began to rock back and forth, knowing no satisfaction as she realized her husband had *never* kissed her the way Mr. Kendrich had just kissed his new bride.

With a huff, Agatha pulled on her spectacles and picked up her needle, stabbing it into the embroidery. It all made sense now.

No wonder Emmalyne Kendrich was in such a hurry to leave.

* * *

Hearing Emmalyne stir, Thayne opened one eyelid and watched as she took in her surroundings, tried to sit up, and then discovered her hand was tied to the wagon wheel.

"Morning." He tipped his hat. She turned away from him and began working the rope. He closed his eye again, resting a few minutes more, secure in the knowledge that she wouldn't be going anywhere.

"I demand you untie me at once."

Her tone was angry, as he'd expected, and he'd be angry too, waking tied up like that. But there wasn't much he could do about it so long as she remained uncooperative. He only hoped that once they reached the Sioux camp and she met Joshua that she'd soften up a bit.

Thayne opened both eyes this time, reached his hands up to stretch, then stood and went to the wagon. Ignoring his captive, he retrieved the makings for breakfast.

"Mr. Kendrich, I insist—"

"Woke up on the wrong side of the wagon, did you?" Thayne chuckled as he scooped oatmeal into a pot. A rock came sailing past his ear.

"I'll scream," Emmalyne said. "Untie me immediately or—"

"Go ahead," Thayne urged. "There's no one around to hear you." He ducked as a second rock flew past, then glanced down and saw she was shivering. He left the oatmeal, grabbing another blanket from the wagon as he walked over behind her.

"Here." He wrapped it around her shoulders. "It's not my intention that you be miserable."

"Well, you certainly could have fooled me." She sniffed loudly as she grabbed the blanket with her free hand and pulled it tight around her.

"If I could trust you not to run off . . ." Thayne let the statement hang in the air as he walked a few feet away and began clearing the ground for a fire.

"Where would I run?" she asked, looking around.

Thayne watched her from the corner of his eye. She looked so forlorn he almost felt guilty. Almost, but not quite. He had to think of Joshua first, and besides, Miss Madsen wasn't getting such a bad deal, either. Her new situation wouldn't be too different from what she'd have been doing teaching school in Sterling. When all was said and done, Thayne hoped she'd see that he'd been more than fair.

He gathered some kindling, then took one log from the small pile at the back of the wagon. In a few minutes' time he had a nice fire going and their breakfast well under way.

He walked over to Emmalyne again, squatting down in front of her.

"Seems I owe you an apology about last night. I'm sorry."

"Sorry for what?" she snapped. "Kidnapping me again, scaring me half to death the way you drove this wagon in the dark, or—"

"Kissing you," Thayne said. He caught her eye. "I'm sorry about kissing you. I had no right to do that. Didn't think it through too well— just wanted to convince Mrs. Beckett—"

"Of your lie," Emmayne finished.

Thayne stood again. "Guess that's about right. Anyhow, I *am* sorry. It won't happen again. And maybe we could call it even with the lying and try honesty from here on out."

Her eyes narrowed. "I lied out of necessity."

"So did I."

She looked away, pulling the blanket tighter around her. "No. It was entirely different."

Thayne shrugged. "Think what you like, Emma."

She didn't respond, but Thayne thought he saw her lip trembling, and he could tell she was even more upset than she'd been before his apology. "How about this, then? How about we make a couple of promises and then I untie you?"

She continued to look away, studying the wagon wheel as if it were a fascinating piece of art. "I don't believe I can put much stock in a promise made by an outlaw."

Thayne gave a wry smile. He walked over to check on their breakfast. "What I'm wondering is if I can trust *you*. It's mighty nice over by the fire, and I imagine you'd rather eat on your own than have me feed you."

Emmalyne finally looked up, eyes blazing. "I'd rather starve than have you feed me."

"That bad, huh?" Thayne shook his head. "Let me know when you're ready, then. You promise me you won't run or try to scratch my eyes out, and I'll untie you. I'm willing to give you a fair shake at honesty."

"*You'll* give *me*—" She gave a huff of anger and turned away from him again, muttering something about the pot calling the kettle black.

Thayne sat by the fire and ate his breakfast. He expected her to come around soon, but instead, she lay down and fell asleep once more. He knew she wasn't pretending when he bent to pull the blanket over her feet. His hand brushed her foot accidentally, and she didn't stir or kick him. Instead, her toes curled involuntarily, bringing a smile to Thayne's face as he went about the rest of the morning's work.

CHAPTER 14

EMMALYNE ROTATED HER SORE WRIST as she hobbled back to the blanket. Sitting down, she brushed the dirt from her bare feet, then carefully tucked them beneath the hem of her dress. Going without shoes last night was bad enough, but traipsing around with her feet and ankles exposed in broad daylight was entirely improper. To that end, she forced herself speak to Mr. Kendrich once more.

"Might I have those new shoes you spoke of last night?"

"Nope." His head was down, eyes focused on the chunk of wood he held in one hand, his knife in the other.

"Why ever not?" she demanded.

"Didn't buy any shoes," Thayne said, drawing his blade carefully down the length of the piece.

Emmalyne sat in stunned silence for several seconds. "How am I supposed to walk without them? How—"

"Moccasins." He finally looked up, laying the partially carved figure aside. "We'll get you a fine pair once we reach the Lakota camp. The lady's boots at the store in Sidney were just as ridiculous as your old pair, so I saw no sense in buying any. And this way the skin on your feet will have a few days to breathe. Those blisters can heal, and then we'll get you the most comfortable shoes you've ever worn."

Emmalyne brought a hand to her mouth, completely stricken. "No shoes," she repeated forlornly.

"*Different* shoes," Thayne corrected, raising his arm to his forehead, using his sleeve to wipe away the sweat. "Don't fret. There isn't any society in the Hills to concern yourself with. Trust me; the moccasins will do fine." He picked up the carving and went back to work.

Emmalyne let out a huff that said she didn't agree. She turned away from him, picking up the bowl of cold oatmeal he'd set out for her earlier.

Frowning, she pushed the spoon into the grayish mixture. She was hungry to be certain, but *this* hungry?

"Eat it," Thayne admonished.

Peering over her shoulder, she was unnerved to find him watching—waiting for her to take a bite.

"Parritch is good for you," he continued. "Sticks to your ribs, and your ribs could do with some sticking."

"What did you call it?" she asked, looking down at the bowl in her lap.

"Parritch—that's the Scottish name my mother used. Though it's oatmeal hereabouts, I suppose."

Emmalyne attempted to stir it as she tried to imagine Thayne as a little boy with his mother. She didn't want to imagine him that way, didn't want to think of him in any way other than a cruel, ruthless outlaw. She wanted no guilt when she finally escaped—and she *would* escape. Last night had proven the need for that more than ever.

Instantly, she wished away the thought, but it was too late. As it had already a dozen times today, the memory of his kiss returned. Her imagination easily conjured Thayne's arms around her once more, his hands surprisingly gentle, the caress of his fingers at her neck tilting her head up as his lips sought hers.

And she had kissed him back.

Flooded with remorse, Emmalyne squeezed her eyes shut, confused and angry with herself that she could not stop thinking about that one moment. Wilford had kissed her good night on three different occasions, and she'd never even spent one *second* pondering those—not that his lips had performed anywhere in the same realm Mr. Kendrich's had. Kissing Wilford had been like kissing a board. With Thayne, it had been frightening, comforting, and exhilarating all at the same time.

There. That was it. She'd finally admitted it to herself. She had not only allowed an outlaw to kiss her, but she had also *enjoyed* it. Overcome with disgrace, Emmalyne bowed her head, praying for her strength of character to return. *Forgive me, Lord. My defenses are down, and this man is making me crazy.*

A minute later, Thayne cleared his throat. "How long's it take to pray over one little bowl?"

Grateful for the distraction, Emmalyne sat up, eyes open once more. Reluctantly, she brought the spoon to her mouth and took a little bite. It was cold, lumpy, burnt. Her lips puckered in distaste. "This is horrid."

"Missing your cream and sugar?" Thayne asked sarcastically.

"Let me guess," she said in much the same tone. "You used ash from the fire as seasoning."

"Didn't think you'd mind much—after the way you enjoyed that prairie dog the other day." He sounded offended.

"Prairie dog? What are you talking about?" She shifted on the blanket again so she was facing him.

"At the soddie. Before the Martins came." Thayne arched his eyebrows, waiting for her to remember.

She did, rewarding him with a hand to her mouth and widened eyes. "*That's* what you fed me?"

He nodded.

"Oh." Her voice was quiet, much of the color fading from her face.

"Go ahead and eat," Thayne urged, his voice gentler. "A strong wind would blow you away about now. It's important you regain your strength. Back on that train, you were a force to be reckoned with."

Instead of responding, Emmalyne began to eat, obediently placing one bite after the other into her mouth and swallowing quickly. He didn't have to tell her she needed to be strong. The events of the past week spoke for themselves.

At last, she felt his gaze leave her. Seeing his attention once more on carving, she turned her face and took the opportunity to study him. His clothes appeared clean, if not altogether new—save for his battered hat—and he leaned up against the tree, using his hand and arm almost as if his shoulder had never been injured. The way he'd driven the wagon last night had astounded her as well, considering a few days earlier she'd believed she had left him for dead.

"How is your shoulder?" she asked before she could stop herself. It was another thing that should not matter to her. She *shouldn't* care.

"It's on the mend," he said, flashing her a half grin, half grimace, "but it hurts like—"

"Mr. Kendrich," Emmalyne cut in, knowing what would have come next. She lifted her chin and folded her arms across her chest. "May I remind you that you are in the presence of a lady, and as that lady, I must insist you take care with your language." She paused, then added another thought. "I doubt your parritch-eating mother would approve, either."

"My apologies," Thayne mumbled, not sounding the least bit contrite. "My mother is long in her grave, and I haven't been in the company of a lady for quite some time." He sheathed his knife and set the carving aside. Scooting away from the tree trunk, he lay back on the grass, pulling his hat low over his face.

"Are you actually going to sleep right now?" Emmalyne asked, irked that he'd ended their conversation so abruptly.

"If you'll be quiet long enough."

"Aren't you worried I'll run away?"

"In bare feet?"

She detected amusement in his voice. "Yes. I would. I *will*. The moment I know you're asleep, I'll leave."

"No, you won't," Thayne assured her. "You gave me your word you'd stay put, and you will. Might want to run off," he added. "But it goes against your grain to break a promise."

"Well, what of your promise to me?" she asked, indignant. "You said you'd tell me where we are going."

"I've done just that near a dozen times," Thayne said, exasperation in his voice. He rolled onto his side, away from her.

"But you haven't told me *why* I must go with you."

"Isn't it obvious?" he asked.

Seconds passed before she replied. She'd already come to several conclusions—all of them too disturbing to say out loud. "No," she said at last, her voice small again.

"You're a teacher. I need a teacher," Thayne said. "I thought you realized that from the get-go. I did ask you on the train."

Emmalyne tried to recall the scene of her abduction. Everything had happened so fast, and she'd been so terrified. Now that she thought about it, though, it did seem as if he had asked if she were a teacher. *But why not arrange for one in the traditional manner?* Thayne's answer didn't make sense, and instead of calming her, it troubled her more. There was something he wasn't telling her. *Something he doesn't want me to know?*

"Who am I going to be teaching?" she asked. "Is there a schoolhouse in the Hills? And *how* will I teach? My trunk with all of my books and materials is gone. I have nothing with which to work. Even you must realize it is impossible to teach pupils to read without books."

"You don't need to teach reading." Thayne rolled onto his back again, then leaned up on his elbows, looking at her. "I need you to teach language—speech, really. It will be a good long time—if ever—before he's ready for reading."

He? Emmalyne imagined an older boy, the big, burly sort she'd been worried about encountering in Sterling. "And who is this *he* you're referring to?" she asked, trying to keep the fear from her voice. "Am I to have only one student?"

"That's right," Thayne said, plainly ignoring her first question.

Emmalyne pursed her lips as her brow drew together. "At least tell me if I am correct in assuming this individual is at the Lakota camp."

"Yep."

A roiling sensation began in the pit of her stomach. *One student, who happens to be with the Indians. A relative of Thayne's—a younger brother, perhaps? But why would Thayne leave him there when they could have traveled together?* A new thought, more alarming than the first, struck Emmalyne.

What if he's worse than an older, unruly boy? Might he be . . . an Indian? "Why doesn't this individual simply attend school like everyone else?"

"He can't. There isn't a school for his kind," Thayne said, offering no further explanation. "And you're out of questions. I need to get some sleep before tonight. I suggest you do the same."

No school for his kind. *I was right. He's expecting me to teach an Indian our language.* Wrapping her arms around herself, Emmalyne looked down at the ash remaining from the morning's fire. For reasons she could not fathom, Thayne must somehow be involved with their tribe, and in order to have his *something valuable* returned, he had to bring them a teacher.

The panic she'd initially felt returned full force. She was going to be left to live with—and expected to teach—wild Indians, the very tribe who'd massacred Custer and his men not two years before. What would happen if she did not perform her duties well?

Emmalyne clutched her middle, fighting off both panic and nausea, the oatmeal she'd just eaten threatening to come up. She began to gag.

"Are you all right?" Thayne asked, sitting up.

"No," Emmalyne gasped. She rose to her knees, leaned forward over the fire pit, and began to retch. He was by her side in a second, holding her hair back, his other hand steadying her arm.

Another minute passed, and all of her belated breakfast was gone, her stomach settled—momentarily at least. She sank back onto the blanket, head down as she wiped her mouth. Thayne walked across camp to retrieve the canteen. A minute later he returned, handing her his handkerchief, wet and cool.

"Thank you." She took it from him, pressing it to her face.

"You worry me, Brownie," he said, squatting beside her.

She looked up, her brown eyes meeting his blue ones. "Then let me go. *Please.*"

Regret reflected in his eyes. "I can't," he said quietly. He reached behind her, pulling the bonnet up over her hair to shade her face. "I'm sorry, but I can't."

* * *

Dusk settled over the prairie as Thayne announced it was time to start out again. Emmalyne felt numb as she took his hand and climbed up onto the wagon seat. She'd slept away most of the day and still wanted to do nothing but the same. Sleep seemed her only escape from the nightmare she was living.

Thayne handed her the blanket, and she wrapped it around herself—prevention against the chill she knew would come.

"Here." He held out a pair of thick wool socks that she gratefully took.

She turned away from him, slipping the socks over her feet as inconspicuously as possible. When she was through, she faced forward in the seat again, hand gripping the side in anticipation of another wild ride.

He looked at her speculatively. "I wish there was room enough in back for you to sleep. As it is though, I barely fit everything we need into the wagon. But it's better to bring it all now. Once we're in the Hills, no sense in heading out again for supplies."

Emmalyne followed his gaze to the wagon bed, taking in all that was stored there. She hadn't noticed last night, nor had she paid much attention to it today, but now she looked with interest at the sacks, barrels, crates, and—*trunk* wedged tightly in the space. Her eyes widened, and she twisted in the seat, looking closer.

"Is that mine?"

"It is," Thayne affirmed as he lit the lantern he'd rigged to hang out the front of the wagon.

"How—where did you—"

"Granny," he said with a wink. "Seems your claim stub was in the valise she borrowed, so she went ahead and helped herself to your trunk too."

"Of course," Emmalyne said, the briefest smile crossing her face at the prospect of being in possession of all her belongings once more. "Did you go through my trunk too?" she asked, remembering his earlier trespass through her valise.

"Only glanced to make certain it was full to the top," Thayne reassured her. "I've no interest in perusing your intimate articles, Miss Madsen. Not that you'll have much use for such frivolity in the Hills."

"No," Emmalyne said quietly, her moment of delight spoiled by the reminder of where they were headed. As Thayne drove the team slowly toward the road, she found comfort in the sight of the bleak and endless prairie. So long as the land remained desolate, there was always a chance she could escape and find her way back to Sidney. She wondered how many days it would be before they reached the Hills and turning back would become an impossibility.

"Why exactly are we traveling at night again?" she ventured to ask, though she was fairly certain she knew the answer.

"Simple. Don't want to meet up with anyone, and the road from Sidney to the Hills is well traveled."

"Are you a wanted outlaw?" Emmalyne asked bluntly. "Are there posters advertising a reward for your capture?" She glanced at his profile, imagining a charcoal sketch of his face tacked to the wall in a sheriff's office.

Thayne chuckled. "Posters? No. Wanted? Likely very soon by the Martin brothers, as I paid the sheriff in Sidney a visit and gave him all the information I could regarding their whereabouts."

Emmalyne turned away from him, looking straight ahead at the horses plodding steadily along. She was grateful Thayne was not driving like a madman tonight. She wondered at his comment and whether he had actually gone to see the sheriff. Why would an outlaw do such a thing? It didn't make sense. But then, nothing had from the moment he'd taken her hand and pulled her from the seat on the train.

She shivered, then wrapped the blanket tighter around her shoulders.

"Cold?" Thayne asked, looking over at her. "We could stop and get another blanket from the back." He paused. "And you should scoot closer." He nodded at the space between them.

Emmalyne swallowed uneasily at his suggestion. Sitting closer was the last thing she should do, yet some traitorous part of her instantly admitted she liked the idea. In the oddest sort of way, it was comforting to be close to him. After all, he *had* saved her life numerous times now.

And that's all it is, she reasoned. *Nothing more. Thayne—Mr. Kendrich— makes me feel protected from the other dangers surrounding us.*

"I'm fine," she lied. "Plenty warm."

He shook his head. "It's not just that. Last night you got so tired you nearly fell out of the wagon. Tonight I want you to lean against my shoulder if you think you're falling asleep. It's a great deal safer."

That would be anything *but safe.* Emmalyne tried to discern Thayne's expression in the darkness. Likely the offer of his shoulder meant nothing to him other than a means of keeping his captive alive and whole. She needed to remember that, remember that he was her enemy. Mostly though, tonight she had to remember to stay awake.

CHAPTER 15

EMMALYNE PICKED FUZZ FROM THE toe of her sock as she looked at Thayne lying in the grass a few feet away, hat pulled low over his face. "How long have you been an outlaw?"

"'Bout six weeks," he said casually, as if such a choice of profession were no big deal at all.

"Hmm." She speculated on what it would take to reform him, to save him from a life of sin and misery. She'd seen glimpses of a good man inside, and she couldn't help wishing and wondering what Thayne could be like if he changed his ways and lived up to his potential. "That's not long at all. No wonder you're so bad at it."

"What's that supposed to mean?" Thayne grunted.

Waving a hand in the air, she said, "Oh, you know. You didn't bring any food or water when you kidnapped me. Then you only had three bullets and so lacked the confidence to use them that you gave the gun to me."

He lifted his hat, turning to look at her. "I gave you the gun to save both our hides. Had all six of the Martins come after us, the only thing three bullets would have done was ensure we both got killed."

Emmalyne completely ignored his defense, instead feeling inordinately pleased that she'd gotten his dander up. *Just get him riled enough that he'll agree to let me wander around a bit.* "And then there was the matter of you forgetting the sack of gold on the train."

"I didn't forget it." Thayne lowered his head again. "I never had any intention of stealing—joined up with the Martins' train robbery only on the chance I'd find a teacher I could borrow."

"*Borrow?*" Emmalyne choked out. "Is that what you call this? And for how long am I to be on loan?"

"Till you get the job done," he groused, pulling his hat over his eyes. "Aren't you tired? You were up all night same as me."

"Not really." She shrugged. "I can't seem to sleep today." *I'm too worried. We're getting too far from civilization and too close to the Hills.*

"Well, *I* can." He rolled away from her, signaling the end of their conversation.

Emmalyne sat quietly for a few minutes, biding her time until she knew he'd almost drifted off. She watched as his breathing changed and he exhaled slow and deep. Smiling to herself, she spoke up again. "Does your family know about this? Are they aware their son has taken to—"

"Gagging women who won't keep quiet so a man can sleep?" Thayne sat up quickly, turning to her, glaring with bloodshot eyes. "Miss Madsen, so help me, if you don't stop your yapping, I'm going to pull those socks off your feet and stuff them in your mouth—right after I tie you up again."

"Well," Emmalyne huffed. "I've never in all my days heard of a schoolteacher treated so rudely." She lifted her head a notch. "Fine. Have your nap. I shall—I shall go see the horses for company." She rose from the grass, brushing the dust from her skirt.

"You do that," Thayne said. "Pet them. Feed 'em some apples, talk to 'em real quiet if you like. Just give me an hour or two of peace."

"Those animals are treated better than I am."

"They're also a mite more cooperative and a great deal quieter." He brought his hand to his chin, rubbing the stubble there as he studied her thoughtfully. "But if feeding you apples and patting your head would make you more pleasant, I'd be happy to oblige. Though with your sour disposition, maybe sugar cubes are required."

Emmalyne's fists balled at her sides. She'd intended to irritate him, but somehow he'd managed to turn the tables, throwing barbs her way. "Mr. Kendrich, *you* are what has rendered my disposition sour. Before being forced to endure your company, I was wholly pleasant. But you—you have ruined me."

"Careful with your words, Miss Madsen. Even out west a ruined woman means one thing. And you and I are both aware that nothing of the sort has happened. Nor will it ever."

With her face scarlet, Emmalyne turned on her heel and walked toward the wagon. *As if anyone will believe* that *if I survive this ordeal.* She retrieved two apples from a barrel near the back. Slowing her pace, she moved toward the horses that were tethered a short distance away.

"Emma," Thayne called.

"What?" she snapped, stopping midstride.

"Don't get any ideas about running. It's dangerous out there, and I'd find you anyway. Promise me you won't run."

"I give you my word." *For now.* She didn't consider lying to an outlaw a real sin.

Her show of bravery ended as she continued toward the horses. She placed one apple in her pocket but kept the other one ready. When she was near enough, she reached out tentatively to touch the first horse.

It nickered, lowering its head to take the apple from her other hand. Emmalyne released the breath she'd been holding and felt her heartbeat slow as she realized the animal was quite gentle. She stood there several minutes, nose to nose with her means to freedom. She'd hoped Thayne would agree to let her walk around a bit so she could escape on foot. But *this* was even better. Leaning to the side, she studied the horse's back, calculating the height, deciding how she could best mount it. A smile curved her lips as she glanced over her shoulder at Thayne, already drifting off to sleep. She looked at the horse again and whispered.

"Oh, I most definitely won't *run*."

CHAPTER 16

EMMALYNE WAS RIGHT. I AM a lousy outlaw. Thayne ran across the prairie, eyes trained on the ground as he tried to follow the faint hoofprints on the dusty earth. He couldn't believe he'd let Joshua's teacher escape again— this time on horseback.

He studied the ground and noticed when she'd stopped walking the animals and begun riding one, leading the other. The way the tracks edged off the road onto the grass, he figured they had to belong to Emmalyne's horse. No sane or skilled rider would weave such a ridiculous path. He'd bet his hat Emmalyne was neither. Likely, she'd never even been on a horse before.

Twice he stopped to catch his breath and consider leaving her to her own fate. Twice his conscience warned him he could do no such thing. Aside from needing her for Joshua and needing the horses she'd taken, a real worry for her well-being weighed in his heart. Like it or not, Miss Madsen was his responsibility. If anything happened to her, he'd never forgive himself. It was one thing to disrupt her life for a year or so, but it would be entirely different if he were the one responsible for ending it.

That, added to the other guilt he already carried, might well do him in. And this time, he'd have no one to shift the blame to. It was he who'd been so unkind today. He who'd told her to be quiet and leave him alone. For once, it appeared she'd done just as he had asked.

Thayne struggled on, ignoring his tired muscles and empty stomach. His parched throat demanded he stop for a drink, but he ignored the pain and continued moving. If he was thirsty, she was near dehydration. If his legs hurt from running, hers were likely stiff and sore from an afternoon spent clinging to the back of a horse. If he felt wary, alone out in the open, she was completely vulnerable—defenseless against any animal or human that might do her harm.

He remembered, all too well, the scene he'd come upon during his first visit to the Hills. A store clerk, intending to set up shop closer to the miners to make his fortune that way, had packed up two wagons full of merchandise, his wife, and his two daughters, and had headed out alone on the road from Sidney.

Fool, Thayne thought, not for the first time, though he'd refrained from calling the grief-stricken man that the day he'd found him weeping beside his dead wife on the side of the road. His daughters were nowhere to be seen. A lone man traveling these parts with three women was akin to walking willfully into a den of lions. The family hadn't stood a chance, and two days outside the Hills a gang like the Martins had put a heinous end to their adventure.

A chill gripped Thayne's heart as he thought of Miss Madsen meeting a similar fate. He was just as much a fool as the shopkeeper had been, and if something happened to Emma, it would be entirely his fault.

Five minutes later, he shouted with relief when he saw one of the horses he'd purchased in Sidney grazing quietly in the grass beside the road. Emma'd been smart, taking both animals so he couldn't follow. But at some point, this one must have gotten away, or she was far enough from camp she'd felt it was safe to let him go.

Slowing his pace, Thayne walked quietly to the horse.

"There, boy," he said, patting the animal's side. With caution he mounted and was pleased to see the horse didn't seem overly skittish. Whatever she'd done, it didn't appear Emmalyne had spooked the animal.

Bareback was not Thayne's favorite, but if Miss Madsen could manage, he certainly could too. Urging the horse into a gallop, he followed the road south, hoping he'd catch up with Emmalyne before dark and, more fervently than that, hoping he'd catch her before something or someone else did.

A half hour of hard riding later there was still no sign of Emma. The sun sank lower on the horizon, and Thayne's worry increased. He gazed out across the empty prairie, imagining her hurt, lost, alone—or, worst of all, at the mercy of some other man. At least when she'd left him before, she'd been within a day of town, and she'd had a gun and water. Best he could tell, she had nothing with her now. Nothing except an animal that had to be weary and her own misguided, stubborn will.

Grudgingly, he admitted to himself that he admired that will, admired her—liked her even. Enough that he'd spent the day trying hard to avoid thinking of her close proximity in the wagon last night or their kiss in Sidney and the possibility of kissing her again.

Last thing I need is another woman. Can't have one anyway—even if I did want one.

He rode on, retracing the path they'd followed the past two days. It was near full dark now, and he missed his lantern, missed Emma, and tried not to give up hope. As the last of the sun dipped below the horizon, it seemed the temperature went with it, and the perspiration across Thayne's forehead brought an unwelcome chill.

The road continued due south, but he had a sudden premonition he should leave it. He was nearing the sand dunes, a part of their journey that had deeply troubled Emma. Perhaps she had ventured off the trail, hoping to find another way around. Knowing full well it was best to trust his instinct, Thayne slowed his horse and moved over to the side of the road, searching the ground for any hoofprint, any clue that Emma might have gone another direction.

Some minutes later, his careful searching was rewarded when he saw unmistakable prints veering off the road and continuing east through the sand. He followed the prints about a quarter of a mile, then saw his second horse standing alone.

"Emma!" Thayne called as he reined in his horse. Before dismounting, he looked all around, eyes straining to see more than a few feet in the dark. He brought his hands to his mouth, cupping them. "Miss Madsen!" His voice echoed across the prairie, but there was no reply.

Thayne slid from his horse and quickly hobbled it with the other near a clump of sagebrush. He began walking a circumference around the animals. It was possible she'd met up with other travelers and left the horse behind. But if so, he reasoned, her horse wouldn't be so far off the road. He walked a bigger and bigger circle—until at last he caught a flash of white in the moonlight. Emma's bonnet lay at his feet. He knelt to pick it up, wrapping his fingers around it as dread curled around his heart.

"Emmalyne!" It was foolish to proclaim his presence so loudly, but he didn't care. Whatever—whoever had her—might be stopped if he made enough commotion. He ran in a staggering pattern back and forth, eyes straining to see anything. His boots kicked up dirt, and low growing brush scratched against his pant leg. He nearly tripped over a stockinged foot sticking up through the foliage.

Thayne dropped to the ground, reaching for her. She lay sprawled on the ground, limbs bent at odd angles, her skirt immodestly high on her calf. His heart lurched. At the least, she'd been thrown. Worse, she might—

"Emma," he whispered, his voice strangely gruff. Placing a finger at her neck, he felt a pulse, slow and steady. He pulled the canteen from his waist and unscrewed the lid, pouring a little of the precious water between her lips. He spoke her name louder.

Several seconds passed, and her eyes fluttered open. He expelled a sigh of relief and barely checked the impulse to gather her in his arms.

The vivid, painful memory of little Joshua, lying much as she was, flashed before him. Thayne felt relief anew, as he had the moment Joshua had regained consciousness after his fall down the stairs. But on the heels of that relief had come the devastating realization that his son was not all right.

"Can you move?" Thayne asked.

"I think so." She started to nod, then winced, bringing a hand to the back of her head.

His fingers brushed hers as he gently probed the spot she'd touched. "There's no blood," he reassured her. "But you've a fine goose egg to be sure. Must have hit your head when you fell." He held the canteen to her lips while she drank, then helped her lie back down. "Your legs all right?" he asked, trying to keep the worry from his voice.

Slowly, she pulled them together, then reached for her skirt as she realized her calf was exposed.

He'd have bet that even in the dark she blushed as he helped smooth the fabric down to her ankles.

"Thank you," she said and raised both arms to show him they too were fine, save for some scratches.

Thayne said his own silent thanks as he looked around. It appeared they were alone. Nothing else had hurt her. He looked down on her again, his face suddenly stern. Now that he knew Emma was all right, he had to resist the urge to shake her until her teeth rattled. "I told you not to run," he scolded much more gently than he felt.

"I didn't run. I *rode*. And I never promised I wouldn't do that."

Her logic did nothing to appease his temper. "Do you have any idea what could have happened to you?"

"Yes," Emmalyne said, forlorn. "I could have made it back to Sidney if I hadn't fallen asleep."

"Do you mean to tell me you fell off that horse because you were *sleeping*?" Without waiting for her answer, he gave a grunt of disgust and sat back.

"Well, it was difficult to ride, leaning forward like that—and I guess I was a bit tired after all," she sheepishly added.

Thayne shook his head as he looked up at the sky and the stars starting to come out. She was the most accident prone yet fortunate female he'd ever encountered. Who else could survive being pushed off a train, bit by a rattler, *and* thrown from a horse within a few days' time? That kind of luck couldn't hold. She had to quit making such foolish decisions.

He looked over and saw she was lying perfectly still. Perhaps she was hurt worse than she'd let on—or *sleeping* again. Not a good idea with that bump on her head.

"Emma, we need to have a talk."

"Shouldn't we be getting back to camp? What about the wagon?"

"I had to leave it behind," Thayne said sarcastically. "No horses."

In the moonlight he caught the chagrined look that crossed her face, but she didn't apologize.

"I'll have you know," he said, "that if someone takes the wagon and we end up without food and water, this time it will be entirely *your* fault."

"I suppose," she said, struggling to sit up. "So let's go."

Thayne noticed her grimace and put his arm around her, bracing her back. "Something hurting?"

"*Everything* hurts." She clenched her teeth together.

He pulled her against his chest, reasoning it was just so she wouldn't fall back. "Likely you'll hurt for a few days. You might as well relax for now. We're going to be here a while. The horses need to rest." Her head was just below his chin, those brown curls within his reach. He tried not to think about that.

She brought both hands to her face, stifled a yawn, then leaned forward, her forehead resting in her palms.

"Oh no you don't," Thayne said. "The horses get to rest. Not you. Sleeping after a head injury can be dangerous."

She groaned. "I'm sorry. About the wagon."

"You're sorry you got caught."

She turned her head, looking up at him. "*Especially* sorry about that."

"Thought so." He bit back a smile.

She made no reply but kept her gaze locked with his for several agonizing seconds. It was Thayne who finally turned away. *It's a good thing we're almost to the Hills where we'll have some company. I can't take much more of this.*

"I trusted you this afternoon," he said. "Enough that I felt I could rest without worrying about tying you up—got the best sleep I've had in a long while." He hadn't thought about it before now, but this afternoon had been the first time in months—eighteen, to be exact—that he'd slept well. Without his hand on his gun or worry in his heart. That realization, and what it meant, hit him forcefully. "It'd be helpful if you'd trust me the same way."

She scoffed. "Generally, I don't make a habit of trusting men who prod me along with a gun in my back, tie me to wagon wheels, and poison me."

Thayne rolled his eyes. "Of all the backward—I did *not* poison you, and I only tied you up the once."

"And the gun?" Emmalyne asked.

"I had to get you moving, had to get some space between us and the Martins."

Emmalyne pressed her lips together.

Thayne didn't bother asking what she was trying not to say. That she chose to be quiet suited him fine. It was about time she started listening. "Everything I've done since you went and got yourself pushed off that train has been for your protection. Tying you up was even for your protection so you wouldn't go and do some fool thing like you did today. What were you thinking, leaving without food or water? Do you even know how to ride a horse?"

"Of course I do. I had riding lessons—a long time ago. My teacher said I was the worst student he'd ever had, but no matter. I remembered what I needed to today." She lifted her head, and Thayne heard pride in her voice. "And I have an apple in my pocket." Her back stiffened. "Forgive me if I didn't see the need to pack a proper picnic. The most important thing seemed getting away from *you*. You said the road from Sidney was well traveled. I fully expected to find assistance."

"Oh, you'd have been *assisted* all right." It was Thayne's turn to hold his tongue. Grateful she'd stirred up his anger more than the other feelings he'd been fighting, he eased his arm away and faced her. "Do you have any idea what kind of people travel this road?"

When she didn't answer, he reached out and lifted her chin, forcing her gaze up to his. "Miners, gamblers, thieves. That's who you were like to meet. Why do you think we travel at night?"

"So you won't get caught by the law?"

"No." He shook his head, exasperated. "Because that's the best way I know to protect you. I'm only one man, and if we were to meet up with others, there's only so much I could do. There is *no* law in these parts, and the men going to the Hills are a greedy lot, looking to make a fast fortune however they can. Most would be only too eager to take advantage of a skirt passing their way."

"What did you call me?"

"A skirt," Thayne said. "That's all a woman is up here. You'll be a rare sight, and more often than not, the men you meet will think of you as just that—a skirt—and what's beneath it."

She frowned. "That's despicable."

"It is," he agreed, glad for the edge of fear in her voice. "It's a sorry state of affairs up in the Hills—lawless and corrupt. Gold does that to people."

"But not you?" Her words were laced with sarcasm.

"No." He gave her a wry smile. "Though I imagine you'd say different."

"You'd be right." Emma's face softened a little. Being careful to keep her legs covered, she pulled her knees close to her chest and wrapped her arms around them. "Though I must admit you're a rather—unconventional—outlaw."

"Think what you wish," Thayne muttered. "But if you're gonna survive up there, you've got to learn to trust me."

Emmalyne rested her chin on her knees. "I told you earlier: I cannot be expected to trust an outlaw."

"We shouldn't have a problem, then. You're the one who gave me that title. Truth is, you're the only person—or thing—I've ever taken without asking."

"I feel so privileged." She glared at him.

"I can tell," he said dryly. He studied her face in the darkness, wondering what it was going to take to get through her sarcasm and mistrust. *My way with women hasn't improved much.* Not for the first time, Thayne felt misgivings about this errand. *What if she flat out refuses to help Joshua?*

Emmalyne yawned and looked behind her, as if preparing to lie down.

"Oh no you don't," Thayne said, capturing her arm. "Sleep on the way back."

"On a horse? That didn't go too well last time—remember?" She touched the back of her head, gently probing the bump there.

"It'll be safe enough. You'll ride with me."

"I'd prefer not," she said.

"Makes two of us," Thayne said, though he doubted their reasons were anywhere close to being the same. "But since the horses need to rest, you can answer some questions. It'll help you stay awake. What made you decide on teaching? Why not stay home and let Daddy take care of you?"

Emmalyne frowned. "Maybe I didn't want to be taken care of. I'm quite capable on my own."

Yes. I know. Thayne refrained from mentioning the many predicaments he'd had to rescue her from in the past week and a half. "Did your father approve of your decision?"

She hesitated, avoiding his gaze as she turned to stare out at the dark prairie. "He didn't know of my decision. And as I haven't had a letter, I am unsure of his feelings now."

"He's probably worried."

"Angry," she corrected. "By now he's furious."

"I wouldn't be so sure," Thayne said. "What'd you two fight about that drove you away?"

"We didn't—"

"Ah—" Thayne cut her off. "You've already talked some in your sleep, so you might as well tell me the rest."

"I don't see why you've any need to know." She pouted, and her lips pushed together, full and soft, reminding him once again how pleasant kissing her had been.

"Oh, very well," she said at last. "My father and I had a *disagreement* about my fiancé."

Fiancé? Thayne waited for her to go on, though what she'd just revealed unsettled him more than he wanted to admit. He hadn't considered the possibility that she belonged to someone. When he'd first seen her on the train, he'd never in a hundred years have believed there was any likelihood she was betrothed. But then, that woman looked vastly different from the one before him now.

Gone was the severe bun, in its place a disheveled mop of honey-colored hair that fell halfway to her waist. Her skin, no longer pale, glowed from days in the sun, and a delightful sprinkling of freckles had popped up across her cheeks and the bridge of her nose, making her look younger than ever. Thayne reminded himself to ask how old she was.

The blue calico he'd purchased for her was a vast improvement over the ugly traveling suit, showing off her slender figure instead of hiding it.

And her eyes—those deep, expressive eyes—heaven help him. If she ever figured out how to use those to her advantage, he'd be in real trouble. Topping all that off was the knowledge that hiding her sassy mouth and sharp tongue were lips that begged to be kissed.

How on earth had he missed all that at first glance? Looking at her now and seeing the differences, he wondered, suddenly, if her getup had all been a ruse.

"Your father didn't care for your beau?" Thayne prompted when she didn't volunteer more of the story.

She shook her head. "*I* did not care for him. But Papa gave Wilford his blessing. Our engagement was announced at a very public affair. I had no choice but to go along with it or suffer all of us to endure complete humiliation."

Thayne frowned at the picture she'd just painted. He imagined Emma, chin held high, fierce pride holding her emotions in check, as she stood by a man she did not love and endured an evening of congratulations. Was there no one that considered her feelings?

"And your mother? Did she support your father in his decision? Did she feel the same?" Thayne asked.

"My mother is dead," Emmalyne said. "But no, she would not have forced my engagement. She didn't care much about what others thought about society. She was very—"

"Outspoken," Thayne guessed.

Emmalyne's mouth curved in a smile. "No, actually. My mother never gave a speech in her life, never talked to those in the social circles. Yet, in her quiet way, she still made her views known. I've no doubt that I shouldn't have been in this predicament were she alive."

"I'm sorry," Thayne said.

"Yes, well I had to leave," Emmalyne continued, brushing off his sympathy as she brushed at a corner of her eye. "It was the only way out. I found a position as a nanny, but then I saw the advertisement for a teacher in Sterling. It seemed a good solution—the right thing to do. I purchased a ticket and borrowed some clothes from the charity bin at church."

"*Borrowed?*"

"Very well, I took them," she admitted. "It was after the Wednesday evening Ladies' Aid meeting. I took the brown suit and left my own gown behind as replacement. I'm certain the person who got the dress enjoyed it much more than she would have that awful suit."

Thayne chuckled. "Point conceded. Go on."

"And that's all. My friend helped get my trunk to the station, and I was well on my way—until a certain *outlaw* pulled me from my seat on the train." She gave him a knowing look. "*Now* may we go?"

"Not yet."

"But I answered your questions," she protested. "Surely the horses are rested."

Thayne shook his head. "You didn't see how hard I rode trying to find you."

Emmalyne looked longingly at the ground behind her. "At least let me sleep, then."

"Nope," he said without a trace of sympathy. "By answering my questions, you've paid for stealing one horse. You've still got to pay off the other one."

She gasped. "I owe you nothing, Mr. Kendrich. I should like to know how it is *you* intend to make up for stealing my freedom."

"Answer a few more questions, and then I'll tell you."

"Whatever happened to ladies first?"

"You *are* going first." Thayne grinned. "You talk, then I will."

She pressed her lips together and looked away.

"It'll be worth your while," Thayne promised. "You'll be more than fairly compensated for your services as a teacher."

"No amount of money—or gold—can replace freedom." Her voice quavered, and Thayne knew he'd just about pushed her too far. Still, he had to know more about this fiancé. If she cared for this man at all, it'd be better to turn around and put her on the next train home. He needed a teacher with her head on straight, not some female who'd spend the year pining for her lost love. "Why didn't you care for your fiancé?"

Emmalyne looked surprised, then uncomfortable with his question.

"Was he unkind to you?" Thayne asked. "Did he—"

"No. Nothing like that." She waved her hand, dismissing the idea. "Wilford didn't have a mean bone in his body. In fact . . ." She hesitated. "I think that was part of the problem. He was spineless and a *complete* fop, caring for nothing other than his father's bank and social functions—the purpose of which was to make an appearance and outshine one's peers. He was boring, egotistical—"

She caught herself, as if realizing what she was saying and to whom she was saying it. She took a deep breath. "Sorry," she said meekly. "That's more than you wanted to know."

It was *exactly* what he'd wanted to know. He was relieved she harbored no affection for the man and that a life of certain boredom was all she'd fled. Feeling for the first time that he was making some progress, Thayne said, "So, in part at least, you came west for adventure."

"I suppose that's fair," she admitted. "But I think I've had enough now." She gave him a half smile.

His heart twisted. "Would you like to go back? If I offered you a ticket home, would you take it?"

"I'd take it and trade it for a ticket to Sterling."

He hated the hopeful expression on her face. "That's not what I asked. What I want to know is whether you'd rather be home or here—with me."

Her answer was slow in coming, but finally she whispered, "Here." Her expression told him she was as surprised by the admission as he was. "I don't want to go home." Her eyes searched his. "But I want to feel safe again."

"Fair enough," he said. "There are some things you should know."

Emmalyne nodded. She still held her knees close to her chest, and she swallowed nervously. Somehow her confession that she'd rather stay with him than go home had changed things. Looking at her now, Thayne was certain she felt the subtle shift as much as he did.

"For all my poor planning as an *outlaw*, I did not choose you idly from that train. I'd almost say God mighta had a hand in it."

"God wouldn't—"

"I know what you're thinking," Thayne said, cutting off her protests. "God wouldn't lead me to do something bad. But think about this. I was able to learn all about the Martins, their plans, their hideout. Because of me, the law is after them now, and chances are, the gang will be stopped before they can hurt too many more people."

"I don't know what to think about that," Emmalyne admitted.

"Don't think. Just feel the truth of it. I walked up and down the aisle of that train without even looking at the occupants. I knew if I trusted my gut—my God-given instinct—that I'd find the right woman. And I did.

"When I felt it, I looked down, and there you were, a prim and proper schoolteacher with a dictionary in your bag to boot. I knew you were meant to help me."

"That's all well and fine for you," Emmalyne said. "But *I* have no such reassurance. All the while you were trying to get me off that train, I was praying to the Lord to *save* me."

"Seems He did just that," Thayne said.

"I don't see how."

"What would your father do if he knew where you'd gone?"

Emmalyne looked confused at the abrupt change of topics. "I didn't suppose he'd find out until I wrote to him."

"Did anyone else besides your friend know you'd left? A servant, maybe? Because I'd bet someone gave you away. When I was in Sidney, there was an older man with your photograph asking after you."

Her head snapped up. "You think it was my father?"

"Unless Wilford is already balding and has your eyes."

Emmalyne covered her mouth with her hand. "My father *followed* me? I never imagined—I didn't think he would—" She looked at Thayne, confusion in her eyes. "What should I do?"

He repeated his earlier question. "Do you want to go home?"

She shook her head. "I can't. It's too soon. I want to be gone at least a year. But my father must be worried. If he's here, then—"

"I took care of that."

"You did?"

Thayne nodded. "Your father sent a telegram one day—I assume to someone at your home or maybe to your fiancé. I spoke with your father afterward and told him I thought I'd seen you on the train. He left his information with me, and later I paid a young boy to send a telegram to the same address."

"What did it say?" Emmalyne asked.

"You don't remember?" He arched an eyebrow at her. "It was from you, telling your father not to worry. That you'd safely arrived in Sidney and that your plans had changed and you were en route to your *new* position. You promised to write as soon as you were settled."

"I did?"

"Yes." Thayne nodded emphatically. "And you will. In the meantime, you're safe from your boring fiancé, and—" He waited a second then plunged ahead, opening the door for her to ask about Joshua. "And there's a boy who needs you very much."

"You *really* sent a telegram?"

Thayne hid his disappointment. She was still too astonished and upset by the news about her father to recognize the tidbit of information he'd offered. "I've not lied to you yet, Emma." Reaching into his pocket, he withdrew a folded piece of paper and held it out. "Only I didn't send it. *You* did."

Emmalyne took the paper and opened it. Thayne watched as she scanned the writing. She was very still for a moment, then looked up at him, her eyes shining. "That was very—very . . ."

"Thoughtful?" he suggested.

"Kind," she blurted, staring at him, a puzzled expression on her face.

He could tell she was struggling to reconcile his kindness with his other, outlawish behavior.

"If it helps," he said, half teasing, "remember I had ulterior motives. After all, if your father had taken you home, I'd be without the teacher I need."

She nodded, some of the confusion easing from her face. A minute passed in silence. She refolded the paper and handed it back, then lay her head to the side and closed her eyes. "I don't know what to think anymore. You've got me all confused. The line between good and evil, right and wrong, is supposed to be clearer."

"Clearer than what?" Thayne asked.

"Than me sitting in the middle of nowhere, having polite conversation with the man who kidnapped me."

"You're thinking too much," he advised. "Listen to your intuition. What's it telling you? Am I good or bad?" He waited, but she didn't answer. "It's when we don't feel it, when we *don't* listen, that we find ourselves in trouble. It's as simple as you knowing that marrying Wilford would make you miserable."

"My family is different," Emmalyne insisted. "Money and social status govern decisions. There is no need for intuition."

"Deny it all you want, Emma. But something led you here, and you followed."

He reached out, brushing his knuckles lightly across her cheek. She was half asleep and, by her own admission, confused. It was the perfect opportunity to kiss her again. He didn't.

"All I'm asking is that you quit fighting it, fighting me. Trust that I'll take care of you and everything will turn out all right." His thumb caressed her lip.

Emmalyne's eyes sprang open. She lifted her head, looking up at him from beneath long lashes.

His mouth curved in a smile. "Thought I'd kissed you again, didn't you?"

"Yes."

"Disappointed?"

"Maybe."

Her admission both captivated and worried him. It was all but an invitation, and suddenly he couldn't remember ever wanting anything as much as he wanted to take her in his arms and kiss her senseless. It was exactly what he could not do. Emma was to be his son's teacher; anything beyond that was impossible.

"Tomorrow, when you're not sleepy, I've no doubt your answer will be different. You didn't come here for a husband, and I didn't fetch you off that train because I wanted a woman. That line is crystal clear. I won't use you ill, Emma. I'll be keeping my earlier promise."

He rose, then reached out, taking her hands and tugging her to her feet. They stood facing each other in a path of moonlight, her eyes wide as she looked up at him, trusting—finally. Thayne felt emotions stirring to life that he'd long thought dead.

He forced himself to break the spell, keeping one of her hands in his as he pulled her toward the horses. "We'd best be off. It's a long piece back to the wagon."

She followed silently behind, and Thayne was left with the uncomfortable feeling that *he* was the one who'd just completely ignored what fate was trying to tell him.

CHAPTER 17

SITTING IN FRONT OF THAYNE, Emmalyne clenched her teeth against each step their horse took. Its steady gait felt more like a wild gallop, jarring her along one miserable mile after another. For the fifth time in as many minutes, she moved her head from side to side and tried to stretch her aching back and neck muscles.

"It's no use," Thayne said at the exact moment her mind came to the same conclusion.

"I guess not." She sighed and leaned back against his arm, giving in to both the idea that he often seemed to know her thoughts and that she needed his support if she was going to make it back to the wagon. She could barely endure sitting as she was—sidesaddle in front of him—and couldn't begin to contemplate straddling her own horse again.

"Are you sure today wasn't the first time you've ever ridden?"

"No, but it was certainly the *last*," she vowed, grimacing against a jolt as their horse climbed the embankment leading to the main road.

Thayne chuckled. "I'm impressed you held on as long as you did. Must've been two hours of he—" He stopped abruptly and cleared his throat. "You've a powerful lot of determination for such a slip of a woman."

Emmalyne tilted her face up to his, letting him know she'd caught his near blunder. "I was determined to escape."

"*Was?*" he asked. "That mean you've changed your mind?"

"For now." She voiced the truce they'd reached silently earlier in the evening. She still wasn't entirely sure of her feelings, though the knowledge that he'd sent a telegram to alleviate her father's worry had definitely changed things. No longer could she think of Thayne as an outlaw. A true blackguard would never do something so kind. As for Thayne's declaration that he'd had his own selfish motives . . . Emmalyne knew he could have found other ways to get her out of town quickly—or to get rid of her father.

The telegram wasn't the only thing weighing in Thayne's favor. There were other things she hadn't seen or hadn't *wanted* to see before. He *had* saved her life—and likely risked his own—when he'd pulled her out of the way of the train and cushioned her fall. Then there was the not-so-small matter of his climbing down a dangerous well because she'd needed water so badly.

He'd been shot twice while she was hidden safely away with his gun. He'd rescued her from a fire, treated her snake bite, carried her to Sidney, and found a doctor. *He's spent the past two weeks trying to protect me. Why didn't I see it before?*

With sudden clarity, she realized she was no longer afraid but felt safe and secure—content, save for her aches and pains—as they rode, Thayne's arms circled protectively around her. Along with this new sense of security, other feelings bubbled to the surface—feelings she didn't dare examine too closely. Though she knew if being in Wilford's arms had felt half this good, she would never have left Boston.

But she had left, and here she was. In the middle of the wilderness with a virtual stranger—a stranger she suddenly felt she knew better than many of her longtime acquaintances back home. Could Thayne possibly be right? *Did some instinct or higher power lead me here?*

Emmalyne remembered the minute the idea to go west had seized her. By then, she'd already secured a post as a nanny in Virginia, but something about the advertisement for a teacher in Sterling had captured her attention. By the end of the day, she'd made up her mind, making bold plans that would take her over a thousand miles from home. At the time, she'd rationalized that traveling farther made her plan that much better, but now she wondered if other forces had been at work too.

She had imagined teaching a classroom full of children in Colorado versus tutoring the pampered children of a wealthy family in Virginia. There was no doubt she would have a harder time in the West, but the appeal of actually doing something worthwhile was too much to resist. At the time, it had seemed vastly important. It still was.

"You asleep, Brownie?" Thayne asked, interrupting her thoughts.

"No."

"Thought you might be since you stopped your fidgeting."

"Just thinking," Emmalyne said quietly. "Why do you continue to call me that—Brownie? I haven't worn that awful suit for days."

Thayne chuckled. "Doesn't have anything to do with your dress. It's your eyes earned you the name."

Uncertain if he was complimenting her, Emmalyne felt an unsettling flutter inside. That he'd noticed the color of her eyes and commented on them at all was more than any other man had ever done.

Thayne misinterpreted her silence. "If you're not partial to the nickname, I'll stick with Emma—or Miss Madsen."

"Emma is fine," she said, her heart strangely warmed by the liberty he'd taken with her name. Only her closest friends called her Emma. To everyone else—her father and Wilford included—she was always Emmalyne.

"Well, *Emma*, is that your stomach grumbling or mine?"

"I don't know." Her hand went to her middle.

"At least one of us is hungry. You still have that apple?"

"I think so."

"Fish it out of your pocket, then, and let's eat." He pulled on the rope, slowing the horse's pace.

Emma carefully patted the side of her skirt, searching for the apple. Feeling a bump, she ran her fingers over the fabric and located the pocket. She pulled the apple out and held it up to him.

"Here. You can have it."

He shook his head. "We'll share. Ladies first. Take a bite."

Realizing it probably was *her* stomach that had growled—and was doing so again—Emma didn't argue but brought the apple to her mouth and took a big, juicy bite. "Mmm." She caught Thayne's grin as he looked down at her.

"Have you always been so outspoken about your food?"

"What do you mean?" She moved the apple out of his reach.

"You either love it or hate it. You acted like the prairie dog was a gourmet meal, but you whine for an hour about the oatmeal every morning."

"Am I that bad?" she asked, chagrined. "Honestly, I don't think I've said two words about food in all my life before last week. At home, it's served at the same time each day, and we eat in the dining room, making polite conversation. It would be strange—likely considered impolite—to speak of what we're eating."

"Sounds boring," he said. "I guess I prefer you overjoyed or ornery. Keeps things interesting."

"But out here," she continued, wanting him to understand, "I've been hungry for the first time in my life. I never know when or if I'll eat. I guess I no longer take a good meal for granted. That's it." She nodded. "I'm simply being appreciative of a good meal—or piece of fruit, as the case may be." She held the apple up to him.

"Appreciative and *picky*," Thayne corrected, amusement in his voice. "Though I am sorry you haven't had decent food out here. Starving you was never part of the plan." He took the apple from her, turned it in his hand, and took a deeper bite—right where she had.

Emma swallowed slowly as she watched him, appalled her gaze so often strayed to his mouth.

He caught her watching and, once again, seemed to guess her thoughts. "If we eat one side first," he explained, "my hand won't get sticky."

"Of course," Emma said.

Instead of returning the apple to her, he kept it, lowering it close to her lips. "Go ahead," he urged.

Left with no choice, she bent her head forward and took a smaller bite next to the one he'd taken. It tasted even better than the first, but this time she kept quiet.

Thayne lifted the apple, again biting where she had. He held it for her once more. She took another bite, feeling her face flush as her lips brushed his finger. *Thank goodness it's dark.* Against her better judgment, she looked up, watching his teeth sink into the apple. She closed her eyes, head forward.

"Want some more?" he mumbled as he chewed.

Emma shook her head. "No, thank you." She was afraid of what would happen if she ate any more. Earlier, she'd all but asked Thayne to kiss her, and he'd calmly refused—for very logical, *right* reasons. Now, here she was again, barely able to keep her eyes or her thoughts off his mouth.

She groaned.

"Soreness getting worse?" Thayne asked. He finished the apple and tossed the core away. "Lean against my chest and go to sleep. I'll keep you safe."

She knew he would. No longer afraid of him but of herself, she resisted the urge to snuggle against him. But the lure of worry-free sleep combined with the steady plodding of their horse finally lulled her eyes closed.

She was sound asleep when, sometime later, Thayne's arm tightened around her and he bent his head for just a moment. Cheek pressed to her hair, an almost inaudible sigh escaped his lips.

* * *

Bleary-eyed, Emma stared at the fire, trying to make sense of her surroundings, the morning—last night. Snatches of their conversation replayed in her mind, leaving her on edge, her emotions in no better state than they'd been the past several days.

Yesterday things had been simple. Thayne Kendrich was bad. He was the outlaw who'd kidnapped her and committed who knew how many other unlawful acts. But last night he'd shattered that image, telling her what she believed to be the truth—about himself and her abduction.

She vaguely remembered falling asleep, and she was fairly certain she remembered Thayne lifting her from the horse sometime later. It was what she thought happened next that had her puzzled.

He had given her a blanket, and she'd curled up and gone right back to sleep—or had she? Was it a dream, or had Thayne leaned down beside her, tucked her in, and told her he'd wanted to kiss her too?

"But I won't let you down, Emma. And I pray you won't let me down either."

Words remembered or imagined, she wasn't sure.

"Breakfast by the wagon wheel, promptly at sunup," Thayne said, reaching down to hand her a steaming bowl.

"Oatmeal, what a surprise." The words were out before she'd had a chance to think. Emma bit her lip and looked up at Thayne, but if he'd heard or minded her sarcasm, he didn't let on. Vowing to be silent, she lifted the spoon, blew on the oatmeal, and then took a bite.

It tasted delicious. "This is good," she blurted, completely forgetting her vow. She leaned forward, looking around the wagon, teasing about the possibility that someone who could actually cook had joined them in the middle of the night. "Did *you* make it?"

"Added more water and a bit of the brown sugar," Thayne said. "We're celebrating today."

"We are?" She settled back on the blanket and dug her spoon into the bowl again.

"Yup."

Emma noticed he seemed to be enjoying breakfast as much as she was.

"What exactly are we celebrating?"

Thayne rose, went to the fire, and refilled his bowl from the pot hanging there. He turned, fixing a look on her. "You're not running away anymore *and*—" He lifted his face, gazing out at the prairie. "By tonight we should be in view of the Hills."

CHAPTER 18

THAYNE PULLED BACK ON THE reins, bringing the animals to a stop a good distance from the road. Dropping the straps, he raised one hand, stretching awkwardly. Aside from being dead tired, his side was stiff and sore from Emma leaning against him the past three hours.

"Emma. Wake up." Thayne reached over, lifting her head from his shoulder. She barely moved, and though she'd been sleeping, he knew she was at least as tired as he. It was the first night of the past three that she'd fallen asleep, and he'd watched her fight it as long as she could.

Her eyes flickered open, and she looked at him. Thayne recognized her moment of panic as her mind tried to register where she was. The worry etched in the features of her young face caused him a moment of guilt.

Just a couple more days, he thought as he climbed down from the seat. *And then you'll meet Joshua, and everything will be all right.* He hoped—had even offered several silent prayers—that it would indeed be all right. But doubts nagged him. Christina hadn't cared for Joshua, and he was her own flesh and blood. *All women aren't like Christina,* Thayne reminded himself. Emma was, in fact, quite different from her. *Different enough that she'll agree to care for and teach a troubled boy?* He didn't know.

"Careful now," Thayne said. He held his arms up to help her from the wagon. Without standing fully, Emma leaned toward him, took a step, and caught her thick sock on a splintery floorboard. Still only half awake, she lost balance, pitching forward into his outstretched arms.

He caught her easily and swung her down from the wagon, wishing once more that his circumstances were different, or, at the least, that there was an easier way to travel—without Emma in such close proximity.

She steadied herself and murmured her thanks. Thayne was struck again by what a good woman she was. How many women would thank a man for a simple thing like help down from a wagon when they'd been forced to sleep sitting up in that wagon all night because they were being dragged—as Emma had put it—to the middle of nowhere? Not many, he imagined.

Since their conversation several days past, she'd been cooperative, amusing, even pleasant to be around. He felt bad now that he'd told her the horses had a better disposition than she. Turned out, Emma hadn't been lying when she'd told him she was perfectly nice—until he came along. He'd seen the other side of her these past few days, and he liked what he saw. Too much. Several times he'd caught himself laughing with her or telling her more of his past than he wanted, and he'd had to stop himself. There was no sense in getting too close to Emma or any other woman ever again.

Thayne tossed her a blanket, resisting the urge to unfold it himself and tuck her in for what was left of the night. But he'd done that much already and knew the more they shared moments like that, the harder their situation would get. He had hoped their truce would make things easier, but instead, it had only brought new, more serious problems. It would have been simple enough to keep Emma from running away, but it wasn't so easy to keep himself from running to her. A man got lonely, and a fine woman like Emma was a sore temptation.

He turned away, but not before noticing she took all of two seconds to throw the blanket over her and fall back on the grass, exhausted. Her sense of propriety was breaking down in more ways than one. Hunger and sleep deprivation made niceties like a proper table setting and a bed seem less than necessary.

It's good, he thought, *that she's leaving behind her citified ways.* Also fortunate was the fact that Emma seemed to be pulling away from him. While outwardly she was pleasant, Thayne could tell that inside she was worried. He sensed her agitation increasing the closer they got to their destination. He wished he knew what to say to alleviate her fears, but he wasn't certain what that was. Several times he'd started to bring up Joshua, only to back down. Somehow he didn't think telling her about his boy was going to help any. Likely, she was expecting a normal student—the kind she would have had in Sterling.

Still, Thayne reminded himself, Emma'd all but been dropped in his lap—quite literally when she was pushed out of that train—and he felt strongly she was the right one to help him.

He tended to the horses, then took his bedroll from the seat and spread it out a good distance from her. A sliver of moon hung low in the sky, and Thayne took comfort in knowing it wouldn't be half full before he held Joshua again.

* * *

The endless knoll of black—as it had appeared from a distance—gradually turned into a forest of deep green as the wagon rolled from the barren prairie up into the pines. Despite her fear over what lay ahead, Emma couldn't help but enjoy the change. Fields of wildflowers, rushing creeks, and tall pines surrounded them—right up to the very edge of the road in some places. The Black Hills *were* beautiful, and reflecting on the one and only time she and Thayne had talked about Indians, she suddenly could not fault the Lakota for wanting to keep this land to themselves.

Still, dread grew in her heart as did the silence between her and Thayne as they traveled. He'd hardly spoken two words to her today. He was lost in his own thoughts again, and that troubled her all the more. That and the fact that they were traveling by day now. Thayne had announced it safe to do so two days back when they left the main road toward the gold fields and Deadwood and headed northeast toward the Touch the Clouds Agency— one of several Indian agencies within or around the Black Hills.

If she'd thought the sand on the road outside of Sidney made for rough traveling, she was wrong. The roads in the Hills were like nothing she'd ever encountered. In several places, she could hardly tell they were riding on any sort of trail at all. Tall grass surrounded the wagon, and hidden within that grass were hundreds of good-sized rocks, just the sort for upsetting wagon wheels. Her hands ached from clinging to the side of the seat for hours on end, and she wasn't at all certain she'd ever be able to stand straight again after all the jarring and bouncing her back had endured.

"Might you—drive a bit—slower?" Emmalyne ground out as they covered a particularly rough patch of ground and she tottered to the side once more.

Thayne shook his head. "If we continue this pace, we'll cover thirty miles today. Only a couple more days, then."

Her stomach lurched despite its emptiness. She closed her eyes, wishing fervently that this was a nightmare she might awaken from. *Why didn't I tell him I wanted to go home? How am I ever going to teach an*

Indian? And who is this student and why *does he wish to be taught?* If only Thayne would answer her questions, but every time she tried to find out more about her teaching assignment, he brushed her off, telling her he'd explain things when they got there.

Hopefully that meant he wasn't just going to drop her off, turn the wagon around, and leave. Perhaps he might even be staying a while himself. That possibility sparked new hope. She'd grown to depend on Thayne.

Looking sideways at him, she decided to find out. "How long will we be staying in the Lakota camp?"

"Not long," he said, eyes trained on the unmarked road before them.

The stirring of hope grew. She'd purposely said *we* and—

"I've got two dozen head of cattle and a crop to get home to," Thayne continued. "I can't spare but a day in the camp."

Emmalyne's heart plummeted. He'd said nothing about her leaving with him. It was as she had believed all along. She was a trade for whatever it was he needed from the Indians.

Nothing more.

She let her eyes close again and even allowed herself to lean against his shoulder, certain she'd faint if she didn't. A moment passed, and she was surprised to feel Thayne's arm around her. It was oddly comforting and brought to mind the kiss that seemed an eternity ago. This time Emmalyne allowed herself to think of it without shame, knowing it might be one of a precious few memories she would have to hold on to as she lived and worked among a strange people.

CHAPTER 19

"Whoa," Thayne called, pulling back on the reins. He stopped the wagon beside a stand of pines and reached for the hand brake.

"Is something wrong?" Emmalyne asked with concern. Yesterday they'd traveled well past dark, and now they were just a few hours beyond noon. "Why are we stopping?"

"There's something I want to show you, and we're a little ahead of schedule." He climbed down from the wagon and held his hand up to her. "We're going to be at the Lakota camp tomorrow. I know you're worried, but I'd like us both to forget about tomorrow and enjoy this afternoon. We've traveled a hard road already, and it doesn't get any easier from here." His eyes met hers, and she was surprised to see her own concern reflected.

Maybe he feels some of what I do about our parting. Stunned at this possibility, Emma placed her hand in his, stepping carefully to the ground. It was reckless and dangerous to think of nothing beyond an enjoyable afternoon—*and what does he mean by that?*—with Thayne. Yet, that was exactly what she wanted to do.

What will one afternoon hurt? A lot when he leaves me tomorrow.

Ignoring all rational thought, Emma lifted her face to his and smiled. "I would be delighted to spend a carefree afternoon with you, Mr. Kendrich." *Returning to formalities with names is* not *going to return things to how they were a week ago. We've crossed too many barriers.*

"Want me to carry you, or are you going to walk in socks?"

"What I'd *like* is to get my other pair of shoes from my trunk," she hinted hopefully, though she'd made the same request—and had it denied—at least a dozen times in the last week.

"Go ahead," Thayne said, taking her trunk key from his pocket and holding it out to her.

"And while you're at it," he added, "grab whatever else you need or want for a bath."

Emma gave him a wary look as she took the key. "What did you say?"

"You heard right." Thayne grinned. "You were telling me a few days ago how you missed your bathtub back home, so I thought you might enjoy a chance to get clean. Fetch your things."

Hands on hips, she made no move to climb back up to the wagon. "Where do you propose to locate a bathtub? Is there a house—does someone *live* out here?"

He chuckled. "No tub. I've got something better."

She shook her head. "Nothing could be better than a warm bath." *He's lost his mind if he thinks I'm going to bathe in a lake.* "Thank you, but I could never—"

"*Emma,*" he said, his voice mildly exasperated. "Trust me."

She frowned, hating it when he said that. Hadn't she trusted him for a whole week now? She had no other choice, really. And, as Thayne so often pointed out, he hadn't let her down yet. "All right," she said, not sounding the least enthused. *A picnic, a short hike to a breathtaking vista . . . that was more what I'd envisioned.*

"I'll water the horses," Thayne said, walking toward the back of the wagon.

Emma climbed onto the seat, knelt, and then turned around so she could reach her trunk.

She put the key in the lock, turned it easily, and lifted the lid.

A row of unfamiliar cotton fabrics lay across the top. Her heart sank as she stared at them, then she sat down on the seat, unable to hide her disappointment.

"Problem?" Thayne asked as he filled a bucket of water.

"I think you took the wrong trunk," she said, forlorn. "Either that or the old woman had already taken my things from it." Emma nodded to the fabrics piled at the top. "None of this is mine."

"Sure it is," Thayne said. "I bought those for you. Didn't take but a glance to see that fancy stuff you packed wasn't cut out for life in the Hills. I bought you another dress and fabric for a couple more. But your belongings are still in there too."

"You bought all this?" Emma turned in her seat again. She lifted the first layer of cloth from the trunk. It was a deep red calico. Beside it was a pink then another blue similar to the one she wore now. Yards of eyelet and lace were wound in a ball beside a placard of buttons and several spools of thread.

She felt suddenly faint. Beyond embroidery, she couldn't sew! *Heaven help me,* she prayed, vowing silently that she would learn. Somewhere there had to be a book of instructions that could help her make a dress. It was as simple as that. Thayne had been considerate enough to purchase the materials for her, and she would use them.

Will he know if I don't? After all, he's not going to be with me after tomorrow. But he'll have to come back sometime if he's going to keep his promise to send me home eventually . . .

Emma pushed both the fabrics and her troubled thoughts aside. Right now she needed only a clean dress and an afternoon free from worry. Tomorrow would come soon enough.

Below the fabrics, she found a yellow dress with matching bonnet. She lifted those from the trunk and found a cotton chemise and bloomers. To the side of those, strands of brightly colored ribbons were tied together in a bow. She felt her throat constrict as she picked them up.

"Did you—did you buy these too?"

"Didn't know what colors you'd want," Thayne said, sounding almost embarrassed. He walked quickly to the horses and stood in front of them, effectively blocking her view.

Emma was grateful. She needed a minute to compose herself and get her jumbled feelings under control. *How long has it been since anyone has given me* hair ribbons?

Twelve years.

A sharp memory filled her senses, nearly stealing her breath away. It seemed silly that something so simple could unsettle her so much, yet tears pricked the back of her eyes as she sifted the ribbons through her fingers.

The tightness in her throat turned into an enormous lump that she tried desperately to swallow. She brought a hand to her mouth. What would Thayne think if she cried now? With all they'd been through, she'd yet to shed a tear. She would *not* shed a tear because, as her father always said, it never helped anything to cry.

Eleanor, their housekeeper, had often echoed the same sentiment. How many times had she said, "No use crying over spilled milk?" More than once, Emma had longed to ask if *everything* qualified as spilled milk. Was there never a time it *was* appropriate to cry? If so, she doubted now was that time, but it took everything she had to gain control of her emotions.

Taking a deep breath, she gave in to a bittersweet memory. For just a minute, she was ten years old again, enjoying a rare outing with her mother. She remembered watching her mother being measured for a new gown at the dressmaker's. Then they were off to the milliner's, giggling and gesturing to one another as they tried on elegant hats topped with feathers, birds, and ribbons. Emma had loved the ribbons most of all, and her mother had pointed to one of every color, indicating she could have them all. Together they'd created a rainbow for her hair.

The carriage had taken them home, dropping them off near the gate so they could walk, sharing a few more precious minutes together. They'd been skipping across the field, Emma clutching the ribbons in one hand, the licorice stick they'd just bought in the other, when the rain began. The sudden, swift storm seemed to come out of nowhere. They ran home, then Emma—sorely tempted to go out and play in the rain—had left again. When she'd heard the thunder growing closer, she'd run away from her favorite play spot beneath the canopy of trees near their home. But her mother hadn't known that, hadn't realized Emma wasn't there until it was too late.

Oh, Mother. Looking up at the clear blue sky, Emma breathed in deeply. *There is no storm. No thunder. No lightning.* Her heartbeat steadied. *It was a long time ago.* She lifted the ribbons to her cheek, savoring their silky smoothness, treasuring the unexpected gift. Her father had never bothered with such trivialities, and eventually, notwithstanding the great care with which she'd treated them, her rainbow of ribbons had worn out. The edges had frayed, the colors faded—just as the memory of her mother eventually faded from her mind. But right now it seemed to Emma that she held those same ribbons in her hands again, and she could see the love in her mother's eyes as they'd spent that afternoon together.

Of course, Emma told herself, *Thayne could have had no idea when he bought these what they would mean to me.* It was merely a coincidence. But such a thoughtful act required she return equal kindness. She would try her best to be positive about the afternoon he'd planned.

He'd finished watering the horses, and she waited, listening as he fed each animal a chunk of apple and offered praise for their day's work. At last he stepped into her view again. He looked up, likely expecting her to be ready to go and instead found her staring at him, the bundle of ribbons still held tightly in her hands.

"Thank you," Emma whispered. She swallowed, willing her voice to regain its strength. "You didn't have to buy me anything, but the ribbons especially."

"I know women mostly wear their hair up, and I got you some of those pins you use too." He shoved his hands in his pockets. "With all the jostling, they maybe fell to the bottom of your trunk, but I promise they're still in there."

"I like the ribbons," she said, hoping her smile conveyed a portion of what she felt. If she were to express all of it, she would have to jump down from the wagon and throw her arms around him.

"And I like your hair down." His eyes met hers steadily. "You about ready?"

Emma nodded, wishing away the blush she knew was staining her cheeks. She untied the bow and pulled the yellow ribbon free, placing it on top of the clothes she'd selected. These she put in her valise, then placed the other things back in the trunk and closed it.

"Grab a blanket to dry off with, if you like," Thayne suggested. She took two from the back—one to place her clothing on and one to dry off with—then accepted his outstretched hand and climbed down from the wagon.

He took the blankets from her and kept her hand, tucking it into the crook of his arm as they started walking. Belatedly, Emma realized she'd forgotten all about her shoes. Thayne noticed too.

"Change your mind about something?" he asked, looking down at her burr-covered socks.

She shook her head ruefully. "No. I just forgot. I was so overwhelmed by your generosity that finding my shoes completely slipped my mind."

He smiled, seemingly pleased with her compliment. "Well, it's not too far. And I'll carry you on the way back."

Emmalyne bit her lip.

"What's wrong now?" Thayne asked.

"I forgot clean stockings too," she admitted.

He laughed. "Well, then. I guess you'll just have to go barefoot again."

She groaned. "What would my father say?"

"Your father?" Thayne scoffed. "What would your fiancé, *Wallace,* say?"

"Wilford," she corrected him. "And he would be appalled. Barefoot *and* my hair down. Scandalous."

"There's no one I'd rather be scandalous with, Miss Madsen." Thayne gave her hand a quick squeeze then let go. They walked a few minutes more and emerged from the trees into a high meadow. He raised his arm, pointing. "There's your bathtub."

She lifted her eyes, gaping at what she saw. There was a pond, right out in the open, with nary a bush around it for privacy. "Oh no. I couldn't possibly." She took a step backward.

But before she could go any farther, Thayne bent down and swept her off her feet. She shrieked as he carried her toward the water.

"Put me down. *Please* put me down."

"If you can't swim, best stick to the edges. Water's shallow there." He didn't miss a step.

She began kicking her feet and tried to lean forward out of his grasp. "I hate cold water."

"Me too," he said, marching on.

"I'll catch pneumonia," Emma threatened. "You'll lose your teacher."

Thayne captured one of her feet and pulled off her sock. They were almost to the shore.

"Oh, please don't—"

He dropped his arm beneath her legs, and she fell, squealing as her feet hit the water. Thayne's other arm braced her back as she fought to catch her balance and keep her valise dry.

"You—" She looked up at him, astonished. "Why, it's warm."

"Yep." His wide grin told her he was pleased with her reaction. "Natural hot spring—there's a bunch of them in these parts."

Emmalyne bent her head. The hem of her dress floated on top of the water. Beneath the surface she wiggled her toes, relishing the warmth. She sighed. "This is delightful, Thayne." She let go of his arm, held the carpetbag to her chest, and turned a slow circle. "But I cannot *bathe* here. There is no privacy, and I'm not the strongest swimmer."

"Not to worry." He stepped back and set the blankets on the ground. "Stay put just a minute." He turned and ran back in the direction they'd just come. She trudged up to the shore, spread out one of the blankets, and set her bag on it.

Wrapping her arms around her middle, Emma shivered, feeling a chill now that her feet had left the warm water. After a few minutes, Thayne returned, a long branch in his hand.

"You can use this," he said, striding toward the spring. "Poke it down in the water around you, and you'll know how deep it is." He jabbed the stick down through the surface in several places, demonstrating.

"But I—"

"Enjoy your bath, Emma." He handed her the stick and tipped his hat. "You've my word I won't watch, and there's no one else hereabouts to bother you." He turned away, walking back toward the wagon.

"What if I slip?" she called out.

"Just holler. I'll be within earshot. Enjoy yourself," he called back, lifting his hand in farewell.

Her eyes followed him until he had disappeared into the trees once more. She stood there another minute, wringing her hands, trying to decide what to do. The warm water *had* felt sublime. *I really could do with a bath . . . Have I lowered my standards so much that I've taken to shedding my clothes in the middle of the wilderness?*

After an internal battle that lasted far too long, she decided on a compromise. She would bathe—with her clothes on. It wouldn't be a true bath, of course, but it would certainly be an improvement over her current situation.

Emma removed her wet sock and laid it out to dry on the grass. Then she gathered her soap and clean clothes, placing the latter at the edge of the blanket. She knew at some point she would have to change into her dry things, but she supposed if she were very careful she could do that while encircled in the privacy of the blanket.

She untied the strings of her bonnet, then took it off and placed it on the ground. She looked around once more and, confident she was alone, walked the few feet to the shore. Taking the stick Thayne had left for her, Emma stepped into the water again.

It felt even warmer than before. *Bliss. First hair ribbons and now warm water.* A smile spread over her face. Gathering her skirts, she bunched them up to her knees, poked the stick down in front of her, and waded out just a little farther. *This feels so good.*

She stayed there several minutes, gave another hesitant look around, hiked her skirt even higher on her legs, and walked in until the water was nearly to her waist. With one hand firmly on the stick and one trying to contain the bundle of half-wet, half-dry fabric gathered at her hips, she soon realized she was not going to be able to make use of the bar of soap, also in the hand holding up her skirt.

Emma waded back to shore, dropping her skirt as she got there. *Would it be so awful if I took off my dress? There's no one to see, and I can get so much cleaner if I do.*

Deciding it really was for the best, she moved quickly, unbuttoning her dress and stepping out of it. She left the soggy cloth on the shore to be dealt with later and hurried back into the water, reveling in the new freedom that came from discarding her outer layer of clothing.

After indulging in a few minutes of doing absolutely nothing but stand in the waist-deep warm water, she decided to wash her hair. With one hand still on the branch, she leaned forward, attempting to get her hair wet. Unfortunately, her corset made it difficult to bend so far. *I guess it has to come off too . . .*

Her fingers fumbled with the laces before at last the corset came off, and she flung it to shore beside her gown. Sinking down into water up to her chest, Emmalyne laughed out loud as she turned a circle, her arms outstretched, making waves on the surface. *Paradise. And it won't get cold, either.* She'd never been in warm water outside of a bathtub. The few, infrequent trips to the ocean she'd taken while growing up were nothing like this. This was delightful fun, she decided, and she intended to enjoy every minute of it.

She leaned her head back, dipping her long hair in the water until it was soaked. She took up the soap in her hands and began washing. It took several minutes of scrubbing and rinsing before she felt her hair was satisfactorily clean. She moved on to washing her face, then her torso— no easy task while wearing her chemise. But there was no way that was coming off.

She'd simply have to deal with the inconvenience of wearing a chemise and bloomers. *So long as I leave some clothing on, it isn't as if I truly bathed in the middle of the wilderness.*

She closed her eyes, battling some unknown and unexpected demon— this part of her that was having the time of her life, relaxing in a warm lake in the middle of nowhere.

With a sigh of discouragement over her own weak character, she scooped up a handful of water, let it fly into the air above, and then watched as it rained down on her.

A huge splash sounded behind her, and Emmalyne screamed, then clamped her hands over her mouth. She whirled around just in time to see Thayne emerge, facing away from her, at the opposite end of the narrow spring.

"You promised," she yelled accusingly. She sank into the water, making certain nothing below her neck was exposed.

"And I'm keeping that promise," Thayne called. He dove under the water and swam toward her, resurfacing a minute later—facing her this time.

Emma opened her mouth to scream, but the sight of Thayne—wet, tousled hair, his bandana tied over his eyes—turned her choked cry to laughter. "You—you look ridiculous," she blurted.

"Now that's poor manners," he scolded. "Considering I can't even see how you look."

"You can't?" Emma asked. She pursed her lips to keep from laughing anymore. "Are you certain?"

He nodded. "Yep. I'm trying my darndest, but this thing works too well. Still doesn't seem fair."

"You promised," Emma reminded him. "In fact, I believe you promised to stay away until I was done."

"You were taking such a long time," he complained. "I figured it'd be dark before I got my turn. Spring's big enough for two anyway."

"You—you go over there, then," Emma said, lifting her hand and waving her fingers toward the far side, though Thayne could not see her. "You can at least do that. It's bad enough that we're improperly clothed and sharing the same body of water."

Thayne let out a hoot of laughter. "Is that what we are?" He shook his head, water flinging out from his hair. "And here I thought we were taking a bath."

"Oh no," Emma said. "That sounds positively sinful. And besides, it isn't true. I'm finished washing, and I have my clothes on."

"Well, why didn't you say so?" Thayne reached behind his head to remove the blindfold. "In that case, there's no need to wear this."

"Wait. *Don't* take that bandana off. Don't you dare."

He frowned. "But you just said—Miss Madsen, I do believe you've told another falsehood."

"Not a falsehood. Not on purpose anyway. I *do* have my clothes on— just not all of them," she admitted quietly.

A corner of Thayne's mouth quirked up. "Which ones would those be?"

"None of your business," Emma snapped. "Now be a gentleman and go back to your side of the lake."

"Hot spring," he corrected.

"It doesn't matter." She rolled her eyes in exasperation.

"But it does," he insisted. "A lake, river, or stream—and we've passed plenty of those—would be cold. I brought you here especially so you could enjoy warm water."

"I appreciate that," Emma said. "It is lovely to be clean. Now if you'll be so kind as to turn around, I'll be leaving."

"What's the rush? Stay awhile and swim." Thayne flopped onto his back.

Emma squeezed her eyes shut and turned away but not before she'd caught a glimpse of his bare chest.

"Open your eyes, Emma."

"I thought you said you couldn't see." Her brow furrowed. *If he is lying, how am I ever going to get out of the water?*

"I can't, but I know you're not looking. Don't worry. My trousers are on. I'm decent."

Emma laughed at the absurdity of his statement. *This entire situation is anything* but. She slowly turned around. Cautiously, she peeked with one eye. Thayne was indeed *decent. More than decent.* Her other eye opened, and she stared at him floating peacefully in the water.

She squeezed her eyes shut once more. "I need to get out now."

"Wouldn't you like to learn to float like this?" Thayne asked.

She shook her head. "No, thank you."

"Water's warm on your back, shoulders, head," Thayne said. "All the way down to your toes, and it feels like the weight of the world is gone for a few peaceful minutes."

It was a tempting offer. Emma shivered, the wet hair clinging to the back of her neck suddenly making her cold.

"It's an amazing feeling," Thayne said. "Nothing quite like it. You can't float like this in a tub."

Emma bit her lip in indecision. She didn't really want to get out yet, and when in her lifetime would she ever again have the opportunity to float in a warm spring? Perhaps this was some of the adventure she'd come west for. "All right," she said at last, her voice small. She looked at him. *In for a penny, in for a pound.* Thinking of his gift of the hair ribbons, she renewed her vow to be positive about the afternoon.

Thayne smiled and stood up in the water. "Do you want me to come to you, or do you want to use your stick and wade out toward me?"

"Neither?" Emma suggested. "Can't you just tell me what to do?"

"I could try, but it'll be easier if I'm beside you to put my hand under your back."

Too late Emma realized her dilemma. Thayne would literally be touching her back—her wet chemise. "Maybe it's not such a good idea after all."

"What's wrong?" he asked. "Believe me, after all we've been through to get here, I'm not about to let you drown."

"It's not that, it's just . . ."

"Ahh," Thayne said, a slow grin of understanding spreading across his face. "How 'bout I hold your hand instead?"

I cannot believe I am doing this. "Yes."

With broad strokes he swam toward her, stopping a few feet away. "Emma?"

"Right here," she answered, feeling suddenly shy.

He held out his hands, and she took them. He smiled as his fingers closed over hers. "Let's walk out a bit farther. Tell me when it's getting too deep for you."

"All right."

He walked backward, towing her out toward the center of the spring. Emma was surprised how comfortable she felt when Thayne was near. *I trust him. I feel safe with him. I feel . . . more than I should.*

He stopped. "The trick to floating is being relaxed. If your body is stiff and tense, then you'll sink."

"Then I think I'm in trouble," Emma said, only half joking.

"You'll be fine," Thayne reassured her. "Imagine you're lying on a feather bed. You're warm, comfortable, about to drift off to sleep."

Closing her eyes, Emma found the scene Thayne described very easy to picture.

"When you're ready, lie back. I'll only touch you if you start to sink."

She nodded and tried to retrieve the image she'd captured a moment before. It wasn't as easy this time. Each time she thought she was relaxed enough to lean back, it was only Thayne's hand at her shoulder that kept her from sinking. And it didn't help that each time her body rose, she realized her bloomer-clad legs neared the surface.

"Are your eyes still closed?" she asked, praying he really couldn't see anything.

"Yes. Don't give up. Think of something else," Thayne suggested. "Something a long time ago. Think about being a little girl again."

For the second time that afternoon, a vivid memory swept over Emma. Her mother's face came crystal clear to her mind, and she *felt* like a little girl again, *felt* like her mother was there with her, tucking her in for the night as she lay down in her bed. Emma's body began to relax. At her sides, her hands unclenched, fingers limp in the water. Quiet surrounded them. A serenity she'd never felt washed over her, head to toe as Thayne had described. All was calm, secure, peaceful.

"You're doing it," Thayne said quietly.

"Wha-at?" Emma asked. "I am?" Her eyes flew open, and she looked up at his face, mere inches above hers. He held his hands up, showing her she was on her own.

She panicked, arms flailing at her sides as she started to sink. Thayne reached for her, laughing as he pulled her toward him.

"I knew I shouldn't have told you."

"How long was I floating?" Emma asked. "I don't remember you letting go."

"That's how it works." He towed her to the shallows. "You relaxed, and your body did what it is naturally meant to do."

"I'm meant to float?"

"Yep."

His mouth was unsmiling, and she wished she could see his eyes.

"I've no doubt you're meant to do a lot of wonderful things, Emma." He took her elbow, turning her away from him. "Now I'd best leave you alone so someday you'll have the opportunity to do them."

* * *

The rest of the afternoon passed far too quickly as far as Emmalyne was concerned. Thayne left her alone at the spring, and somehow she managed to get dressed with the blanket around her. She was spreading her things out to dry when Thayne returned. He'd removed the bandana from his eyes, and instead he held it, bulging, out to her. Emma was delighted to find it full of berries. They moved the blanket to a spot in the sun and lounged there another hour or so, eating berries and the biscuits he'd made the night before.

"If I had a proper kitchen here, I'd make a pie with these," Emma said, popping another of the delicious confections into her mouth.

"You can cook?" Thayne asked.

Emma laughed. "Don't look so excited," she warned. "The only thing I can make is pie. We used to have a kind old cook who would let me help in the kitchen at Christmastime. She made beautiful pies, and she taught me how." A wistful smile crossed Emma's face. "But that was years ago. Perhaps I couldn't even make one anymore."

"I imagine you can do whatever you set your mind to," Thayne said. "You got away from your stuffy fiancé, didn't you?"

"Yes. I did." She wiggled her bare toes, enjoying the newfound freedom they so aptly signified.

"You've traveled from Boston to the Black Hills, you learned to float on your back today, you're wearing your hair down, and your feet are bare—quite the modern woman I'd say."

She laughed again. "Oh, quite. I'd make the society pages, I'm sure."

Thayne polished off another biscuit, then lay back on the blanket, hands clasped behind his head as he watched her.

She ran her hands down the length of her hair, squeezing at the tips to remove any last, lingering drops of water. Fingering the ribbon holding her curls back, she suddenly turned to him.

"Someday when I am home again—"

"When you're married to Willard?" Thayne teased.

"*Wilford*, and I'm not going to marry him. I left behind a letter encouraging him to find a woman who could truly appreciate his wealth and status." Emma let go of the ribbon and folded her hands in her lap. "I assured him I was not, and never could be, that woman."

"All right, then," Thayne said. "What *will* you do when you are back in Boston someday?"

"I don't know," she said. Truthfully she could not ever imagine herself fitting in at home again—not after her adventures of the past three weeks. "I don't know what I will do with my life." Her eyes met his. "But I do know I will look back on this afternoon and treasure it. Thank you, Thayne."

"My pleasure, Emma."

CHAPTER 20

EMMA HELD ON AS THE wagon crested a hill—the last, Thayne assured her, before they arrived. Rows of Lakota lodges spread out before them, dotting the landscape as far as she could see. Her breath caught.

"How many Indians live here?" she asked in a quavering voice.

Thayne held the reins in one hand and stroked his chin with the other. "If I remember right—I think it's about eight or nine hundred. Those here at the Touch the Clouds Agency were the last to come in from their places in the Hills."

Emma bit her lip. "Does that mean they were the wildest?"

"Suppose you could say that," Thayne said casually. "Though I don't see it quite that way."

Looking over at him, she saw he was leaning back against the seat, a relaxed smile on his face. The road was much better this close to the agency, and Thayne seemed in a particularly good mood this morning. *He's happy*, she realized. *Glad he's almost through with me and will soon get back whatever it is the Indians took from him.*

"Just how *do* you see it?" she demanded, anger suddenly overcoming even her fear.

Thayne turned to her in surprise. "What's wrong?"

She looked away, as much ashamed of her quick temper as she was of the tears pricking the back of her eyes. For the second time in as many days, she felt on the verge of breaking down. But today, it was for entirely different reasons.

Forcing herself to breathe slowly and praying her heart would calm, Emma tried to forget about the Indians for a minute and instead remember Thayne's kindness the previous day. She hadn't imagined the dress she was wearing or the fun they'd had swimming or their conversation late into the evening. He'd kept her safe and shown her kindness these many days, and until she fully understood the situation, she owed him at least civility in return.

Turning in the seat, she looked at him. "I'm scared," she admitted. "That you expect me to stay with people so different from me—people I've heard only the worst of—is terrifying. Please," she implored, taking her eyes from him and looking out toward the encampment. "Help me understand why we're here and who these people are."

"These Lakota are my friends. They are good people, people concerned about their families and survival." Thayne leaned forward, capturing the reins with both hands again.

"How did you come to know them?" Emmalyne asked. She gathered her shawl around her. Despite the afternoon sun beating down on them, the air was much cooler in the Hills than it had been down on the prairie.

"About two years back, near six months after I'd started up my mine near Deadwood, there was a skirmish—one of many, mind you—between some soldiers from Fort Kearny and one of the Lakota camps. The Lakota, led by a man named Crazy Horse, had been leading raids on the mining camps, killing as many miners as they could in the process. Crazy Horse and the other leaders knew they needed to get the white men out of the Hills before it became too late."

"Too late for what? Did they attack you?" Emma asked.

"Too late to keep the white men from covering the Hills. And no, they didn't attack me. At the time, I was wrapped up in the mine and pretty much ignorant of everything else, including the Indians and their plight. I could've been killed back then and deservedly so."

"*What?*" Emmalyne exclaimed.

Thayne held up a hand. "Let me finish. I'll try to make sense."

She nodded and leaned back in her seat, determined to understand his tale.

"The soldiers from Fort Kearny came looking for some Indians—*any* Indians—to kill. That was the government's way to teach the natives a lesson that murdering miners was not going to be tolerated." A bitter edge crept into Thayne's voice as he spoke. "The soldiers came upon a Lakota camp when almost all the men were away hunting."

"What happened?" Emma asked when Thayne had been silent at least a full minute.

He looked over at her. "What do you think?"

She didn't answer but kept her eyes trained on the lodges, growing closer by the minute.

"Kearny's men swept in there with their rifles and killed everyone, everything that moved—women, children, babies, horses, dogs. It was nearly a complete slaughter."

"*Nearly?*"

"A young boy about three years of age was shot in the stomach. His older brother found him and was trying to load him on a drag pole when I discovered the two of them." Thayne led the horses to the side of the road, gradually slowing them until the wagon came to a stop. He turned to face Emma.

"The older boy was maybe seven or eight and so scared out of his mind that he tried to stab me with his knife when we saw each other. I grabbed him, tied him up good, and went to work helping his brother."

"What did you do?" She searched Thayne's eyes and was startled when the pain she saw there left, replaced by a brief smile.

"I did what Kendrichs have been doing for generations," he said, a touch of pride in his voice. "The right herbs, the right place, the right hands, can heal."

"And then?" Emma prompted, caught up in his fascinating story. It was not difficult to picture Thayne in these Hills, kneeling over a small boy, working a miracle. Hadn't he already worked several miracles on her behalf?

"The little one got better. I fed the big one and kept an eye on him. Eventually, we came to an understanding that he was to lead me to more of his people, and I would follow him, carrying his brother."

"So you brought the boys back and became friends with the Lakota?"

"Didn't work out quite like that," Thayne said. "I brought the boys back, all right, but their father shot an arrow through my leg by way of greeting."

Emma gasped, and her hands flew to her mouth. "They shot—"

"Then their uncle stabbed me. Would've finished me off except the older boy rushed ahead and apparently spoke on my behalf, told how I'd saved his brother."

"They let you go?"

Again, Thayne shook his head. "Couldn't really do that on account of the arrow was in deep, and I was bleeding to death pretty fast. Fortunately, the Lakota have a tradition of healing too. I stayed with them for over a month while I got my strength back."

"My goodness," Emma exclaimed. She leaned back in her seat, and Thayne clicked the reins. The horses pulled, and the wagon rolled forward again.

"Turns out, aside from being a healer, I had quite a lot in common with the Lakota."

"Oh?" Emma said.

He nodded. "My ancestors were driven from their homes in the Highlands of Scotland. Those not killed were stripped of their lands, their livestock—even their manner of dress was forbidden."

"The Jacobite uprising," Emma said. She was familiar with that history—the other side of it. "My ancestors were English," she admitted quietly.

Thayne gave her a wry grin. "I won't hold it against you. But it seems nothing much has changed here in our land of the free. The Lakota have been driven from their lands, forced to live in government agencies. They can no longer hunt and follow the seasons as they've done for generations. Many of the brave ones, the protectors, were killed as they tried to drive the snake—white man—from their lodges. And as with the Scottish clansmen, they were unsuccessful."

Emma sat quietly, trying to digest all that he had told her. She understood better now his relationship with the Lakota, but many of her questions had gone unanswered. If Thayne was friends with them, then why had they taken something of his? And why couldn't the United States government provide the Indians a teacher? If what Thayne said was true and the Lakota way of life had been all but wiped out, then why wouldn't the government encourage the Indians to learn the English language and ways?

She had more questions now, unsettling thoughts about Thayne's part—then and now—as an intruder in the Black Hills. If he was so adamantly against what had happened to the Lakota, then shouldn't he feel bad for his part in it?

"Ready for the rest of the story?" Thayne asked, interrupting her thoughts.

"There's more?"

He chuckled. "Oh, you know there's more. I can see the questions and accusations as clearly on your face as they're likely churning in your mind."

She pressed her lips together, holding back a grin. "*No one* has ever been able to read my mind like you do. Is that another Kendrich trait as well?"

"Maybe." He winked.

Emmalyne looked at him, astonished at his sudden lighthearted behavior. "Very well, then, since you know my every thought—"

"Oh, not every one," Thayne said. "Though that would be interesting." He grinned.

"What *is* my question?" Emma demanded, folding her arms across her chest and looking at him. "What is it you think I want to know?"

Thayne paused, a thoughtful look on his face as he considered. "You're wondering how I reconcile being one of those responsible for driving the Indians from their lands?"

Emma's eyes widened, and she nodded silently.

"I don't, completely," Thayne said. "Though when I left that Lakota camp after a month, I felt differently about mining." Thayne slowed the horses and lifted a hand in greeting to a group of Sioux children playing in the creek beside the road.

"Lone Wolf—the man who healed me—speaks English. We spent many hours learning about each other and trying to understand our differences. I came to see the Black Hills as sacred ground, much as the Scottish Highlands were to my own ancestors. Once I felt that way, I knew I couldn't mine the land anymore. To the Lakota, it is akin to rape."

"But you're still here," Emma said.

Thayne nodded. "Yes, but I don't mine anymore. I'm still here, working with the land and working with the government and the Lakota, trying to find a way we can live together." He shook his head dismally. "The Scottish and English never really figured it out. Oh, there's peace in that region now, but things never returned to the old ways for the clans. I guess I see that same future for the Indian tribes that lived in these parts first. The government will never relinquish the land, but perhaps they'll allow the Indians to leave the agencies and work the land as we do. That would be better than what they've got now."

Emma turned in her seat, watching the children stare at them. Thayne's reasons for wanting a teacher were clearer to her, and facing the Lakota, while still a very frightening prospect, now seemed something she could endure. She needed to remember the things Thayne had shared with her. She needed to think of the little boys in his story and remember they were just that, children like those she might have taught in Sterling.

Straightening her back, she sat up in the seat, determined that the only way to get through this was to put her heart into it and do her best. Thayne had said she might go when the job was done. She would hold on to that promise to get her through whatever lay ahead.

CHAPTER 21

THE CHILDREN LINED UP TO greet them as Thayne guided the wagon through the gates. He stopped the team and jumped from the wagon as Lone Wolf made his way past the little ones.

"You are returned, friend."

Thayne clasped the older man's hand firmly. "All is well?"

Lone Wolf nodded. "As well as can be, living as we are here." He leaned down, speaking to the young girl next to him. She listened to his counsel, then ran off toward one of the many rows of lodges pitched in the camp.

"Red Hawk will be pleased to see you," Lone Wolf said. "She has taken quite a liking to your son and would not mind if you were to take her into your lodge as his mother." He looked up at Emma, her face pale as she stood on the wagon step behind Thayne. "Though I see you have found a second wife already."

Thayne turned back to the wagon and held his hand out to Emma. Feeling her fingers trembling, he gave her hand a reassuring squeeze, then turned back to his friend. "Not a wife but a teacher. This is Emmalyne Madsen. She has come to help with Joshua."

Emma gave a perfect curtsey. Lone Wolf frowned as he looked her over.

"I do not think she will last two moons," he said in his native tongue to Thayne. "It is not too late to change your mind and take a Lakota wife."

Thayne tried to hide his amusement. "You know I cannot. I can do more for your people when I keep myself from within these gates. Were I to live here, the government leaders would not take my counsel as seriously."

"You have spoken with the great father on our behalf?"

Thayne shook his head, sorry to be disappointing the older man. "Not the great father but one of his emissaries who will take my message to him."

Beside Thayne, Emma sidled closer as the children crowded around her.

"There is talk of allowing the hunt again," Thayne said. "I can make no promises, but I have tried to convince them that it is better for all if the Lakota provide for their own instead of relying on annuities from the east."

"It is well," Lone Wolf said. "Though I know not what we would hunt for this many together and with the buffalo gone."

Thayne nodded. Privately, he agreed with Lone Wolf and was very much afraid his words had fallen on deaf ears. But he couldn't give up, couldn't bear to think of these brave, proud people living as they were for years to come.

"There is something else," he said, venturing to bring up the other possibility he had discussed with the agents. "It may be possible in the near future for some—a few at first— to come live and work the land as I do—to raise cattle and plant crops."

Lone Wolf frowned. "We know nothing of your way, your cows, your houses—"

"Not now," Thayne said. "But you could learn. Is it not the role of Lakota men to provide for and protect their families?"

Lone Wolf nodded.

"The white man's way is different, but the result is the same. Our families eat and are safe. I cannot return things to the past for your people, but we can both work toward something—better than this. Think on it as the agents are."

"We will enjoy your visit then," Lone Wolf said, ending the conversation for the time being, though Thayne suspected they would speak of such matters long into the night. The Indian turned and spoke to the children clustered around Emma. They scampered off as a woman came toward them, a towheaded little boy held in her arms. Thayne rushed forward and took him from her.

"Joshua." Thayne hugged his son for a long moment, then pulled back so he could study the toddler's face. Thayne laughed as little hands went instantly to the stubble on his chin and cheeks. His heart was full as he pressed his son close again. *Never,* he promised silently. *Never again will we be apart as we have been.*

"We have changed his name," Lone Wolf said, amusement lighting his face. "He is no longer Light Hair Who Shows His Bones but Light Hair Who Eats Much."

Thayne laughed as he patted Joshua's belly, hanging round and full over the breechclout he was wearing. "You're right. He has grown." Thayne looked at Lone Wolf, appreciation in his eyes. "I owe you much, my friend, for keeping my son safe and well."

"No more than I owe to you, Takes An Arrow."

* * *

Emma clasped and unclasped her hands nervously as Thayne and the old Indian continued to talk. She edged closer, studying the little boy in Thayne's arms—*his* little boy. That much was obvious. They were the exact image of each other. *He is what the Lakota took from Thayne.*

Blue eyes as brilliant as Thayne's peered at her over his shoulder, and Emma couldn't resist smiling at the toddler. He did not smile back but continued to look at her curiously. She reached out, brushing her finger across the top of his fist clutching Thayne's arm. *He's hardly more than a baby,* she realized. *Where is his mother? No wonder Thayne joined up with outlaws and took me from the train. If this were my child, I'd have been that desperate too.*

Her heart constricted as she pictured Thayne leaving her tomorrow, taking this darling little one with him and going home to his wife. She had never asked if he was married. Though when she thought about the things he'd said, the way he'd apologized for kissing her, and how he'd resisted the opportunity again, it made perfect sense.

Everything did. His son, his purpose in taking her—even his kindness yesterday as he prepared to leave her behind. She felt tears building and knew that this time she would not be able to keep them at bay.

The young woman who had brought Thayne's son to him came closer, indicating Emmalyne was to follow her. She nodded and, head down, made her way past Thayne and Lone Wolf, still deep in conversation. It was better this way, she told herself. Better that he didn't see her cry.

CHAPTER 22

THAYNE WATCHED AS THE CEREMONIAL pipe made its way around the circle. *At least the government hasn't taken* that *from the Lakota,* he thought, studying the elders as each took his turn. Lone Wolf had presented Thayne's ideas, and heated discussion—both for and against—had followed. Thayne realized he hadn't solved any of their problems, but he was grateful to have at least conveyed possible solutions. If nothing else, perhaps he'd brought hope for the future.

Outside the lodge where they were gathered, Thayne glimpsed Red Hawk beckoning to him. Out of respect, Thayne looked to Lone Wolf for permission to leave. The older man frowned at Red Hawk and shook his head. She retreated, and Thayne's attention returned to the men surrounding him and his son, asleep in his arms.

Thayne knew the other men considered it strange that he had not yielded the care of Joshua to Red Hawk, Emma, or any of the other women in camp. But after being separated from his son so long, Thayne was more than reluctant to let him go. Before bringing Joshua here, he'd nearly lost him—twice. It was both difficult and unwise to forget those times—or to ignore the possibility that they might happen again.

Thayne stroked Joshua's damp hair away from his brow as he thought of all he still had to explain to Emma and all he was asking her to do for him. In truth, he was hoping for a worker of miracles much more than a schoolteacher. He worried over her reaction when she realized the depth of his problems, plans, and hopes. He decided tomorrow was soon enough to speak with her. Hopefully, she had enjoyed the day free of travel as much as he, but since this morning, he had seen her only from a distance, wearing new moccasins and helping some of the other women carry water.

Lone Wolf looked up at the doorway again. Thayne followed his gaze and saw that Red Hawk had returned.

"Red Hawk is worried about She Who Cries Much," Lone Wolf said. His mouth twisted in a smile. "Perhaps I was generous in saying she would last two moons. Maybe you should reconsider my offer before you leave tomorrow."

"Are you speaking of Emma?" Thayne asked, looking from Lone Wolf to Red Hawk. "She doesn't cry much—in fact, I can't remember her crying at all since I've known her." He returned Lone Wolf's grin. "She gets angry."

Lone Wolf shook his head. "Not the woman you brought here today. Go and see for yourself. It is troubling Red Hawk."

Thayne lifted Joshua to his shoulder and rose from the ground. He left the lodge, following the silent woman as she wove through camp, past fires, food boxes, and sleeping dogs. Above them, the half-moon lit their path.

After several minutes, she stopped in front of a lodge that was set apart from the others. Pulling the buffalo hide back, she indicated Thayne should enter. He nodded his thanks, then ducked inside, still holding Joshua close to his chest.

The covering fell back over the entrance, leaving them in near dark. Thayne blinked, then waited patiently for his eyes to adjust. Across the space, he heard soft, unmistakable crying.

"Emma?"

He moved quickly toward the bed of furs he saw along the opposite wall. He made out Emma's shape, curled in a ball, draped in the pale yellow gown, moccasined feet sticking out at one end, a tangle of honey hair at the other.

"Emma," he said again, touching her gently.

She jumped up, backing herself as far away from him as possible. Even in the dim light he could see her eyes were puffy and her face was red from crying.

"What's wrong?" he asked, alarmed at her appearance.

"Thayne?"

He heard relief in her voice, but it was quickly followed by a fresh spurt of tears. She pulled her knees up to her chest and buried her head in her arms, sobs wracking her body. Thayne moved closer.

"Are you hurt?"

Her crying grew louder.

"Did someone frighten you? Tell me what happened." Thayne juggled Joshua to a better position and reached for her with his free hand. He touched her arm.

She didn't pull away, nor did she cease her weeping. Uncertain what to do, Thayne decided to wait her out. Sooner or later, she'd run out of tears and have to talk to him.

He felt suddenly guilty that he'd left her alone all day. Before their arrival, she'd made it clear that Indians terrified her. He'd hoped his story had eased her fears somewhat, but thinking about it now, it probably hadn't been such a good idea to tell her about getting shot by an arrow and stabbed by the same people they were staying with. Maybe the part where he'd been cared for and everything turned out all right hadn't really sunk in.

He remembered the children's curiosity this morning, and he wondered if she'd spent the day having her hair and dress mauled by children and adults alike. *What a fool I am,* he chastised himself. *She'll be in a fine mood now to learn the details and difficulties of her new pupil.*

Waiting for Emma to stop crying took longer than he anticipated, but finally—just when he was starting to nod off himself—her tears dried up. She lifted her head and looked at him with red-rimmed eyes.

"I'm sorry for leaving you alone all day," Thayne said.

"I thought you'd left for good."

He frowned. "Why would you think a thing like that?"

"Because it would be easier for both of us." She took a deep, shuddering breath.

"What are you talking about, Emma?"

"I understand now." She tried to smile but wasn't quite successful. "I understand, and I forgive you. I would have done the same thing in your place."

"You would?" Thayne asked, perplexed. He was starting to think the stress of the trip had finally gotten to her—just when he needed her most. The arm holding Joshua had fallen asleep, so Thayne carefully moved him to the other side. When he looked up again, he caught Emma bestowing a tender gaze on them both.

"I never imagined you had a son. He's beautiful." She reached out to touch Joshua's cheek. "And I'm so glad he's safe—oh, Thayne, the anguish you must have felt these past weeks, knowing Indians held him hostage."

"*Hostage*? I brought Joshua here for protection." Thayne's eyes met hers, full of questions.

"I don't understand—I thought—" Tears welled again, and she looked away.

Oh no. "You thought what?" Thayne asked quietly. He brought a hand to her chin, tipping her face up to his.

"Isn't—wasn't your son some sort of ransom until you brought the Lakota me—a teacher—in exchange?"

"I told you that very first day you weren't going to be a trade." He searched her face, trying to see if she remembered. "I take it you didn't believe me."

She shook her head. "You said a lot of things, many of which pointed to my staying here. You told me I needed to teach language and speech. If not the Lakota, then who *am* I to teach?"

Thayne sighed and brought his hand to his head, running his fingers through his hair. "This *whole* time you've thought I was bringing you here to stay with the Indians?"

"Yes. Why do you think I kept trying to escape?"

"If that's what you thought, then why did you *stop* trying to run off?"

She shrugged and looked away. "You convinced me to trust you." Her lip trembled. "I told myself you'd make sure I was safe, and you *had* promised I could go home when the task was done. I really thought I could be brave, but then today I saw you with your son, and I thought you'd left and gone home to your family and I was all alone." Her hands came up, and she buried her face in them, shoulders shaking as she began to cry again. It was not a slight, feminine cry but a ghastly wail, followed by great gulping sobs.

Astounded at what she'd just said, by what she'd believed all this time, Thayne sat in shock for a few seconds before his protective instinct kicked in. He laid Joshua at the end of the fur bed and gathered Emma in his arms.

"Emma." He stroked her hair. "I'm sorry. I should have told you everything at first. I should have trusted you with the truth about Joshua, the same way you trusted me." He pulled her closer. She clung to his sleeves, soaking the front of his shirt with her tears. Thayne didn't care. It was the least he deserved. With her fear of Indians, what a hellish three weeks she must have suffered.

She lifted her face to his. "*Why* am I here?"

"My son," he began, then looked over at Joshua, asleep. "I need you to teach my son."

She looked confused. "He's little more than an infant, Thayne. School is years away for him."

"He'll be two next month," Thayne said. "And I'm expecting—*hoping*—you'll be able to perform a miracle." *A few of them, actually.* He rushed on before she could interrupt or he could lose his courage. "Joshua doesn't talk—ever. He doesn't babble or make cooing noises. He can't walk or crawl or play as a child his age should. Other than the way he looks, there's not much about him that is—normal."

Thayne held his breath, surprised at how anxious he felt about her reaction. Emma pulled away from him and wiped the last of the tears from her face.

"His mother?"

"Gone." Thayne knew he should tell Emma all of it, but he couldn't bring himself to do that right now. Revealing Joshua's abnormalities was difficult enough. Telling her what the woman he'd loved had done was more than he could bear at the moment. "I tried working with Joshua myself, but it was all I could do to keep him fed and dry and carry him around all day while I tended to the chores. I can't raise a boy myself and care for a farm and livestock. And I knew Joshua wasn't right. I knew he needed someone special to help him."

"So you went searching for a teacher on the train?" Emma shook her head in disbelief. "I attended school at the Academy for Young Ladies in Boston. Along with reading and arithmetic, we studied things like serving tea and making polite dinner conversation. I don't suppose those areas of expertise will do either of us much good." She rose from the bed and stood facing him.

"Conversation might," Thayne said. *Shoulda had* this *conversation with her about three weeks ago. Of course, then she wouldn't have come.*

"There was never a class about helping children who don't walk or talk." Emma looked at Thayne, tears glistening in her eyes once more. "I'm not the miracle worker you were hoping for."

"I'm just asking you to try." He hated the pleading in his voice, but keen disappointment filled him. She was telling him no, rejecting his boy, just as Christina had.

Emma stood there a moment longer, then walked around Thayne and knelt beside Joshua.

"You brought me *all* this way—to care for your little boy?"

"I did." Thayne felt a flicker of hope as he watched her take one of Joshua's tiny hands in hers. "Teach him. Help him." *You can't do worse than I have. Chances are, you'll do much better.* He feared the worst as he watched yet another tear slide down her cheek.

"And if I can't?"

"I believe you can." Thayne held his breath as she pressed Joshua's hand to her cheek, almost lovingly. *The way a mother would—the way his own mother never did.*

"He's never spoken?"

"No. As an infant, he babbled some, but after a while that—stopped. He needs a teacher, someone who can understand him, get through to him."

Emma brushed the hair away from Joshua's brow, then stood and faced Thayne. She held her hands at her hips and her brows knit together in a stern, scolding expression he'd yet to see from her. But when she spoke, her voice was warm—soft.

"Would've saved us both a heap of trouble if you'd just said so in the first place. But—"A smile lit her face. "I accept the position."

CHAPTER 23

"Aaaaaaa—apple," Emma repeated. She took Joshua's finger and traced the letter on the open page of the primer she held in her lap. Before they left, she'd insisted on taking it, along with a picture book of animals, from her trunk. Now, at midmorning, she was on her third time going through the book with Joshua and was showing no intention of stopping anytime soon.

Thayne could hardly keep his eyes on the road, and he *couldn't* keep the smile from his face.

Early this morning, he'd awoken in the Lakota lodge to find his son a few feet away and Emma next to Joshua on the other side. The two were sleeping curled up together, Emma's arm protectively cradling Joshua against her body. Thayne wasn't sure how long he'd lain there fascinated by the picture before him, but he'd been very aware of the havoc such a scene was causing him internally.

He'd told himself their afternoon of leisure two days before was all for Emma, that she needed to be calm and rested before they reached the Lakota agency and she met Joshua for the first time. But by the day's end, Thayne had been calling himself a hundred times a fool for even entertaining the idea that he could be alone with her at the hot spring and keep his distance. There, in the warm water, he'd been playing with fire, and he knew it. Each day he cared for her more. Each night he reminded himself she could never be his.

This morning, watching her sleep holding his son, Thayne's torture entered a whole new realm—one even more difficult to face than the physical attraction he felt toward Emma. Already, she was fulfilling his wishes and dreams—acting like the mother Joshua would never have. Thayne had wanted her for himself, and now he wanted her for Joshua. It was one thing for a man to live a life devoid of love and affection, but how could he deny his child such things?

Pushing troubled thoughts of the future to the far back of his mind, Thayne concentrated on the road before him and the hope Emma had already brought. This morning she didn't seem the least daunted by the tasks ahead but was enamored with Joshua and refused to listen to a list of what he could not do, insisting instead that he had only to be taught the right way to learn.

After her flood of tears last night, she seemed a new woman, changed overnight with the worry of the past three weeks lifted. Her enthusiasm was infectious, and Thayne found he could not remember a day he'd ever felt happier. They were in the hills he loved, and their wagon was rolling toward home. His son was safe, and a beautiful, vibrant *teacher* had agreed to be a part of their lives.

* * *

Thayne cast a worried glance in Emma's direction. She held Joshua on her lap as he slept, two blankets shielding him from the driving rain. Thayne and Emma were not so fortunate. His hat and her bonnet did little to protect them from the cold, stinging drops. Lightning flashed ahead of them, and Emma cringed. Thunder shook the dark sky a few seconds later. Thayne was certain he heard her whimper.

"Storms like these don't usually last more than an hour or so," he said, hoping to reassure her.

"Is there nowhere we can go to get out of it?" she shouted. "No place that might offer us protection? Think of Joshua," she urged. "This is dangerous."

"Best to keep going," Thayne said. "I don't know any of the miners in these parts, and I'm afraid we might get offered more than hospitality."

"I think it's worth the risk," Emma said. She leaned over Joshua, lowering her head as the rain intensified.

Watching her shiver, Thayne felt terrible. *Maybe we should find a place to stop.* But looking around them, he knew the road was safest. While the thick trees might shelter them from the rain, they would also be a target for lightning. Urging the horses to go faster, he wished the storm had held off until tomorrow when they were closer to home and he knew a few places they might have found shelter.

Thunder boomed a second later, ricocheting off the narrow canyon.

"Thayne, *please*," Emma cried, turning to him, terror in her eyes. "I've got to stop. I've got to get out of this."

"Emma, there's nowhere—"

She stood up in the wagon, Joshua still clutched in her arms.

"Sit down," Thayne barked. "All right, we'll stop." He guided the horses to the side of the road, seeking what little cover an outcropping of rock offered.

As soon as the wagon stopped, Emma started to climb down. Thayne jumped off his side and ran to take Joshua from her. She shook her head but allowed Thayne to help them down. Her feet no sooner touched the ground than she fell to her knees and, heedless of the mud, scooted under the wagon.

Thayne wiped the water from the brim of his hat and squatted down beside the wheel.

Shivering, Emma huddled under the wagon. Methodically, she rocked Joshua back and forth, the look in her eyes a hundred miles away. Worried about her state of mind and Joshua's safety, Thayne crawled under the wagon box, hunched over as he sat beside her.

"It's just a little rain," he said, putting his arm around her.

She looked at him at last, the fear in her expression palpable.

"No," she said. "It's not."

Thayne wasn't sure if she was trembling from cold or anxiety. He decided it was time for drastic measures, betting that if he could get her good and angry, she'd be all right. "You're not going to cry on me again, are you? My shirt's still wet from two days past."

"Your shirt is wet because you've got us stuck in this awful storm. And *no*, I am not going to cry. I seldom do."

"Could've fooled me, what with the way you carried on the other night. Lone Wolf predicted there'd be nothing left of you by morning."

"He did not."

"No," Thayne admitted. "But he did tell me you wouldn't last two moons in the Hills. He offered me Red Hawk as your replacement."

Emma scowled. Lightning illuminated their shelter, and Thayne felt her tense. He squeezed her shoulder as the thunder sounded, farther away this time.

"Storm's moving on," he said.

"Not fast enough," Emma replied, but her voice was steadier.

"We get a lot of storms up here. And a lot of snow in the winter. Maybe this isn't going to work out. Maybe I should turn around, put you on a train, and send you right back to Wendell."

This time Emma didn't bother to correct his misuse of her fiancé's name. "You wouldn't dare. You said yourself I've been too much trouble already, and besides, you need me to teach this darling boy to talk." She pulled the blanket back and peeked at Joshua, miraculously sleeping through the torrent above them.

"True," Thayne said. His hand brushed against her ice-cold fingers as he helped tuck the blanket around his son. "You're freezing. Give me your hand."

She obeyed, and he took her slender fingers in his and began rubbing. Though his intent was to warm her, he was affected by their touch as well. What a pleasure it was to hold a woman's hand, to feel the simple touch of another human being. He'd been without for so long. After a few minutes, she closed her eyes, a slight smile on her lips.

"That feels so much better. Thank you."

Thayne was again reminded of the day he'd fed her the prairie dog and she'd acted as if she had arrived in paradise. Funny how a simple thing like warm hands or a piece of burnt meat seemed to fill her with such gratitude and something as ordinary as a thunderstorm got her so upset.

He took her other hand and began warming it too. They sat in companionable silence for several minutes until Thayne realized the rain had slowed considerably. "I think we're good now." He crawled from beneath the wagon and reached for Joshua.

"Can't we wait until the storm has completely passed?" Emma anxiously peered out at the sky. "Sometimes when it seems one is over, the second wave passes through."

Thayne shook his head. "We should go. I don't want to spend the night in this canyon, and that's exactly where we'll end up if we don't get going and cover some miles."

Emma glanced at the sky once more, then finally leaned forward, placing Joshua in Thayne's outstretched hands.

Careful to keep his son covered, Thayne placed Joshua on the center of the wagon seat, then returned to help Emma.

"My dress," she moaned, looking down at the mud-stained fabric as she grasped Thayne's hand. He pulled, took a step backward, and felt his heel sink into a hole in the road. He sat down hard, inadvertently jerking Emma forward.

The soles of her moccasins slid on the wet grass, and her free hand flailed in the air before she toppled toward him, landing half on Thayne and half in a rather deep puddle on the muddy road.

"You all right?" Thayne asked, taking her arm and guiding her to a sitting position.

"No, I am not *all* right," she snapped. "I'm a mess. Just look at me." She pushed aside a strand of hair plastered to her face.

"I am looking," Thayne said, unable to keep the laughter from his voice. "In your pink dress with mud up to your elbows, you—you remind me of the little piggies after they've been rolling around in the mire."

Emma's eyes narrowed. She started to fold her arms across her chest then realized that would only make her dress worse. Instead, she wagged a finger at him. "What a terribly rude thing to say. A *pig*? Really, Thayne. And you're one to speak. Why—with your hair that needs to be cut, your unshaven face, and your muddy hands and knees, you look like a great grizzly bear that's just woken after a long winter of hibernation."

Her mouth pressed into a thin line—a feeble attempt, Thayne decided, at looking stern and reprimanding. Her twitching lips and the spark of amusement in her eyes gave away her true feelings.

"If I'm a bear who's been hibernating—" He stroked his chin, accidentally spreading the mud to his face. "Then it's likely I'm . . . *hungry!*" He lunged for her, catching her around the waist as she shrieked.

"And there's nothing a hungry bear likes more than a delicious pink pig."

"Thayne, don't," she begged, laughing as she tried to wiggle from his grasp. "We're already a muddy mess. "But if you pull me in again—"

He continued to try. She managed to free one hand and brought it to his chest, attempting to push him away.

He was again reminded of the strength she possessed when she really wanted something—whether it be pushing him from a train, riding a horse bareback, or shoving him in the mud. He decided to let her have her way. After all, his ploy had already worked. Now, instead of fear in her eyes, he saw mischief.

Emmalyne shoved with all her might and sent him sprawling into the puddle she'd fallen in just moments before. He still held her hand though and pulled her with him, thoroughly soaking the arm that hadn't gotten muddy the first time around.

She gasped, shaking her fingers, flinging dirty water all over both of them as she knelt, panting and breathless, beside him.

Thayne pulled out his bandana and wiped his eyes. Still chuckling, he offered it to Emma.

Yanking it from him, she attempted to dry her hands, then suddenly looked up.

"*What* are we doing?"

"Wrestling in the mud like a couple of pigs?" he offered.

She frowned.

"Don't like that?" he asked, raising an eyebrow. "Well then, how about getting your mind off the storm?"

"I hate storms," Emma said softly.

"I noticed." He took his bandana from her and used it to wipe a spattering of mud from the tip of her nose. "But the thing about a storm is there's often a reward at the end." He rose from the ground, then reached down and gently lifted her to her feet. Walking carefully, they made their way to the wagon.

He helped her up to the seat, then pointed at the sky to the north of them, a faded rainbow arcing across. "You know the promise of the rainbow, don't you?"

"No more floods." Emma scooted over, careful not to touch Joshua with her muddy gown.

Thayne climbed up beside her. "How about you promise me we'll continue on now and there'll be no more floods of tears like we had a couple days past?"

Emma lifted her chin. "And what shall I get in return?"

"Two days from now—a hot bath and a roof over your head."

"Just two more days?" She sounded ecstatic.

"Promise." He clicked the reins.

Her smile was back. "You've got yourself a deal."

CHAPTER 24

Emma leaned forward over the wagon seat, bouncing Joshua happily on her knee as she took in their surroundings. Today the sky was clear—unlike the afternoon of the thunderstorm two days earlier. She wore her last clean dress—one she'd brought from home that was far too fancy to be traveling in—and she'd washed her hair this morning in a frigid stream near their camp.

Thayne had watched her as if she'd lost her mind, and then he'd told her as much, but Emma felt it was worth the sacrifice of being chilly to be well dressed and as clean as possible when she saw her new home for the first time.

Careful, she warned herself as that thought crossed her mind once again. *It isn't my home. I'm going to Thayne's residence to teach his son. Nothing more. Yes, but I* am *going with him. He didn't leave me behind.* Her heart soared with joy, and nothing, not even another storm, could tamp it down. The relief she'd felt when leaving the Lakota camp, coupled with the knowledge that their long, arduous journey was nearly over, made for high spirits. And the little boy perched on her lap only added to the happiness she felt. She knew Thayne worried that Joshua would quickly become a burden to her, but he was wrong.

Deep inside, and with good reason, she was confident she could help. The doubt she had felt that first night had quickly been replaced with hope, thoughts, and ideas she was almost sure could help Joshua. Doing just that, while living and working side by side with Thayne, seemed better than any other teaching position she could have imagined. It appeared he was right. Some divine fate *had* led her here.

She watched as Thayne guided the horses into a canyon narrower than those they'd traveled already. Faded ruts made out the markings of a rough road, and Emma sat back in the seat, one arm firmly around Joshua while her free hand grasped the side rail.

Yesterday afternoon and this morning they'd passed a half dozen homesteads—or claims, as Thayne referred to them. She had yet to see another woman, but several scraggly looking men—one clad only in long underwear—had waved at them as their wagon rolled past. Since noon, though, she had seen no one. When she questioned Thayne about it, he'd told her simply that when he built his home he'd wanted to be alone and far away from the mining areas. He was interested in raising cattle and crops, and the best way to do that, he insisted, was to find a good chunk of land away from other people.

"The last hour or so is rough," he'd told her by way of warning.

He'd been right, of course; though by now, Emma was somewhat used to being jostled about in a wagon. What Thayne hadn't mentioned, however, was how beautiful this part of the Hills was. On either side of them, mountains of pine sloped upward, beds of colorful shale at their base, towers of granite framing their tops.

Purple wildflowers lined the way, poking up through the knee-high, late summer grass. Chipmunks scurried over fallen logs; birds trilled above the steady creaking of the wagon wheels. Though it was only the second week of September, autumn had already arrived. Wild berry bushes blazed with color, and golden aspens fluttered in the breeze. Emma was thoroughly enchanted. No matter what Thayne's home looked like, she simply knew she was going to like living here.

After what she guessed to be an hour or more on the rough canyon road, the valley began to gradually widen. In the distance, Emma could see the mountain curve around, marking the end of the canyon and their journey.

"We're almost there?" she asked.

"Almost," Thayne confirmed, though he didn't sound nearly as enthusiastic as she'd expected him to. Emma suddenly remembered how she had chastised him about the soddie they'd sheltered in on their journey through Nebraska. He'd told her his home was somewhat *different*. Uneasily, she wondered what that meant.

She knew many miners lived in large canvas tents. Perhaps Thayne did as well, and that was what had him looking worried. The possibility bothered her too. It had been one thing to sleep in such close proximity on their journey and at the Indian agency, but it was entirely another to continue such an arrangement. She'd hoped and looked forward to the possibility of her own room. Privacy now seemed the utmost luxury. Though, she supposed, life in a tent with Thayne and Joshua was far better than life in a Lakota lodge with people she didn't even know.

That she was even entertaining such an idea was absurd, yet that was what had become of her reality. She thought of Wilford and what he would likely say if he could see her now. She giggled once, then bit down on her lip as Thayne shot her an accusing glance.

"What's wrong now?"

She shook her head, eyes wide as she tried to look innocent. "Nothing. I was just thinking."

"About?" he prodded.

"Not now."

"Hmmph." Thayne's attention returned to the road. "I imagine Wilford lives in a grand house, drives a sleek carriage, and has an assembly of servants to do all the household chores."

"As a matter of fact, he does," Emmalyne said. "He also would never take me anywhere as beautiful as this, swim with me in a hot spring, or give me the opportunity to do something worthwhile with my life." She looked down at Joshua and noted that his eyes were trained on the picture book in his lap. "B—bear," she said, pointing to the page. "Grrrr. Grumpy bear," she added, glancing at Thayne. "If you're worried what I'll think of your homestead, you needn't be. I'll happily live in a tent so long as—"

Emma stopped abruptly, her mouth partway open as her eyes took in the sudden change in scenery. The wagon had turned sharply and was winding up a gravel drive. To the right, backed up to the canyon wall, a large red barn stood between two good-sized, plowed fields. To the left, a garden had yet to be harvested, and rows of pumpkins and squash littered the ground. Directly in front of them, at the end of the drive, a stately, two-story white farmhouse waited to greet them.

An older black man sat in one of two rockers on the front porch. Seeing them, he rose from his chair and started down the steps, a huge grin on his face.

"He's *not* a servant," Thayne warned her as he pulled the wagon to a stop in front of the porch.

"Well, I'll be," the man said, walking toward them. "You actually did it. You actually found yourself a woman willing to come back to this here desolation."

"Good to see you, Marcus," Thayne said as he climbed from the wagon. He held a hand up to Emma. She passed Joshua into his arms and climbed down herself.

"Emma, this is my good friend Marcus. He lives here and has been doing double duty while I've been gone. Marcus, I'd like you to meet Miss Emmalyne Madsen. She came from Boston to be a teacher."

Emmalyne smiled warmly as she held her hand out to Marcus. His stooped posture made him almost a whole head shorter than Thayne. "It's a pleasure to meet you. And, actually, I'm here because Thayne kidnapped me off the train."

Marcus stepped forward and clasped her hand. "The pleasure's mine, Miss Emma. You say this man stole you?" He shot Thayne a disbelieving glance.

"Yes," Emma said. "Though I've forgiven him."

Marcus laughed as he dropped her hand. "I like her already," he said to Thayne. "You'd best treat her fine and pay her well."

"I intend to," Thayne growled.

Emma couldn't quite tell if he was enjoying the exchange or not.

"I pay you well enough, don't I?" Thayne demanded of Marcus.

"Yes indeed." Marcus looked at Emma again. "I got myself a gold mine just for watching a couple of cows and putting up some corn these past months."

"How—nice," Emma said, completely confused. She glanced at Thayne as he handed her Joshua. "I thought you didn't mine anymore."

"I don't," Thayne said. "But when a friend can do some good with gold that's already been found and is just sitting there, I'm happy to pass it on." He turned to Marcus, clamping the other man in a firm hug. "It's good to be home. Any problems—or visitors—while I was away?"

"Not a one," Marcus said.

Emma watched the worry ease from Thayne's face. She felt her own relief, knowing that whatever had been troubling him seemed to have been resolved.

"And I hope you were joking about only tending to a couple of cows." Thayne walked to the wagon and lowered the backboard.

"Don't fret none," Marcus assured him. "You got two dozen, more or less, roaming the land hereabout. I counted just last week. Figured I'd give 'em another few days on the range; then, if you weren't back, I'd go round 'em up myself."

"No need," Thayne said. "I look forward to doing it."

"That's good, then," said Marcus. "'Cause I got me some news of my own."

"Oh?" Thayne lifted the water barrel from the wagon and set it on the ground.

"My boy Samuel pulled a nugget this big," Marcus held up his fist, "outta your mine three Saturdays past."

"*Your* mine," Thayne corrected.

Marcus nodded. "Well, we cashed it in over at the bank in Deadwood and—" He paused, flashing a huge grin Emma's way. "My Pearl is coming. I had a letter from her two weeks ago, and we wired her the money. She'll be here by the month's end. For the first time in seven years, I'm gonna be with my wife."

"How wonderful," Emma said sincerely.

"That's great," Thayne agreed. "I can't think of a man and woman more deserving. You two are welcome here as long as you like. It may be a bit crowded this winter, but come spring, we'll build you as fine a house as can be found in these parts."

"That won't be necessary," Marcus continued. "Frandsen called it quits, and I bought his property—house, barn, cows, and chickens—right down to the last egg in the henhouse, the table in the kitchen, and the curtains at the windows. My Pearl's gonna have a home of her own for the first time in her life."

The old man beamed proudly, and Emma's curiosity rose. What was his story, and how had he and Thayne come to be friends? Had Thayne really just given away a *gold mine*?

Thayne and Marcus unloaded everything from the back of the wagon—including her trunk, which they made an exaggerated show of straining over as they lugged it to the porch.

"I'm going to take care of the horses," Thayne announced. "I don't suppose you need an extra team and wagon, Marcus?"

Marcus scratched his head. "As a matter of fact, I could do with a wagon. I already got me one fine horse, though."

"Well, think about which of these other two you'd like," Thayne said. "And consider the horse and wagon payment for the extra couple of weeks I was gone. Come with me to the barn?"

"'Course," Marcus said.

Emma watched as he climbed slowly up to the seat. She'd already wandered around the yard and garden while the men were unloading, so she decided to wait on the porch. She was desperate to see the inside of Thayne's home but knew it would be impolite to go inside without him. Instead, she settled into a rocker with the picture book and Joshua and began reading to him—as she already had several times today. This time though, she began using her hands to make the signs of the letters after she had pointed to the printed letters and made the sounds for each. It had been years since she'd used her hands this way, yet they still seemed to know what to do. The language of the deaf was as ingrained in her as was English. After all, she'd grown up with both from the time she was a very little girl.

"You really take her off a train?" Marcus asked as they pulled out of the yard.

Thayne shrugged. "Sort of. It's a long story."

Marcus kept his eyes on Emma, watching her interact with Joshua. "Well, whatever it is, it must be good. Already I can see you've chosen well."

CHAPTER 25

Marcus led one of the two horses to a free stall in the barn. "Where you planning on having her stay?"

"Joshua's room," Thayne said, unconcerned. "How much corn would you say you harvested?"

"Enough," Marcus said. "Your cattle should be nice and fat over the winter. You gonna sleep in your old room, then?"

"No," Thayne said, sharper than he intended. "I figured you could stay there. I don't need a room. I'll sleep in the parlor on that fancy pull-out settee Christina insisted on having." He peered over the gate at the milk cow and her calf, considerably bigger since he'd seen them last.

"Miss Emmalyne gonna be all right with that?"

"Why shouldn't she be?"

"Girl from Boston got to think about her reputation."

Thayne left the cows and turned to Marcus. "Exactly what is it you're getting at?"

"Apparently not much," Marcus grumbled. "Not much going on in that head of yours if you can't see clear as day what I'm talking about. You can't have no pretty, young, unmarried woman live with you."

"I wasn't planning on it being just the two of us. I expected you'd be here as well." Thayne scooped oats from the barrel and poured them into the feed sack. "But it will still work out. I have a son. She's his tutor. It's as simple as that."

"No, it ain't," Marcus insisted. "She's gonna be shunned everywhere she go. Other women will talk behind her back. And the men—the men in these parts gonna think she's offering something she ain't."

"We're not going to be around anyone else," Thayne said. "And besides, she's only here until Joshua catches up. Once he's able to walk and talk. When he's a little older and—"

"And what if he never does those things?"

"He will." Thayne looked away, pretending he was occupied with checking the wick on the wall lantern.

"I believe that myself," Marcus said. "But it's gonna take some time, and you got to think about that young woman back there. You got to be fair to her. More and more, people are coming to the Hills every day. I know you think you're out here a ways, and you are, but Myersville ain't so far. And womenfolk, they're different. One finds out another is anywhere within a day's ride, and they got to go a callin'. All it takes is one woman, Thayne. Just one coming out here and finding Emma ain't your wife . . ."

"She'll never be my wife," Thayne said bitterly.

"Never say never," Marcus warned.

Thayne gave him a wry grin. "In this case, I'd say it's justified. I can't have *two* wives."

Marcus looked around exaggeratedly. "I don't see that you got *any* right now. How you know Miss Christina is even alive, and if she is, what are the chances she'd ever darken your doorstep again?"

"Oh, she's alive," Thayne said. "I feel it. She's just biding her time until she chooses to make my life miserable again."

"Well then, I'd say you got yourself a bit of a problem. What you gonna tell people about Miss Emma?"

"The truth," Thayne suggested. He grabbed a pitchfork and started tossing hay into the last stall.

Marcus shook his head. "Nope. You've got to think of something to protect her."

Thayne leaned on the fork. "All right, we'll say she's my sister. Satisfied?"

"If you think she's gonna pass as your sister, I might as well sign up as your long lost daddy." Marcus laughed. "You two look about as much alike as we do. Her eyes are brown; yours are blue. Your hair's light; hers is darker. She's pretty. You're ugly."

"I get your point," Thayne said. "How about cousin, then? I can say she's my cousin come to help with Joshua."

"Hmmm." Marcus considered as he emptied the bucket of oats. "I suppose that might do—for now." He glanced behind to see if Thayne had heard, but he'd already left the barn to retrieve the other pony.

"Though it ain't gonna last," Marcus predicted. "Unless it turns out she's a kissin' cousin after all."

CHAPTER 26

THAYNE RETURNED FROM THE BARN alone and grumpy again.

"You could have gone inside," he said to Emma when he saw her still sitting in the porch rocker.

"I thought I'd wait for you to give me the grand tour," she said, bestowing a smile on him in hopes of lightening his mood.

"Nothing grand about it," Thayne mumbled. "It's just your basic farmhouse."

He was wrong. Emma walked ahead of him into the entry while he held the door for her. An ornately carved mahogany table stood to the right, a matching oval mirror hanging above. Beside those stood an oversized hall tree, completing the ensemble and looking entirely out of place. The hall tree had enough hooks and knobs on it to supply storage for an entire men's club, Emma guessed, and she couldn't imagine why Thayne had chosen it for his home. A tasseled rug covered the bare pine floor and led to a staircase.

Beyond the hall tree was a doorway Emma couldn't yet see into. To her left, opened double doors led to a spacious kitchen. Thayne nodded his head, indicating he'd show her that first. Eager to see everything, she handed him Joshua and went into the kitchen, stopping in front of a large round table that looked like it had had little use.

Thayne walked past her and stopped at an enormous cast-iron stove. "Should you get the hankering to try your hand at a pie someday, this is one of the best stoves to be had. Took four horses and went through six wheels getting the thing up here."

"I can imagine," Emma said, thinking of the impossibility of toting such an iron beast across the same bumpy roads they'd traveled.

"Dishes are there in the cupboard."

Emma's eyes traveled to a lovely hutch along the far wall.

"You'll find the silverware and oilcloths in the basket," Thayne continued. "I don't expect you to do any cooking—unless you want to, that is."

Had she imagined the hint of suggestion in his voice?

"Right now, everything we eat has to be fresh every day. I didn't get much ice cut last year because I was busy looking after Joshua. As soon as the temperature drops and the creeks freeze over, I'll plan a day or two to go cut some blocks. That'll make it easier to keep butter, cream, and the like a bit longer."

Thayne brought a hand to his brow and rubbed it as if he were upset about something. "I didn't figure on Marcus getting a place of his own. Last year the two of us managed to prepare and set aside what we needed. I brought some preserves with us from Sidney but not near enough to get us through . . ." He looked at her hopefully.

Understanding dawned. "You want me . . . Oh my." Her hand flew to her throat. First sewing and now this. "Thayne, I don't know the first thing about preserving food," she admitted.

"I didn't suppose you did," he said. "But between myself and Marcus, we could maybe teach you, and then we'd all work together. Truth is, a lot of these chores should have been done weeks ago. But I was gone so long Marcus didn't get to them. I hadn't planned on you pitching in so much, but if we're going to survive the winter here, I'll need your help—besides your work with Joshua, of course."

"Hmm," Emma considered. "Would I get a raise?"

"Of course." Thayne didn't seem happy with her answer.

Emma laughed. "I was teasing. Of course I'll help—or I'll try anyway." She walked over to him, placing a hand on his arm. "Be warned. You may be sorry you asked." She grinned.

Thayne returned her smile. "I appreciate your willingness. Once winter sets in, there will be long hours when you can devote all your time to teaching Joshua."

"I shall look forward to those too," Emma said.

He led her across the entry hall to the other doorway she'd seen. Inside, she was surprised to find a modern parlor, with furniture as fancy as many of the homes in her own neighborhood in Boston had. Two stiff wingback chairs were arranged in front of the window, and a curved settee sat against the opposite wall. An oval table rested on a patterned oval rug at the center of the room. A tall, stately grandfather clock towered in the corner. Everything appeared as if it had hardly been touched. A thin sheen of dust covered the furniture and even the rug. Emma wondered if it had ever been walked on.

A fire crackling in the fireplace struck her as the only warm and welcoming thing in the entire room. As with the furniture and rug in the entryway, everything seemed out of place, as if someone had tried—and failed—at importing an East Coast townhouse to a country farm. She doubted she would spend any time in here. The last thing she wanted to do was sit in a parlor and endure required social visits. She'd had enough of that back in Boston.

Though Emma could not cook, the kitchen was more to her liking, and she much preferred the rockers on the porch to the uninviting chairs in the parlor.

"If you don't mind too much, I'll keep my things in here," Thayne said. "I'll sleep on the porch so I'm close by, but I won't disturb Joshua's sleep when I go out to the barn early."

"That sounds very agreeable—if *you* don't mind the inconvenience."

"No inconvenience," Thayne assured her. Joshua squirmed in his arms, and Thayne leaned over, setting him down on the dusty rug. "I hope you don't mind sharing with Joshua. There's only the one room that can be used upstairs. The other belonged to my wife, and I'd prefer to leave it be."

"Of course." Emma felt a peculiar pinch at her heart. *You had a wife once. Joshua had a mother. I am just his teacher.* Knowing already that she wanted more—and could not have it—she wandered closer to the fireplace. Thayne followed.

"It's better I'm down here for other reasons too," he continued. "Marcus thinks we need to tell people you're my cousin—so they don't get the wrong idea. If I keep my things down here, and you take the room upstairs—"

"Are you suggesting we *lie*, Mr. Kendrich?" Emma tried her best to look appalled.

"Only to protect your reputation, Miss Madsen. If you are unconcerned, then I see no reason to say anything."

I'm concerned all right. Though it's my heart I fear for more than my reputation. Emma pretended to be considering as she took a crystal candlestick holder from the mantel. After a moment, she held it up as if she were toasting with a glass of champagne. "To lying." *And lots of other wrong things like running away from home, sleeping under the stars, walking around in bare feet, bathing in a hot spring . . . falling in love.*

Thayne picked up the matching piece. The crystal clinked, and their eyes met.

"To lying."

* * *

Sunlight streamed through the upstairs window by the time Emma woke the following morning. She yawned, stretched, then lay perfectly still, enjoying the luxury of the feather tick. Though it sat on the floor—Thayne promised he would build a bed frame soon—she felt better rested than she had since leaving home.

Better rested and *clean*. Last night she had shut the kitchen doors and spent a lovely hour soaking in a real bathtub. While she had enjoyed her last bath at the spring, there was something about a warm kitchen, a scented bath, and a clean towel, that made her feel feminine once again. If only her clothes were as clean. Emma groaned, thinking about the pile of laundry that awaited her.

Throwing back the covers, she walked to Joshua's cradle and was surprised to find him gone. *Did someone come in here while I was sleeping?* Pulling on her robe, she went out to the hall, down the stairs, and into the kitchen. Thayne sat at the table, a spoon held in his hand as he fed Joshua, who was seated in a baby chair she hadn't noticed yesterday.

"Did he—did he get out of bed by himself?" she asked.

Thayne looked over at her, a corner of his mouth lifting as he took in her disheveled braid, wrapper, and bare feet. "I got him up, but he *was* fussing. You sleep like the dead, Emma."

She blushed. "And a good morning to you too. I'll get dressed and be back down to help."

"You do that."

She ran up the stairs, into the bedroom, and closed the door, leaning against it as her heartbeat steadied. *What was I thinking to go down looking like this? Why is this so difficult—already?*

She crossed to her trunk and dug a clean shirtwaist from it. She'd have to wear a dirty skirt until the wash was done, but that was the least of her worries at the moment.

Thayne always seemed to guess what she was thinking or how she felt. It would never do to have him knowing her feelings now. She had to get herself under control, had to quit thinking about the man downstairs and start concentrating on his son—the little boy she'd come here to help.

The reason I'm here, she reminded herself. It was going to be a very long year if she couldn't do that, couldn't quit acting like a schoolgirl who felt her heart go pitter-patter each time the boy she liked smiled at her across the school yard.

CHAPTER 27

Dearest Father,

I am sorry to have missed you in Sidney, but I am now arrived safely at my new position. While on the train from Chicago, I met a gentleman in need of assistance with his young son. The pay is twice what I would have made in Sterling, and I am eager to work with this pupil, as I believe he suffers from some of the same difficulties Mama had. It is a joy, Papa, to think of helping this child by teaching him the language Mother taught me.

Please forgive me for leaving without telling you, but I could see no other way to convince you I could not marry Wilford. Tell him I wish him the best.
I shall be in touch again soon.

All my love,
Emmalyne

Emma read over the short letter once more, then folded the paper and placed it in the envelope. She picked up the seal, pressed it into the wax, and stamped her initials over the fold. She was grateful she'd thought to bring her stationery set—perhaps seeing the familiar paper and hearing from her would be enough to convince her father that all was well.

"Shall we go for a walk, Joshua?" she asked the little boy sitting on her feather tick. She'd set him there a quarter of an hour ago, giving him one of her baubles to play with. It was encouraging to see him touching the jewels and showing interest in his surroundings. "It seems your hands work just fine," she commented as she worked the bracelet from his grasp. "Now if we can just get you to use them more and get you walking." She made the sign for walk with her fingers. "Walk," she repeated, pointing to her legs as she moved back and forth across the floor in front of him.

"Joshua walk." Kneeling, she picked him up and tried to stand him up in front of her. His little legs buckled. "Joshua," she said sternly. "You're a big boy. You need to use those legs." Rolling up his pants, she pointed to his legs. "Walk. Legs wal—" Emma gasped. A terrible scar wound its way around the back of Joshua's calf, unsightly stitch marks scoring the leg. She shuddered, wondering what on earth had happened to the boy. Her eyes filled with tears, imagining the pain he must have suffered.

Since they'd picked up Joshua from the Lakota camp, Thayne had been more than dedicated in the care of his son, changing his nappies, feeding him at mealtimes, dressing him. Now she wondered if there was more than fatherly love behind his actions. *But why would he hide this from me? He wants me to help his son.*

Her curious eyes met Joshua's, still focused on the bracelet she'd placed just out of his reach. "Maybe we'll walk out and see your daddy." She stood, then gathered Joshua in her arms. "He's been so busy playing with his cows these past few days that he hasn't had much time to talk to me, and I think he needs to explain a few things."

She marched downstairs, wrestled Joshua's coat and her shawl from the hideous coatrack, and went outside. Standing on the porch steps a moment, she looked all around the yard but could see no sign of Thayne or Marcus, though she knew one of them, at least, was nearby. Thayne had promised her that either he or Marcus would always be within earshot and she was to yell for them if there was ever a problem—*any* problem, he'd emphasized.

When Emma had asked what he meant by that, the only thing he'd told her was to always keep Joshua in sight. She was not to leave him alone for a minute—not even in the next room while she stirred the soup or brought in the wash. His order had left her somewhat perplexed, though now that she'd seen Joshua's scar, she better understood Thayne's request. But it was time, Emma decided, that she and Thayne had a long talk. Though she'd only been here a week, there were a dozen or more questions she wanted answered.

Carrying Joshua, she walked down the drive to the barn. Marcus was just outside, loading baskets of berries and bushels of apples into the wagon to transport them to the house.

"You about ready to do some canning, Miss Emma?"

"Ready as I'll ever be," she said, eyeing the overflowing containers. "Did you pick all those berries, Marcus?"

"That I did." He beamed. "And I hear you make a mean pie. Any chance of getting one of those tonight?"

Uh oh. "I'll try," she said feebly. "But it has been a long time, and I'm sure you've noticed about the only thing I've mastered cooking in the last week is hotcakes."

"And fine hotcakes they are." He winked.

"Have you seen Thayne?" she asked, hoisting Joshua to her other hip. "I was hoping he might tell me about the scar on Joshua's leg."

Marcus set the last bushel in the wagon. "He might tell you. Might not. But I wouldn't ask if I were you."

"Why not? If I am to teach Joshua how to walk, I should know his limitations. I need to know what has happened in his past."

"Nothin' good, that's what," Marcus said. "Nothin' good happened to his daddy, either, and that's all you need to know to help them both. I seen you with Joshua. You know them finger movements for words and stuff. You're teaching him to talk that way, ain't you?" He removed his hat and wiped the sweat from his brow.

Emma nodded. "I'm trying."

"You go to a special school to learn that?"

"No." She didn't offer any other information. If the men intended to be so tight-lipped about the past, then she could do the same.

Marcus wasn't going to let her off so easy. "Well, where'd you learn it, then? It's plain as day you know exactly what you're doing with that boy."

"I know because I grew up speaking that way. Thank you, Marcus. I'll get the kitchen ready." She turned away and walked back to the house, more curious than ever about the little boy in her arms and his father, who she couldn't seem to keep from her thoughts.

CHAPTER 28

SETTING THE LAST BATCH OF jam on the table to cool, Emma sank down into a chair, brushing the hair from her face. She touched the sagging bun at the nape of her neck and knew all of her must appear pretty much the same—tired and worn-out. *Who knew putting up preserves could be so much work?*

The past four days that was all they had done—she and Marcus, that is. Thayne had gone to round up his cows. Emma missed him and was cranky from being on her feet, laboring over a hot stove for hours on end. Still, looking at the rows of jars lined up in the cabinet and on the table, she felt a sense of satisfaction she'd never known before. Because of her labors, they had applesauce to enjoy and jam for their bread this winter. *Bread. Oh no.* She had yet to learn to make that, and when Marcus left to fetch Pearl next week, Emma had a sinking feeling that task would be hers as well.

Right about now, a nap sounded divine—and well deserved after all her hard work. She knew Marcus had gone out to the barn to do the afternoon chores, so there was no one around to see her being lazy.

No one except Joshua. With wide blue eyes, he looked up at her from his place on the floor. Emma was pleased to see he'd scooted himself several feet in order to get to the shimmering tortoiseshell combs she'd placed well out of his reach. He *was* progressing. Each day she spent an hour or more playing with him, moving his legs, helping him try to stand.

But she hadn't had much time to practice the sounds with him, or more importantly, to test her theory about his hearing. Deciding that now was as good a time as any, Emma moved Joshua to the doorway where she could watch him while she got things ready.

Starting near the stairs, she rolled up the long entryway rug. Once it was out of the way, she swept the bare floor clean then lugged the hall tree into Thayne's parlor. She couldn't understand what had prompted him to purchase such a distasteful piece of furniture when simple hooks along the wall would have done just as well and suited the entry so much better.

Save for the small table, the entryway was bare now and large enough, she thought, for her experiments. Taking Joshua with her, she ran upstairs, retrieving several blankets and her pillow. Dragging all these back to the entry, she made a throne for him to sit on. She wanted a true test of his hearing and knew that if he felt vibrations on the floor they would interfere. Placing him on the pillow and blankets, she handed him the combs. Hurrying to the kitchen, she quickly gathered several pots, pans, and utensils.

Joshua did not look up at her as she came back into the room. *Not unusual,* Emma mused, *if he really can't hear me.*

Sitting on the floor, two feet behind him, she quietly spoke his name.

Nothing.

"Joshua," she said louder.

Still no response. Emma clapped her hands. She wasn't certain, but she thought his head might have moved a little. Leaning to the right, she picked up a kettle and spoon and tapped it lightly. Joshua turned her way.

She grinned. *Good boy.* Scooting farther back, she repeated the pattern. This time she had to hit the kettle a bit louder. Again, Joshua's head turned around to follow the noise.

Over and over, Emma did the same thing, striking the pot, calling his name, tapping on the floor and doorknobs. She moved as far away as the parlor and kitchen, hastily scribbling notes on a piece of paper after each sound she made. Looking around the kitchen, she spied the grinder. Wondering if that was a range of sound Joshua would be able to hear, she quietly took it from the table and lay down on the floor with it. Hiding behind the half-closed door, she waited a few minutes more, in case Joshua had noticed her. It didn't appear he had because he was busily engrossed in pushing the teeth of her combs together and pulling them apart repeatedly.

She cranked the handle on the grinder once. He didn't look up. *Come on, Joshua.* Making sure there were beans inside, she turned the handle again. She thought she saw him flinch. She cranked it twice more. He looked over at her and smiled.

Emma felt her heart melt. He not only heard her, but he was responding with emotion. She crawled over to him and scooped him in her arms, kissing his cheeks. "Good boy, Joshua," she praised him. "Good." She motioned with her hands, then hugged him again. "I knew you could hear a little bit. I knew it."

The front door opened and Thayne entered, taking in the unusual scene—rug and hall tree missing and in their place Emma and Joshua, pots, pans, spoons, and blankets.

"What's going on here?" he asked.

Seeing his disgruntled look, Emma laughed out loud. "We're playing, Thayne. And the most marvelous thing happened. Joshua can *hear*. He can't hear everything," she cautioned immediately. "And his left ear is definitely better than his right, but he *isn't* deaf. I'm going to be able to help him." She beamed at Thayne, then turned to Joshua and kissed his cheek once more.

Thayne stood silently, staring at them, an unreadable expression on his face. "That's good," he said at last. Tipping his hat, he backed out to the porch, closing the door behind him.

Emma felt her joy deflate. *Have I done something wrong? Why isn't Thayne as happy as I feel? Joshua is his son.*

Confused and hurt, she placed Joshua back on his makeshift throne and set to cleaning up the mess she'd made. She returned the pots, pans, utensils, and grinder to the kitchen, placed her notebook and the blankets on the stairway to take upstairs later, put Joshua in his chair, and unrolled the rug.

But when it came time to put the hall tree back, she decided against it. So long as that atrocity remained in the parlor, the long entryway was the perfect place for Joshua to learn to walk. Deciding that having the beastly thing take up his space was the least Thayne deserved for his ornery, unappreciative behavior, Emma left it there and shut the door.

Feeling some of the exhilaration from her success with Joshua return, she went to the kitchen and decided she would bake a berry pie to celebrate.

CHAPTER 29

HANGING HER APRON ON ONE of the new hooks Marcus had installed before he left, Emma stopped to pick up Joshua, then hurried out to the porch. The wagon—Marcus's now—rolled up the drive, and Emmalyne waited anxiously for her first glimpse of Pearl. Marcus had done nothing but speak of his wife for several days before he left to get her, and Emma felt she knew the woman already.

Watching as the wagon drew closer, Emma saw that Pearl did indeed match the picture she'd painted in her mind. She guessed Pearl to be about fifteen years her senior, and from what Marcus had told her, Emma knew the woman had vast experience in everything from midwifery to working the fields.

Even from far away, Emma could tell Pearl's weathered face held kindness. Rising up on her toes, Emma strained to see over Marcus to the lovely woman who, she hoped, would take over the stove for a few days at least.

Even Thayne had come from the barn for the occasion, though he stood several feet away, surveying the vegetables in the garden that were long overdue to be picked. Since their arrival, nearly a month past, he had all but avoided Emma. The closeness she had enjoyed on their trip was a fading memory, and she understood why he had tried to make it clear she was here only as Joshua's teacher.

Emma knew she should be content—especially given all that Thayne was paying her. Last Saturday, they'd sat at the table together and he had listened while she described Joshua's progress. When she'd finished, Thayne had told her she was doing a fine job, then he'd handed her a pouch containing more than she would have made teaching half a year in Sterling.

Ignoring her protest that it was too much, Thayne had left for the barn, not to be seen the rest of the day. Though he had not treated her unkindly, Emma felt her heart breaking a piece at a time. She told herself over and over again that it was better this way. Eventually, she would have to go home, and leaving Joshua would be difficult enough. If she could recover from caring too much for Thayne before the time came for her to leave, she might survive the separation that already filled her with dread.

Pasting a smile on her face, she walked down the steps to greet the stout woman Thayne was helping from the wagon.

Marcus, hat in his hand, stepped up proudly. "Pearl, this here's Thayne Kendrich and Miss Emmalyne Madsen. Miss Emma, Thayne, I'd like you to meet my Pearl."

Emma stepped forward, Joshua in one arm, her other hand extended to Pearl. "Welcome," she said. The sight of another woman lifted her spirits considerably.

Pearl took Emma's hand in hers and squeezed. She looked up at Thayne. "Mr. Kendrich, I don't know where to begin with thanking you. I'd all but given up hope I'd ever be with my Marcus and Samuel again."

Hands in the pockets of his overalls, Thayne shifted uncomfortably under her praise. "You've a couple of fine men, and it's high time you were able to join them."

"It never would have happened without your help," Pearl continued. "Samuel would still be in Virginia, and I'd a likely died on that plantation I just left. Our family is indebted."

Emma watched with curiosity as Thayne's face turned a deep red. He didn't say anything but moved over to the wagon, his attention on the horses.

Hoping to rescue him from his obvious discomfort, Emma asked, "Would you like to come inside, Pearl? Thayne and Marcus can see to your things."

"Nothing to see to," Pearl said in a matter-of-fact tone. "All I need is these clothes on my back. Left the rest for the others to use."

"Of course," Emma murmured, guilt stealing over her as she thought of the trunk full of clothing and fabric she had yet to use sitting upstairs.

Thayne and Marcus took the horses to the barn, leaving the two women alone. Emma led her guest into the kitchen. Seating Joshua in his chair, she went to the hutch to get two cups and plates for tea.

"I'm so glad you're here," she said when she'd served them both a piece of pie and sat down herself. "Marcus has probably told you I'm in desperate need of some assistance."

"Only thing he's told me is that you're working miracles with Thayne's boy." Pearl looked over at Joshua, who was busily mashing a piece of bread. She took a bite of pie and nodded approvingly. "This is a fine crust."

"Thank you," Emma said. "I'm afraid baking pies is the limit of my culinary abilities, though."

"Who taught you to make pie like this?"

"One of our cooks," Emma said, embarrassed that she'd been raised with such extravagance when this woman had likely spent her entire life serving others. "It was a long time ago."

Pearl nodded. "Well, whoever she was, she done a good job. Crust is one of the harder things to learn. Where did you say you're from?"

"Boston." Emma looked down at her plate. *Snooty Boston. We may have fought against the South, but that doesn't mean we treated our servants a whole lot better than slaves were treated.*

"Well, I been in South Carolina these past twelve years. And I'm telling you, it's nice to have a change of scenery."

"It is," Emma agreed. "Did you enjoy the train ride?"

"More so than you did, I bet." Pearl chuckled at her own joke. "Quite a tale Marcus told me about you and Mr. Kendrich."

"Quite," Emma agreed. She and Marcus had spent hours together, cooking berries, peeling apples, baking bread. Gradually, he'd pulled the entire story from her.

"And what is your plan now, Miss Emma?" Pearl looked at her pointedly.

"I—" Emma froze, the fork halfway to her mouth. "What do you mean?"

"You know what I mean." Pearl clucked and shook her head as if she were disappointed Emma wasn't fessing up to some misdeed. "You got yourself a little boy and a fine man needs caring for. How you planning on doing that?"

Emma remained speechless.

"Well, sitting there with your mouth open isn't the way, that's for sure." Pearl rose from the table. "I got my own boy to get home to. I can't be staying here more'n a couple of days, so let's get to work and you tell me what it is you want to know."

* * *

"Oh, dear," Emma exclaimed. She brought a hand to her mouth.

"What'd you do now?" Pearl demanded. Walking around the table, she frowned as she watched Emma try to push her arm through a sleeve she'd sewn shut. Pearl brought a hand to her forehead and let out an exasperated sigh. "Isn't that your fourth time?"

Emma nodded solemnly, lips pressed together. "I don't know what I'm doing wrong. When I pin it, everything is fine, but then I sew it up and—and somehow I *sew it up*."

"Land sakes, girl. I hate to say this, but you're hopeless."

At this declaration, Emma burst out laughing, the defective sleeve flopping gaily at her side. Her laughter was contagious, and after a second, Pearl's severe frown melted, and she joined in with an unfeminine snort and hearty chuckles that echoed around the kitchen.

"You'd best take some of that money Mr. Thayne paid you and find yourself a seamstress. 'Cause at the rate you're learning, you're all gonna be naked before you figure it out."

Emma found this terribly funny and said so.

* * *

In the other room, Thayne looked up from the book he was reading to Joshua. "What are they doing in there?" He exchanged a worried glance with Marcus.

Marcus shrugged. "Don't know, and that's probably best."

"I hope so." Thayne scooted to the far side of the settee, catching a glimpse of Emma as she danced around the kitchen, bent over in hysterics. Her hair was down, tied back prettily in one of the ribbons he'd given her.

With difficulty, he resisted the urge to join her and see what was so amusing. He missed Emma. Though they lived on the same farm, he made a point of avoiding her as much as possible. *No sense in putting either of us through the torment.*

Thayne watched as Emma, still laughing and wiping the corners of her eyes, ran up the stairs.

"No sense at all, right, Josh?" Thayne asked, shortening his son's name as Emma had done. It was easier, she'd explained, for Joshua to learn to speak and discern single syllables. It was also easier for him to hear when he was spoken to in his left ear.

Proving both her points, Joshua tipped his head back, looking up at Thayne.

Such a simple response from his son brought a flood of emotion. That Josh made frequent eye contact and responded when talked to now filled Thayne with hope. Emma was truly working a miracle—many of them. It had been all he could do that day he'd watched them playing on the floor together to keep from breaking down right there. By proving that Joshua wasn't deaf—as Thayne had feared—and working with what hearing he did have, she had given Thayne back his son. Possibilities for the future filled his mind. Josh would go to school and learn to read and write. He'd grow tall and strong, with every opportunity afforded other boys his age.

But right now, he just wanted a story.

Making an indecipherable gurgling noise, Josh rocked forward, pointing to the page in front of him.

"Bear," Thayne said, looking down at the picture. "Grrrr." He remembered the way Emma had teased him about looking like a grizzly fresh from hibernation. Though he was no longer covered with mud, Thayne doubted he looked much better these days. He was too busy to shave more than once a week, and his hair had grown even longer in the month they'd been home.

He stroked his stubbled chin, wondering about the possibility of getting Pearl to cut his hair before she and Marcus left tomorrow. Deciding he would ask her, Thayne finished reading the story to Joshua, then handed him to Emma for tucking in as she came back down the stairs.

When he was certain she had returned to her room and was out of earshot, Thayne went to the kitchen and made his request of Pearl.

"I'll say you need a haircut," she clucked, looking him over. "'Bout time you started caring what you look like." She finished cutting a piece of fabric and stood, waving the scissors at him. "Got a lovely young woman living here, and you're hanging out with the animals in the barn. Smelling like them and starting to look like 'em too."

Such a tirade from anyone but Marcus's wife might have made Thayne angry. Instead, he was amused. Over the course of their friendship, Marcus had spoken of Pearl so many times that Thayne felt he knew her long before her arrival. That she told things as she saw them and harbored strong opinions on just about everything and everyone came as no surprise. Still, Thayne felt the need to defend himself.

"Those cattle are our livelihood."

"And it ain't gonna be very lively until you start sharing your affections with something other than those animals," she retorted. "Now go wash up. I'll clear this mess off the table." She waved him out the door.

Thayne walked to the well, drew up a bucket of water, and washed his face and hands. Leaning forward, he dumped the rest of the bucket over his head, then shook the excess water from his hair.

Above him, the night was clear and cold, lit by the moon and a spattering of stars. The smell of the woodstove filled the air. Trees were quickly shedding their leaves. Thayne guessed it wouldn't be long before the first snow. He was grateful this was his last night sleeping in the barn.

Not yet ready to face past ghosts in the other bedroom upstairs, he'd given up the parlor and settee for Marcus and Pearl. And though the barn was warm enough for now, he didn't sleep well out there. Being so far from Joshua and Emma worried him more than he cared to admit.

Just as he'd worried the Martin gang was following them those first days in Nebraska, Thayne felt apprehensive now. Though his sources in the Deadwood saloons had not seen or heard from Christina for some time, he couldn't get past the feeling in his gut that told him to beware. She was out there somewhere, and it was likely only a matter of time before they'd meet up again.

Shaking his head once more, Thayne cast a last glance around the yard, then walked back to the house. Entering the kitchen again, he found Emma alone, shoving another piece of wood into the stove.

Hearing him, she turned around. "Hello, Thayne." She wiped her palms on the front of her apron in a nervous gesture. "Pearl said you wanted a haircut."

"I—do, but . . ." Thayne took a step back and looked toward the parlor. The door was shut tight, and an exaggerated snore came from the other side. *There lies the devil and his mistress,* he thought. *I'll get you back later, Marcus.* Thayne turned to Emma, considering his options.

"I guess I am looking pretty bad—like a grizzly bear, if I remember correctly."

"I didn't mean that."

"And you have absolutely no resemblance to a pig."

"Thank you." She pulled a chair out. "Shall we start?"

He eyed the pile of fabric scraps at the end of the table. "Let's hope you're easier on hair than you are on cloth."

She laughed. "I don't think I can be worse. Pearl has suggested I use some of the money you've paid me to find someone to take care of our sewing needs."

"Oh?" Thayne raised an eyebrow.

"She suggests I confine my limited talents to teaching Joshua and baking pies and hotcakes—and occasionally bread, if we're very desperate." Emma sighed. "I'm so sorry I can't make better use of those beautiful fabrics you bought for me."

"It doesn't matter." Thayne walked toward her. "I shouldn't have assumed you could sew."

She looked at him anxiously. "Would you mind terribly if I send them along with Pearl tomorrow? She has only the one dress and could use—"

Thayne held up a hand, stopping Emma. "I won't mind at all. If I could afford to give away a successful mine, I'm sure we can spare a few yards of fabric."

"Did you really do that?" Emma stepped back so Thayne could sit in the chair.

He pulled it out a bit farther and sat. "I did. And don't go thinking it was any great sacrifice. After my month with the Lakota, I just couldn't rationalize working the mine any longer."

"But you knew it still had gold in it?" she guessed.

"Lots of gold." Thayne looked up at her. "And Marcus had lots of need. He's helped near twenty people come to a better life with that money—all without increasing the mine's size. And there's still plenty in the existing tunnels."

"What a good feeling that must be to help people like that." She took a clean, folded towel from the hutch.

"You're doing something pretty good yourself," Thayne said. "Everything I had hoped for and more with Joshua. He's making noises and trying to crawl."

"He is a bright little boy." Emma unfolded the towel and tied it around his neck. "I could probably help him even more if I knew what his first two years were like."

"Are you planning to choke me if I don't tell you?" Thayne brought his hand up, trying to wedge a finger between the towel and his neck.

"Sorry," Emma exclaimed, blushing as she worked to untie the knot. "Better?" she asked a moment later.

"Much," Thayne said. He swallowed just to make sure. "I believe you were about to tell *me* how it is you know so much about teaching children who can't hear."

She hesitated, one hand on the comb, the other reaching for the scissors. "All right. If you promise to answer some questions in exchange."

"Fair enough."

"If you want to look better than those scraps over there, you'll have to hold still," she warned, placing one hand on the back of his neck as she searched for his part.

Thayne closed his eyes. *This is dangerous—on a whole different level than you were thinking of outside.*

"How did Joshua come by that scar on his leg?" Emma asked.

"Fell down the stairs and broke his leg. Bone came right out through the skin."

Emma gasped. "How long ago? *Those* stairs?" She looked toward the flight that led to the second floor.

Thayne nodded. She placed a hand on either side of his head. "Careful. I *want* to do a good job."

"You'd best be the one answering the questions, then. Where did you learn sign language?"

"From my mother. How did Joshua fall down the stairs? I thought you said he'd never walked or crawled."

"He hasn't," Thayne confirmed. "How come you learned to sign?"

"You didn't answer the whole question," Emma reminded him. "But I'll be the lady and go first." Bending Thayne's head down, she began snipping at the hair in back. "My mother was deaf."

"Your mother—" Thayne turned his head, trying to see her face.

"Ah, ah," Emma scolded.

He looked down again. "But you hear fine."

"I do." *Snip. Snip. Snip.* "Not all hearing loss is inherited. My mother's was from an illness she had as a child."

He waited, hoping she was cutting evenly and would offer more information. The scissors clicked away, and from the corner of his eye, he watched hair fall to the floor. Still, Emma remained silent.

"Head up, please," she said.

Thayne obliged. "When we spoke of her before, you never mentioned it."

"I told you she wasn't outspoken." Emma smiled briefly at the memory, then her face clouded. "I don't speak of her much. She died when I was ten."

"You still miss her?" Thayne guessed.

Emma nodded. "Yes. More so recently. Signing reminds me. I've been glad to find it's still second nature, almost as easy as speaking aloud." Emma took a step back, critiquing her work. "Your turn. Tell me about Joshua's fall."

Thayne hesitated. There was no easy way to have this discussion, but Emma was right. After all she had done for Joshua, she deserved to know what had made him the way he was. "Joshua was dropped—by his mother. I didn't get there in time. I tried, but—"

"Oh, Thayne." Emma stopped working, scissors held in midair. She sank into the nearest chair, bestowing a look of the deepest pity on him. "Was she very ill?"

"Ill?" Thayne realized Emma had already reached the same conclusion others had in the past—the doctor who'd tended Joshua, for one. No mother would purposely drop her child down a flight of stairs.

Except Christina, and she *wasn't* ill. Though she hadn't looked too well after Thayne shot her less than a minute later.

He ran his fingers through his hair, still uncut on top. "Listen, Emma. It's complicated and long, and I'm not up to telling the whole thing tonight. Let's just say that Joshua wasn't normal before the fall, and he was even worse afterward. It was about nine months later that I took him to the Lakota camp, and you know the rest from there."

Emma looked down at her hands, clasped around the scissors in her lap. Another minute passed, and Thayne reached out, placing his hand over hers.

"Looks like we've both faced some difficult things in the past."

"I think yours was worse. To lose your wife and see Joshua hurt like that—" Her eyes filled with tears.

He knew he ought to correct her, tell her the truth about Christina. *If only I had lost her.* "Hey, no more floods, remember?" Thayne gently chided. "All that laughing in here earlier was already enough to have me good and worried."

She forced a smile and stood again. "I promise to keep a straight face and steady hand while I finish." She began cutting the side where she'd left off.

Thayne closed his eyes, allowing himself the pleasure of feeling her gentle touch. The kitchen was quiet, save for the snip of her scissors, and he let his mind drift over all they'd just shared.

He remembered when he'd first had the idea to find a teacher for Joshua. Marcus told him he'd lost his mind, and even Thayne had to agree that it seemed a poor plan at best. What were the odds that he'd find a woman willing to travel to the middle of nowhere to teach a troubled boy? But, like his worrying spells, it had been a notion he couldn't let go of. So on little more than his impulse and faith, he'd taken his son to the Indian agency for protection and started off on his search.

Now, sitting here with Emma—a woman not only willing but also well qualified to help his little boy—Thayne felt overwhelmed with gratitude. That there was a higher power in this than his own he had no doubt.

"Turn to the side, please," Emma said softly.

Thayne complied.

"You were right, of course," she said.

It took Thayne a moment to realize their thoughts were running along similar lines.

"I knew it that first night I met Joshua and you told me all the things he could not do." Her hand brushed Thayne's cheek as she studied his sideburn.

Ignoring instructions, he looked up at her, then reached up to touch her hand.

"You were meant to come here."

She met his gaze and nodded solemnly. "It appears that I was."

CHAPTER 30

THAYNE SAT ON A STOOL inside the doorway of the barn, head bent, scraper in his hand as he worked, intent on removing caked mud from the shoe of his horse. A shadow crossed his path, and he looked up to see his nearest neighbor, Orville Grady. Orville was scratching his neck vigorously as if some sort of pest had invaded his shirt collar. *Probably has,* Thayne thought, based on the infrequency most men in the Hills exhibited when it came to washing both themselves and their clothing.

"What can I do for you, Orville?" Thayne gently set the horse's foreleg down and rose from his stool.

The scratching continued. "I—I understand you got a woman living here."

"That so?" Thayne looked past Orville, noting the indisputable evidence of the claim. Freshly laundered clothes—including a woman's garments—hung on the line, and Emma herself was in plain sight, working in the garden. "Who'd you hear that from?"

"David Williams, Hank Evans, Charles Fuller. They say she's been here since September."

"True enough," Thayne said, surprised it had taken this long for word to spread. "I needed some help with my boy."

"David and Hank say you already got a wife."

David and Hank should mind their own business. "Emma is my cousin. She came from Boston to work with Joshua for a spell. She's a teacher."

Orville nodded and turned, following Thayne's distracted gaze across the yard to the very object of their discussion. "I was wondering," he began, "if maybe she might like to get out and meet some other womenfolk—especially if she's from the East and used to parties and such."

"What womenfolk would you be speaking of?" Thayne asked. Making sure the horse was still tethered, he left the barn and stepped out into the cool autumn air. "Because the only kind I can think of who are available to socialize certainly wouldn't make fine company for my cousin."

"Oh no." Orville's face turned a bright shade of red, matching the area on his neck where he'd been scratching. "I'm talking about the Harveys' barn raising. There's gonna be a dance after."

Frowning, Thayne looked up at the sky. "They'd best hurry. Nothing much is going to get raised once the snow comes." Checking his overall pockets for nails and wire, he started toward the chicken coop.

Orville looked taken aback by Thayne's brusqueness. "It's this Saturday." He walked quickly to catch up. "We'll start building early, and that'll leave evening for supper and the dance. Even if it snows between now and then, there'll only be a couple of feet on the ground at most."

Greenhorn. I'll make sure we talk after you've survived your first Dakota winter. Thayne guessed what Orville was hinting at and didn't like it, but he also knew there was no way he could take Emma to a dance. He'd barely survived the close contact with her when she'd cut his hair a few weeks back. Since then, the smell of her, the feel of her hands on his skin, the understanding that something larger than both of them had brought them together was near all he could think about. Holding her in his arms while dancing would do him in for sure.

"I'm sorry, Orville. I'm sure the Harveys need help with their barn, but I was gone from July to the middle of September fetching Emma, and I'm still behind. If we're going to be ready for winter ourselves, I just can't spare the time."

Orville scratched his arm. "Well then—maybe—seeing how she's your cousin—*I* could take her to the Harveys for a spell?" He rushed on. "Not all day, mind you, but I could be her escort for supper and dancing."

Thayne stopped midstride, fighting the impulse to hit Orville and then pick him up and literally throw him off his property. Thayne narrowed his eyes, looking at the man in a different light. He was young and inexperienced, but he'd had good luck with his claim. Aside from his scratching, he seemed a normal sort of man—normal enough to chase a skirt all the way out here on the basis of hearsay. Thayne's fists clenched at his side.

Orville noticed and took a step back. "*Is* she your cousin?"

"Yeah. And I got a right to protect her from a bunch of lonesome prospectors. You think I'm going to send her into a den of lions like that?"

"Ain't no saloon we're talking about," Orville said defensively. "It's proper folk, homesteaders like yourself. Families. It was Mrs. Harvey's idea in the first place. Her married sister will be there too, and they'd be pleased as punch to have a few more females in attendance. That's how come I offered to come here."

Thayne brought a hand to his forehead. *Marcus was right. I'm going to cause problems for Emma if I'm not careful. But I'll cause problems for us both if I get close to her again.*

"Well, maybe I could spare her for the evening." *Might be for the best. The way she looks at me lately doesn't help matters any. Maybe it will be a good thing to remind her there's nothing permanent between us.*

The itch had spread to Orville's other arm. Thayne decided he had better introduce Emma quick before Orville scratched half his skin off.

"Come on," Thayne said. "You can meet Emma yourself and ask her how she feels about dancing."

* * *

Emma sliced another squash from the thick vine and set it in the basket beside her. She glanced over at Joshua, playing contentedly in the dirt a few feet away.

"Someone is going to need a bath tonight." Lifting her hands, she looked ruefully at her fingernails. "And I wasn't just talking about you, Josh." Rising, she brushed the soil from her skirt and walked to the front porch. She reached across the steps and retrieved her cup of water, along with the toy horse and rider Thayne had carved for Joshua.

Emma tilted her head back and took a drink, careful to leave plenty for Joshua. She rejoined him in the garden, squatting down to help him hold the cup.

When he'd finished, she turned it upside down. "All gone."

He ignored her, instead digging his fingers gleefully in the dirt again. Emma gently tilted his chin up, getting his attention.

"All gone," she repeated slowly, showing him the inside of the empty cup once more. "Gone."

"Gm," he mimicked.

Emma smiled. "That's right. Gone." She scooped the cup through the dirt, then showed Joshua how to dump it out, making a little mountain for the horse and rider to climb. "Giddyap," she said, moving the figure over the mound. She clicked her tongue, making the sound of hoofbeats.

Just as she opened her mouth wider, intending to teach Joshua how to move his tongue and make the sound, she heard footsteps behind her. She looked up, feeling a blush heat her face as she saw a man she did not recognize standing beside Thayne.

Dropping the toy, she stood and wiped her palms across the front of her apron. "Hello."

Thayne stared at her, unsmiling. Her gaze drifted from him to the stranger, a feeling of uneasiness beginning to flutter in her stomach.

"Emma, this is Mr. Grady. His place is about six miles from here. We passed it on the way in." Thayne turned to him. "Orville, my cousin, Emmalyne Madsen."

She gave Mr. Grady a hesitant smile and took his extended hand. "Pleased to meet you, Mr. Grady." *Who are you? And why is Thayne upset?* They'd passed several homesteads on their way from the Lakota agency to Thayne's property, but she couldn't remember one man from another who'd waved and called hello—not even the one who'd been clad in nothing more than long underwear. *Could it have been him?*

"Please, call me Orville."

She nodded but did not repeat his name.

"Orville has some news," Thayne said.

Emma's heart lurched, and she sought Thayne's eyes. "A letter? Has something happened to my father?"

"No. Nothing like that," Thayne quickly reassured her, his expression softening.

"There's going to be a barn raising at the Harvey place this Saturday— and a dance," Orville blurted. He began scratching the back of his neck.

"Oh," Emma brought a hand to her heart, feeling its beat slow to normal as relief washed over her. *News in the Hills is not the same as news at home,* she reminded herself. "A dance." She almost laughed. "How delightful."

Thayne's scowl deepened. "I got work to get back to." He tipped his hat. "Good day, Grady." He turned on his heel, heading back toward the barn.

Confused, Emma watched him go. She looked to Mr. Grady for some explanation. He had his hat off and was twirling it nervously in his hands.

"Miss Madsen, I was wondering if you'd do me the pleasure of accompanying me to the Harveys' dance."

She opened her mouth, but no words came out.

"I got a wagon I could take you in," Mr. Grady continued. "And all the womenfolk for miles around are gonna be there. You'd have a chance to meet up with 'em and make some friends. It ain't right how we're all so far apart out here—so *alone*."

Understanding dawned. *So that's why Thayne seemed angry. I wonder why he didn't just tell Mr. Grady to leave.* She glanced toward the barn again and caught Thayne looking her way just before he disappeared around the side. Perhaps he wasn't as unaware of her as she thought. She forced her attention back to the man in front of her, intending to let him down as gently as possible. After all, six miles was no small distance to travel to ask someone to a dance.

"It sounds lovely, Mr. Grady. Truly, it does, but I cannot accept your kind offer. I am here to care for Thayne's son, and I couldn't possibly leave him for that long."

"Thayne said it'd be all right. Said you could go." The hat was still in Mr. Grady's hands, his fingers clenched tightly over the brim.

Emma wished she had something to grab on to as well. The hope she'd felt only a moment ago had fled, her emotions plummeting back to earth. "He said I could go—that you . . . you could take me?" *There must be some misunderstanding. Surely Thayne wouldn't send me off with some other man.*

But Mr. Grady was nodding vigorously, a hopeful expression on his face.

Emma prayed she was masking her feelings better than he—difficult though that was, considering it felt like she'd just been punched. If only it were Thayne who'd come to her and suggested they go to the dance. *Instead, he thinks it* good *I go with another man?* What else could she do now *but* go? To refuse would be to put her heart on her sleeve even more than she already had. This was likely Thayne's way of telling her she needed to stop hoping he'd ever see her as more than Joshua's teacher.

Clasping her hands in front of her, she pasted a smile on her face. "In that case, Mr. Grady—Orville—" She brightened her smile. "I would be most pleased to accompany you."

"You would?" He reached out, taking her hand again, pumping it up and down. "That's swell. Just fine. I'll come for you around four. It's a little more than an hour's drive, and there's to be a dinner before the dance."

"I shall bake a pie for it." She tugged her hand away, wishing the sorry state of her nails might have been a deterrent to Mr. Grady's enthusiasm like his scratching was to hers.

But he plunked his hat on his head and nodded twice more to her, his grin stretching nearly from ear to ear. "Good day, Miss Madsen. Till Saturday."

"Until Saturday." She lifted her hand, wiggling three fingers at him. At last he turned away, walking in the direction Thayne had gone.

Emma looked down at Joshua, his attention no longer on the cup and figure but on the basket of squash. Dropping to the ground, she blinked back angry tears and scolded herself for feeling hurt. Then she picked up the tin cup and filled it with dirt.

Raising it high, she dumped the whole thing over the miniature cowboy's head.

CHAPTER 31

EMMA LOWERED THE CURLING TONGS with one hand and picked up the oval mirror with her other. She sighed as she studied her reflection. The ringlets framing her face did little to lighten her mood. She'd taken more pains getting ready tonight than she had for the fanciest ball back home. And why? All in the hope that Thayne might so much as glance her way before she left.

Realizing there were only a few minutes more until Mr. Grady came for her, Emmalyne gathered her things from the kitchen table and put them in the basket to go upstairs. She tied an apron over her dress and went to the stove. She stirred the stew, sliced and buttered the bread, then went to the cupboard to get the plates.

Two apple pies—one to take and one to leave home—sat cooling beside the stack of dishes, and Emmalyne wondered again if she should have made only one. Surely Thayne would have minded missing out on her pie. *And it would serve him right for sending me off with Orville Grady.* But likely Thayne wouldn't have missed her pie enough to change his mind or at least come to the dance himself. And Joshua liked her pie too. She saw no point in punishing him because his father didn't care for her as she cared for him.

Emma set one place at the table and put Joshua's tin beside it. She'd hoped seeing her place empty would bother Thayne, but she was dismayed to find it was her heart that felt heavy as she looked at the table. Turning around quickly, she untied her apron and was hanging it on the peg when Thayne walked in.

Barely trusting herself to speak, she didn't look at him. "Supper's on the stove, and I'll leave a pie for your dessert. If you'll read to Joshua and give him my good night kiss . . ."

Outside she heard the unmistakable sound of a wagon and team. Grabbing her cloak, she took a pie from the shelf and hurried past Thayne.

"Good night," she called and walked out the front door.

Thayne shoved his hands in his pockets and looked out the kitchen window, watching as Orville helped her up to the wagon seat. He climbed in beside her, sitting closer than he should have, Thayne thought, scowling. A second later, a corner of his mouth lifted as he watched Emma scoot away.

Wisely, Grady didn't move any closer. After talking with Grady in the barn the other day, Thayne had no real worries about Emma's safety. After all, Orville was a member of the Citizens for Law in the Hills committee. The dance was being held just over in the next valley, and the folk who were going to be there were more recent settlers—homesteaders like himself, looking for places to raise their families. Grady was strong enough to protect her from any miner who came looking for a skirt.

When the wagon was out of sight, Thayne left the window and went to the stove. He lifted the lid on the pot and inhaled. The stew smelled delicious, but he wasn't hungry. He turned to Joshua, busy smashing crackers and potatoes on his tray.

Thayne walked over, ruffling his son's hair. "Not hungry, either?" He lifted Joshua from the chair. "How 'bout we play blocks, then I'll give you that story and kiss from your mo—" He caught himself. "Emma promised."

Less than a half hour later, Thayne heard the sound of wagon wheels crunching over leaves outside. Scooping up Joshua, Thayne hurried to the front door, concerned something terrible had happened to have Emma home so early. He felt both relief and disappointment when he opened the door and saw it was Marcus helping Pearl down from their wagon.

Thayne raised a hand in greeting as his friends made their way to the porch.

"You were right, Pearl," Marcus said by way of greeting as he walked past Thayne into the house.

"Right about what?" Thayne asked as he handed Joshua into Pearl's outstretched hands.

"'Bout you not hearing of the barn raising and dance," Pearl said. She headed straight for one of the wingback chairs and settled into it, a squirming Joshua in her lap. "We got word of it clear up our way, but you're so far off the beaten path . . ."

"We heard," Thayne said. He sat next to Marcus on the settee. "Emma's there right now."

"What?" both Pearl and Marcus asked at the same time, their mouths hung open in astonishment, with a disapproving glint in Pearl's eye.

Thayne shrugged. "Orville Grady asked her to go with him. She took a pie," he added lamely.

Pearl and Marcus exchanged a glance. Sensing one of Marcus's lectures coming his way, Thayne stood up. "She left one here too. I'll get us all a piece." He practically ran into the kitchen.

Thayne took the pie from the shelf and set it on the table. The lattice-trimmed top was a perfect golden brown, and his mouth watered in anticipation. He looked up to find they'd followed him.

"Let me get this straight," Pearl said. "Your gal is at the dance with some other man?"

"She's not *my* gal," Thayne said. "We all know that."

"Nuh uh," Pearl said, wagging a finger at him as Joshua watched, seemingly entranced by her animated movements. "Emma don't know she isn't your gal. She *wants* to be and don't know why you won't let her."

"She knows what she needs to," Thayne grumbled. He cut the pie and set out two plates beside the one Emma had already put at his place. "You want some supper too?" he asked, looking at Marcus. "She left some stew and bread."

"Pie'll be fine," Marcus said, sitting at the table and reaching for a plate.

Pearl set Joshua in his chair and went over to the stove. She lifted the lid, peeking at the simmering mixture. "Mmm. Smells good. My, that girl learns fast."

"She's not a girl; she's a woman, and she's here to help Joshua. *Nothing* more." Thayne sat at the table, picked up a fork, and took a bite just as Marcus began to gag.

Instantly, Thayne understood why. A briny taste burned his tongue, and he bent over the plate, spitting chunks of apple out of his mouth.

"Whatever is wrong with you two?" Pearl demanded.

"Water," Thayne choked out, pointing to the pitcher at the far end of the table.

Pearl picked up the pitcher and poured water into the cup Emma had set out earlier. Thayne pushed the cup toward Marcus, then lifted the pitcher and drank straight from it.

Joshua squealed and clapped his hands.

Marcus continued to gulp down his water.

Thayne rose from the table, took the plates of pie, and dumped them back into the tin.

"Land sakes. *What* is wrong?" Pearl marched toward Thayne, pulled the tin from his grasp, and stuck her finger in the pie. Putting the finger in her mouth, her lips puckered in surprise. She let out an indelicate snort that quickly turned to full-on laughter.

"Salt!" she hooted. "Clever girl used salt instead of sugar." Pearl's mirth increased, and she pulled out a chair and sat down, slapping the table.

"Clever?" Thayne asked. "There's nothing clever about it, and I'm sure it was a mistake."

Pearl only laughed louder, shaking her head as Marcus reached for the pitcher and poured himself another glass of water.

"I don't see what's so funny," Thayne grumbled. "Wasted the apples, the flour, salt. And she'll be mortified when she realizes what she's done. Have you forgotten she brought a pie to the dance?"

Pearl's mouth snapped shut. She pulled a hankie from her sleeve and dabbed her eyes.

"Apple, like this one?"

Thayne nodded.

"Oh my," Pearl said. Elbows on the table, she leaned forward, her face serious now. "You realize what this means."

Thayne shook his head. "I don't see how it means anything, other than Emma made a mistake."

"That's a possibility," Pearl said. "But it ain't the only one. Emma may have made a good pie and left the bad one for you, or she could have made a mistake and made them both with salt quite by accident." A sly look crossed Pearl's face. "Of course, she could also have done it on purpose."

"That's the most ridiculous thing I've ever heard," Thayne said. He reached for the pie, intending to take it outside and dump it.

Pearl slapped his hand away. "Not ridiculous at all if she meant to get your attention."

"How so, Pearl?" Marcus asked. He'd finally stopped gulping water, but his voice was hoarse.

She looked at her husband. "Well, if Emma's upset with Thayne for not taking her to the dance, salt in his pie might've been how she vented her anger."

"Why should she be angr—"

"*Or,*" Pearl continued, interrupting Thayne. "She mighta put salt in both pies, hoping to lure Thayne to the dance."

"Your wife's gone daft, Marcus," Thayne said. "How would salt in a pie get me to go anywhere?"

"Did Emma mention anything about the pie before she left?" Pearl demanded.

Thayne nodded. "Yes, but she also mentioned supper."

"I'm not touching that stew," Marcus said.

Pearl shot him a stern look. "But aren't you concerned about the reaction when everyone tastes Emma's pie?" she asked Thayne.

He stuck his hands in his pockets and shifted uncomfortably. "Well, of course," he said. "I don't want her to get her feelings hurt or be humiliated."

Pearl nodded. "*Exactly.* Were that to happen, why, she might just up and leave these parts, which would leave you in a pickle again, now wouldn't it?" Pearl nodded, answering her own question. "Which is why you're gonna march in the other room right now and get ready for that dance. If you hurry, you just might spare your gal some embarrassment."

"She's not *my* gal," Thayne reiterated. His proclamation fell on deaf ears.

"Pearl's right," Marcus said. "You'd best hurry. We'll stay and watch Joshua. He's better company than you anyway."

Thayne ran his fingers through his hair as he looked from Marcus to Pearl then back to Marcus again. "I can't go to that dance. Emma will be all right. She's with Orville Grady. He'll bring her home if anything happens."

"And on the way, he'll put his arm around her and pull her real close so she can cry out her humiliation on his shoulder," Pearl said, painting a picture Thayne didn't care for.

"Emma doesn't cry easy," he said. "A little thing like a bad pie isn't going to upset her that much."

"You sure?" Pearl asked.

Marcus looked skeptical too. "You never can tell with women, Thayne. They seem tough on the outside, but underneath they're soft and sensitive when you least expect it."

I find that hard to believe if you're talking about your wife, Marcus. "You know why I can't go," Thayne said.

"Didn't say you had to dance with her or anyone else." Marcus leaned back in his chair, hands clasped behind his head. "Emma doesn't even have to know you're there. Just get the pie and leave."

Get the pie and leave. Thayne stroked his chin thoughtfully. "Maybe." If there were a way he could spare Emma the humiliation of bringing a terrible pie and also spare them both the awkwardness of dancing together . . .

"All right, I'll do it."

He left the kitchen and went to his dresser in the parlor. Removing a clean shirt from the top drawer, he looked in the glass, wondering if he needed to shave since he was only going to retrieve a pie.

Back in the kitchen, Marcus and Pearl exchanged silent, victorious looks as they listened to water being poured in the basin.

"Good thing we got to the Harveys' early and heard Orville Grady boasting about bringing the prettiest gal in the Hills," Pearl whispered.

Joshua banged his spoon on his tray like a judge slamming his gavel in agreement.

Marcus nodded. "Good thing, all right."

CHAPTER 32

THE SOUNDS OF FIDDLES PLAYING and feet stomping reached Thayne as he pulled into the Harveys' yard. He parked the wagon close to the cabin and didn't bother with unhitching the team, as he planned to stay only long enough to retrieve Emma's pie.

Across a small field, he could barely make out the new barn rising up in the dark, and he felt a moment's guilt that he hadn't come to help with the building. Under normal circumstances, he'd have been more than happy to lend both his time and tools, but the worry of the dance afterward had kept him far away.

Until now.

Thayne climbed the porch steps and walked quickly through the open door of the cabin. The long, narrow room was crowded, and a wall of men, their backs to him, kept the dancers hidden from view. A good thing, he thought, as he made his way toward the table laden with pies and cakes. It appeared the desserts were being saved for later in the evening.

It took him only a second to spot Emma's lattice-top pie with the apple and leaf design on top. She'd done a fine job on the crust, if nothing else. Standing by the table, Thayne tried to look as nonchalant as possible as he stuck his finger in her pie, then pulled it out quickly and brought it to his mouth.

Salt.

Snatching the pie off the table, he held it close and, with his back to the crowd, made his way to the door. Once there, he strode across the porch, then out past the field and the new barn. Deciding he'd gone far enough, he flipped the tin upside down, beat on it a couple of times, and watched as the pie fell in chunks to the ground. Likely, a deer or some other animal would think the salted apples tasted just fine.

So she didn't ruin mine in anger. Thayne made his way back to the cabin, relieved to discover the whole thing really had been a mistake. He didn't for one minute buy Marcus and Pearl's notion that Emma had done such a thing on purpose to lure him to the dance.

Tossing the pie tin under a blanket in the wagon box, Thayne climbed up to the seat just as a shrill whistle came from the cabin, accompanied by several hoots and hollers. The hum of fiddles increased to a frenetic pace, and a bucket on the porch vibrated from the steady stomping.

Hands on the reins, Thayne hesitated. It all sounded innocent enough . . . but how many women were really in attendance? What if this was the start of the men getting out of hand? Telling himself he was just going to check to make certain Emma was safe, he jumped down from the seat and went back inside. Pushing his way through the wall of men, Thayne stopped, seeing immediately what held them so entranced.

He counted six women—all of them dancing, weaving in and out of the circle with the six men in the center of the room.

"Allemande left," the caller shouted, and the dancers changed directions.

Thayne caught a glimpse of Emma's face, flushed and smiling, as she was pulled forward by the man in front of her. Her yellow gown swept a wide arc on the floor, and Thayne noticed the matching ribbon in her hair. When she'd left this afternoon, the ribbon had been tied around a neat bun, and only a few curls were by the sides of her face. He'd thought she was pretty then, and he'd had to hold back telling her so. But now, with her hair hanging down her back, flying with the ribbon as she turned, he recognized what every other man in the room must have.

She was stunning.

He forced his gaze from Emma and took notice of the other women in the circle. One was Nathan Harvey's wife. Another, who looked like she was about to give birth any minute, kept waving to a small child every time she went past. No doubt she was married too. That left only four eligible women to dance with. Thayne lifted his head, scanning the room, estimating the number of miners packed in the tight space. Four women to at least *eighteen* men. And three women—one with more than a couple of front teeth missing—who couldn't hold a candle to Emma.

"Bow to your partner and do-si-do," the caller yelled. The circle dissolved back into couples.

Thayne watched in astonishment as the men beside him swarmed forward, shoving each other out of the way to get to the dancers. Those who got there first tapped the men already dancing on the shoulder, and those men stepped back, making way for the new partners. Thayne noticed Orville Grady's scowl when he succeeded in getting not Emma but the toothless woman next to her.

Returning his attention to Emma, Thayne noticed her smile vanish, replaced by a wince when the man dancing with her stepped on her foot. Looking at her feet peeking out from beneath her skirt as she swished past, Thayne realized that getting stepped on probably wasn't her only problem. She'd worn her city shoes—as he called them—and after near two months of wearing moccasins, her feet had to be pinched.

Not two minutes passed before Thayne found himself jostled, an elbow to his arm and a shove from behind pushing him out of the way as more men crowded onto the dance floor. He noticed at least five men vying for a chance to take Emma's hand. Again, Orville was unsuccessful, and he slunk back to the side, a pathetic look on his face.

Thayne felt much the same, and he decided that since he was already here, he might as well see if Emma felt all right and find out if she wanted to stay or leave this melee behind.

When the couples fanned out in two rows, he rushed forward with the next wave of men. Determined, he moved quickly, snatching Emma's hand as he tapped her partner on the shoulder. The man moved back, and Thayne took his place as she rose from her curtsey.

"Thayne! You came." Her smile was back, bigger than it had been before. His heart seemed to miss a beat, and Thayne knew he'd made a grave mistake. This was exactly what he'd wanted—*needed*—to avoid. But it was too late now. He took her other hand and swung her around.

"Ya doin' all right, Brownie?"

She laughed and nodded. "Let me guess. I *look* brown because I'm so hot from all this dancing. We haven't stopped in over an hour. What I'd give for a drink of water and some fresh air." She stepped forward, and Thayne wrapped his arm around her middle, his other hand high in the air as they turned again.

"Let's do it, then," he said. "Come on. I'll—"

Someone tapped him on the shoulder and took Emma from him in the same movement. It was Orville. Apparently he—and several other men—had taken the cue from Thayne, because they were now all "tapping and taking" a little too early in the song. The competition was fierce.

Emma looked over her shoulder at him and shrugged as Orville whisked her away. Thayne held up his index finger, indicating he'd be back in a minute. Wending his way through the crowd, he returned to the table and found a bucket of water and a cup. When he'd filled it, he held it high above his head and made his way through the throng once more. On his way back to Emma, he stopped near the musicians.

"You got some women ready to pass out," he warned them. "You might want to slow it down a bit."

One of the men nodded. "Will do. This piece is almost over."

"Thanks," Thayne said. He walked closer, planning the best strategy to reach Emma again. Good as their word, the fiddlers hit a grandiose finale then cut off abruptly. An uproar—from all but the women—immediately followed. Thayne pushed forward, touching Emma's arm just as a waltz was announced.

He handed her the cup of water, and Orville glared at him, none too happy to have lost his partner.

Ignoring him, Thayne steered Emma away from the other dancers so she could rest a minute and take a drink.

"Thank you." She brought the cup to her mouth, drinking until every last drop was gone. Afterward, she licked her lips, reminding him of their first day on the trail. Thayne suddenly wished he could have those days back again, when it had just been the two of them and their situation hadn't become so complicated.

Another man ventured near, and Thayne warned him off. "She's resting."

"Once again, you swoop in and save me." Emma laughed and shook her head. "And I'd thought those days were over."

Never, Thayne wanted to say. *I'll always be around to watch over you.* Instead, he shoved his hands in his pockets. "No problem."

"So why *are* you here?" she asked. Her forehead wrinkled with concern, and she raised up on tiptoe, looking around the room. "And where is Joshua?"

"At home with Pearl and Marcus," Thayne said. "It was their idea I come. Practically shoved me out the door."

"Oh." She seemed disappointed. "Shall we at least dance, then? You did come all this way."

Thayne shrugged. "You really want to? I thought you were tired."

"I'm tired of spinning and turning and getting my arms pulled out of their sockets." She looked away as if suddenly shy. "But a nice slow dance with you sounds heavenly."

A very bad *idea.* "Then step right this way for a piece of heaven." He placed his hand at her back, leading her toward the door instead of the center of the room. From the corner of his eye, he saw another man approaching them. Emma saw him too.

She leaned across Thayne and, just as the man was about to tap Thayne's shoulder, placed her empty cup in his outstretched hand. Smiling sweetly she said, "Would you mind terribly holding this for me, Mr. Roberts?"

"I, uh—'course not, Miss Madsen." He tipped his hat.

Thayne nodded as they walked past. He led her behind the musicians and somehow avoided any other demands for her attention.

Emmalyne paused at the dessert table. "Those look so good. And I'm starving."

"Let's dance first," Thayne suggested. "Or we might not get the opportunity. Then I'll fend off your would-be suitors while you eat."

"They aren't suitors." She was frowning at him. "Just lonely miners looking for an evening of fun and companionship."

"*That's* what I'm afraid of." Thayne led her out the door.

"I don't see my pie," Emma said, looking over her shoulder.

"Maybe it has already been eaten," he suggested. *A real possibility, considering the critters that live out in these parts.*

"Did you get any of the one I left at home?"

"Yep. Had myself a piece. You bake a right fine pie." *Usually, that is.* "I imagine by the time we're back Marcus and Pearl will have taken care of the rest of it." *And with a little luck, they'll keep their mouths shut about the whole salt incident.* He led her to the far end of the porch—away from any men who might be lingering by the doorway but close enough they could still hear the violins.

Facing Emma, Thayne lifted her hand, kissing the top of her knuckles lightly as his eyes met hers. *You're in it already. Might as well enjoy.* He pressed her palm to his, his large fingers closing over her slender ones. *A perfect fit. Everything about this woman is a perfect fit for me.*

Her other hand rested lightly on his shoulder. He touched her waist, pulling her closer than he should have. She didn't resist.

"Porch is narrow," he offered by way of an excuse.

She nodded. He watched her swallow and recognized it as a sign she was nervous. It was one of a dozen little habits of hers he found endearing.

He hadn't danced in forever, but the steps came back easily. There would be no stepping on toes so long as he was her partner.

She noticed, sighing in contentment after a few turns around the porch. "For a cowboy, you dance very fine. Am I to suppose you practice all those hours you're out in the barn or in the hills rounding up cattle?"

"Now that would be a funny thing." He grinned. "Actually, my mother taught me. It's in my—"

"Blood," Emma finished with a smile that matched his. "I've decided if more people had Scottish ancestry, the world would be a much better place. The Scots have great intuition, miraculous healing powers, compassionate hearts, *and* great dancing skills."

"Aye, lass. I believe you've the truth of it," Thayne said in an exaggerated brogue, silently pleased by her assessment. He steered them too close to the railing and took the opportunity to pull her closer.

Emma's hand crept farther up his shoulder, perilously close to the back of his neck. She tilted her head back, looking up at him, her brown eyes shining in the lantern light. He wondered if she could hear his heart beating, or was that hers? *It ought to be yours . . . together.* He was getting lost in those eyes. Suddenly, he wasn't so certain of his ability to stay off her toes or away from her lips or—

"Hey! You can't keep her all to yourself." An insistent finger jabbed him in the shoulder.

Thayne turned around to find a man he didn't know glaring at him.

"Dance is inside, mister," the man said, jerking his head toward the doorway. "And it's my turn now. I get her next."

"We've been interrupted twice already," Thayne said, holding his temper in check. He stepped in front of Emma, gently pushing her behind him. "The lady was overheated and asked for a few minutes of fresh air. She'll go back inside shortly."

"Then I'll dance with her out here," the man said. "Rules is rules, and when you get tapped, you gotta give up your turn."

"The lady—" Thayne began.

"It's all right, Thayne." Behind him, Emma squeezed his fingers. "We can go back inside now." She tucked her arm through his and started forward.

The disgruntled prospector stared at them a second then preceded them to the door. Just inside the cabin he paused, watching them enter.

To make certain we do, Thayne thought, his irritation growing. As they walked past, the man looked at Emma and muttered under his breath.

"I can *see* she's overheated."

Thayne pulled his arm free from Emma's, turned abruptly, and landed a punch square on the man's jaw. He staggered backward into the dessert table, knocking a layered cake off onto the lap of another miner.

"What—who?" The man with the cake in his lap stood and caught two others laughing at him across the table. He picked up a pumpkin pie in one hand and a tart in the other and sent both sailing toward them. Both missed their targets and hit a third man standing behind.

The miner Thayne hit was on his feet again. His lip was bleeding, and he looked angry enough to kill someone.

"Get outside, Emma," Thayne ordered. He ducked as the miner swung at him. The punch caught the ear of one of the men on the outskirts of the circle.

Men on either side of the dessert table were grabbing up pies and cakes, plates, cups, and forks, and throwing them at each other as fast as they could. A fork hit one of the fiddlers just as someone bumped him from behind. The fiddler lifted his bow and promptly jabbed it in the ribs of the man beside him.

The women started screaming. Somewhere a baby cried.

"My china! Not my china," Mrs. Harvey wailed.

Thayne supposed he'd better offer to pay for the damage, seeing how he'd started the fight. *Worth every penny, no matter what it costs. Been a long time since I've had a good brawl.* He spun around, barely avoiding a kick to the head, and punched his attacker in the stomach. *Maybe this'll get my mind off Emma for a while.*

Across the backs of two men bent in a headlock, Thayne hollered to Orville, who didn't look too inclined to try and enforce any sort of law just now. "I'm taking her home, Grady."

He shook his head. "I brought her. I'll take her home."

"Don't make me hit you too," Thayne yelled. "She's mine, and I'm taking her home."

He turned toward the door, throwing one more punch—just for fun—and stomped out to the porch. Emma was sitting prim and proper, hands clasped in her lap, on the wagon seat. Thayne climbed up beside her, half expecting a lecture. Instead, she leaned over and threw her arms around him in an impulsive hug.

"Thank you."

"You're not mad?" he asked warily.

She shook her head. "On the contrary. I'm grateful. I heard what that man said and was thinking of punching him myself. You saved me breaking a finger or two."

Thayne laughed. "You surprise me, Brownie." He realized he should have known she'd not mind the fight, after all the complaining she'd done about her *spineless* fiancé. Thayne guided the horses out of the yard—before the fight spread outside and someone came after them. He glanced at Emma, looking tousled and tired after a long night of dancing. "You know, for such a citified girl, you do continue to surprise me."

CHAPTER 33

"How was the dance last night?" Marcus asked, stretching as he sat down at the table.

Emmalyne left the stove to set out plates. "It was delightful. Thayne started a fight."

"*What?*" Pearl asked as she stomped into the kitchen. She hung her coat on a peg and blew on her hands. "I'm thinking twice about my decision to come north. A body could freeze up here."

Thayne came in carrying Joshua.

"What happened at the Harveys'?" Marcus asked.

Still pleased with how the evening had ended, Thayne looked over at Emma and grinned. "One of the men insulted Emma. I was defending her honor."

"That so?" Marcus said, his eyebrows raised.

"That is exactly what happened," Emma confirmed. She pushed a row of jars to the far end of the table and carried over a pan of bacon.

"You still haven't found a place for that applesauce?" Pearl scolded. She turned to Thayne. "You got to get this woman a cellar built—somewhere to store your food besides this table and the floor." She looked pointedly at the jars lined up against the wall on either side of the hutch. "The place Marcus bought has a fine room built right into the side of the mountain. It's just a few steps outside the door, and it's big, with lots of shelves. I can go out—see what I got—anything I need's in there and kept nice and cold too."

"I'll get right to work," Thayne said sarcastically. He set Joshua in his chair and began spooning oatmeal into his bowl.

"Defender of virtue by night, builder of pantries by day." Emma giggled.

"And while you're at it," Pearl continued. "Fix that outhouse of yours. It was bad enough a month ago, but now that it's so cold—" She shuddered. "A body could find herself frozen to the seat in no time at all—specially someone like Emma, who don't have much in the way of padding back—"

"Pearl!" Emma brought her hands to her face, already pink with embarrassment.

"What's the problem with the outhouse?" Thayne sat down beside Marcus.

"The middle board in the back is loose—flaps like a kite in the wind," Pearl said. "And I don't enjoy no breeze when I'm about my business."

Emma sank into a chair, leaned over the table, and buried her face in her arms. Thayne couldn't tell if she was embarrassed or laughing or a little of both.

"Well then, Marcus. You going to be around for a bit today?" Thayne asked.

"Can't." Marcus said. "Only four more days this quarter, and I've got to spend at least two of them at the mine to keep my claim."

Thayne nodded, understanding. "Too bad," he said. "Because it looks like I have a fun-filled day ahead of me, building a storeroom and fixing the privy."

* * *

"Bye, now," Pearl called, waving from the wagon seat. "We'll look for you early on Christmas Eve."

"Yes," Emma called excitedly. "I can't wait."

Standing beside her, Thayne said nothing. The last thing he wanted was to spend Christmas anywhere near Deadwood, but Emma had seemed so eager to accept Pearl's invitation that he hadn't told her no. *Maybe we'll get snowed in,* he thought hopefully. *Though, maybe it is better if we do spend the holiday with others instead of here at the house, just the three of us.*

He'd watched this morning as Emma had handed a letter to Marcus and asked him to please mail it for her. Thayne had noticed she seemed a bit weepy when she made the request. *Maybe she's finally getting homesick. And being with Pearl at Christmas might be the thing to keep her spirits up.*

Emma carried Joshua into the house, and Thayne went to the barn for tools. He knew just the location to build a root cellar into the mountain as Pearl had suggested. It was a little farther than a few feet from the house but almost visible from the kitchen. It would be the perfect place for storing not only Emma's preserves but also the deer he hunted and butchered that would see them through the long winter.

Envisioning the shelves he would build laden with plenty, Thayne noticed one snowflake and then another floating in the air around them. A sense of urgency came over him, and he decided to work only half a day on the cellar. Thus far he had avoided leaving Emma and Joshua completely alone for any length of time, but beginning today that would have to change. If they were to eat this winter, it was time he looked to the land and animals that lived there to provide what he, Emma, and Joshua would need in the coming months.

CHAPTER 34

THAYNE PAUSED TO WIPE HIS eyes as the dust from the last charge settled. Bandana tied over his face, he made his way back to the entrance of the mountain storeroom. A new four-foot pile of rock and debris littered the ground, and for the next thirty minutes, he loaded cart after cart, wheeled them well out of the way, and dumped them. Finally, there was only the small debris at the rear of the tunnel left to shovel. When that was finished, he had the walls to smooth so Emma could begin whitewashing tomorrow.

I don't miss mining one bit, Thayne realized as he worked. *I'll take riding these hills and rounding up cows any day over the backbreaking labor of excavating a mountain.*

The mountain in question was proving to be nearly solid rock. Fortunately, he'd only planned to extend the now five-foot-wide storeroom about twelve feet. Heavy timbers braced the walls and ceiling, though as solid as the mountain seemed, he doubted even that was necessary.

Thayne dug in the shovel once more and turned to the cart behind him. As the dirt and rock slid to the floor of the cart, something caught his eye. Thinking it was his imagination, Thayne pivoted away and scooped up another load. Again, he turned to dump it but this time could not ignore the familiar color glimmering amid the rock and dirt.

Laying the shovel across the cart, he bent for a closer look. His fingers pawed through the soil, and within a minute, he'd collected three thumb-sized nuggets in his palm. Thayne let the remaining dirt and rock sift through his fingers into the bed of the cart. His fist closed around the nuggets, and he closed his eyes, suddenly wishing he had never started the cellar.

Stepping outside, he opened his hand once more and stared at the rocks in his palm. The shine he'd caught in the lantern light was reduced to a dull bronze out in the sunshine, and Thayne felt his last hope vanish. *Not fool's gold, then.*

He pocketed the nuggets and returned to the near-finished storeroom. Holding the lantern in his hand, he walked along the back wall, becoming more disheartened by the minute as the evidence of his discovery became clear. He hadn't made a cellar at all. He'd started another gold mine.

Immediately, he started calculating how best to cover it up. The past two weeks of work were for naught. The jars would have to remain stacked against the kitchen wall this winter. Using the storeroom wasn't worth the risk of having someone discover the gold.

Indian legend said that he'd be punished for taking from these sacred hills, and Thayne had no doubt it was true. He'd already seen firsthand what havoc could be wreaked upon a man's life—all from a simple nugget of gold.

* * *

After making sure Joshua was asleep, Emma came out into the hall and saw that Thayne was still waiting for her. Smoothing her skirts, she descended the stairs, stopping about halfway down and sitting carefully. Three steps below, Thayne leaned against the rail, a disconcerted look on his face.

"You wished to talk?" Emma asked. This was out of their routine, and it had her worried. Usually, the only times she could count on Thayne for conversation were when they ate meals together, and even those times had become infrequent of late because he had been hunting every few days.

He glanced up the stairs at her. "There's a problem with the storeroom."

"All right." *What can possibly be so worrisome about that?* "It really isn't as necessary as Pearl made it sound. We can move the jars elsewhere—the parlor perhaps?" she suggested, purposely baiting him. She knew he hated that she'd put the hall tree in there. At least once a week, she heard him muttering under his breath—or worse—when he caught his shirt on one of the obnoxious hooks as he walked by.

"I'll attach a lean-to on the kitchen next summer," Thayne promised. *Will I be here next summer?*

"In the meantime, I'm going to seal up the root cellar and do my best to make it look like it was never there. I don't want anyone—not even Pearl or Marcus—to know it's there."

Bewildered, Emma looked at him. "Why? Is it dangerous?"

"Very." Thayne reached into his pocket and withdrew a small pouch. He handed it to her.

She untied the string and pulled it open. Turning the pouch on its side, she dumped the contents into her hand. Her eyes widened, and she looked again at Thayne.

"Is it—"

"Gold," he confirmed. "More dangerous than you can imagine."

"You found this here—there—just outside?" She turned a nugget over in her fingers and brought it closer to her face for inspection.

"I did. This afternoon."

"Are there more like this?" she asked.

He nodded.

"A lot?"

"Looks that way."

Is he saying the gold itself is dangerous, or did something else happen? "Was there a cave-in or a slide?"

"No. Though I imagine you might think that from looking at me right now." Thayne slapped his pant leg and dust flew in the air. "That isn't the kind of dangerous I'm talking about."

Emma folded her arms and sat back against the step, waiting for him to elaborate.

"When gold the size of those nuggets is discovered, word travels like a wildfire. And before you know it, you've got a boom mining town like Deadwood sprung up around you. That'd ruin what we got out here for sure, Emma."

We? "Why does anyone need to know?" she asked calmly, though he'd sent her heart to racing with that one simple word.

"You think I can drop by the store in Myersville and pay for the flour with a gold nugget?"

"Well . . . no, but—"

"No buts. Aside from the rush it would start, it would also put you and Josh in constant danger. Wealthy miners and their families are targets. And that's not a risk I'm willing to take."

Families. "But what about your other mine?" she argued. "You've done so much good with the proceeds. I hate to see these," she picked up the nuggets and rolled them in her hands, "go to waste."

"The mine up north belongs to Marcus now, and he does as he sees fit. As for me, I want no part in the business."

"But why close up the cellar?" Emma asked. "No one has to know about the gold, and we could use it, Thayne."

He shot her a disappointed frown and held his hand out, waiting until she'd returned the nuggets and pouch. "I'm sorry you feel that way, Emma. I know this place isn't fancy like what you grew up with, but since we've been home, you've had food to eat and everything else you need to get by. It's my experience that much more than that tends to make a man—or woman—go bad."

Emma returned his look with an angry glare of her own. "Don't you dare insinuate that I'm selfish. I wasn't talking about using that gold for myself. It's Joshua who needs it."

"What do you mean?" Thayne's brow furrowed as he pocketed the pouch once more.

"I can only do so much for your son," Emma said. "His speech is coming along, and he knows enough signs that we can both tell what he wants, but I can't fix his legs." She paused until Thayne finally looked up at her again.

"He's trying so hard, but the leg that was broken just won't support his weight. I think it's healed wrong, and it hurts him terrible just to stand on it. There are doctors back East who could help him."

Thayne leaned forward, elbows on his knees, as he considered what she'd said. He'd come to accept that Joshua was never going to hear well. The constant earaches he'd suffered as an infant, coupled with Christina's abuse, made it very likely that Josh would always struggle. But the thought that he might never walk . . .

"What do you know of the procedures and doctors you speak of?"

"Not much—yet," Emma admitted. "In my last two letters home, I've asked my father to research for me. Though, as I haven't yet given him a return address, I don't know what he may have found out." Her voice was soft, the anger she'd displayed just a minute ago all but gone.

"The travel alone would cost a lot of money, and staying in a big city and putting Josh in the hospital—it would all be very expensive," Emma continued, pleading her case. "I've saved every penny of the money you've paid me—and I intend to return it so Joshua can have what he needs, but even that might not be enough. If there is a way to help him sooner . . ." Placing her hands on either side of her, she scooted down the stairway until she was only one step above Thayne. "Promise me you will at least consider it. If I was meant to come all this way to help Joshua speak, perhaps you were meant to find the means to fix his leg. It isn't wrong, taking what God has offered." *What I'm offering.*

Thayne reached over and took her hand in his. "Unfortunately, Emma, sometimes it is."

CHAPTER 35

THE SLEIGH BELLS JINGLED MERRILY as Thayne guided the horses to a halt in front of a modest cabin a few miles south of Deadwood. With an apron tied around her ample waist, Pearl ran out to greet them, waving a wooden spoon as she came.

"You're late," she scolded Thayne, pointing the spoon in his direction. Reaching into the sleigh, she took Joshua from Emma.

"It's not my fault," Thayne insisted. "Emma had to finish baking her pies early this morning."

"Uh oh," Pearl said, exchanging a knowing glance with Marcus as he and their son, Samuel, walked up, each with an armload of firewood. "You didn't use more than a pinch of salt in those pies, did you?"

"Of course not." Emma looked from Thayne to Pearl and Marcus, wondering what in the world they were all grinning about. Thayne helped her down from the sleigh, took her mittened hand in his, and led her inside. Though her cheeks were rosy from hours in the cold, the simple gesture warmed her heart.

The afternoon was pure delight, and Emma decided she could not remember ever having such a tasty Christmas feast. Pearl was as fine a cook as could be found, and Emma begged her to come stay with them again soon.

"There are only so many ways to make hotcakes, stew, and pie," she said. "And I should love to know how to dress a turkey and make gravy as you do."

"Oh no," Pearl said, shaking her head vehemently. "I ain't letting you do nothing that invovles dressin'. We've already tried that, and it just don't work for you, honey." Emma laughed along with the others at this good-natured teasing.

After that, she rocked Joshua and listened as Marcus and Pearl took turns telling tales of the old days before the war. Though many of their stories were sad, Emma could see those times were a part of what made them the fine people they were now, and she found herself admiring Thayne's choice of friends all the more.

Nightfall came all too fast, and Marcus, Pearl, and Samuel, and Thayne, Emma, and Joshua bundled up for the ride into Deadwood for its third annual midnight celebration. Thayne had given no details about their excursion, and Emma imagined a peaceful church service with a singing choir. She was shocked instead to find hundreds of prospectors jammed into the street in front of the city's largest establishment—the Grand Central Hotel.

"My *real* cousin works in the restaurant," Marcus said, pointing to the sign. "You should ask Thayne to take you there for supper sometime."

"I don't think he likes Deadwood very much," Emma said, practically yelling in Marcus's ear so he could hear her above the noise of the crowd. "We almost didn't come today. He seemed very worried about it."

Marcus nodded. "That's understandable."

Emma was about to ask him why when the crowd around them started to hush. She looked over at Thayne, standing beside Pearl, Joshua bundled tight against his shoulder. He was staring in the same direction as everyone else—at an enormous pine tree set high on a stand some distance from the crowd.

Rising up on her toes, Emma strained to see if there was something— or someone—beside the tree. Perhaps they were going to sing outside, gathered around the tree—as she'd seen nothing resembling a church on their walk through town. A few general supply stores, the post office, and the Grand Central appeared to be the only buildings not dedicated to one vice or another. They'd passed numerous gambling houses, bawdy theaters, and houses of ill repute. There was a saloon on nearly every corner, and judging by the look—and smell—of the men around them, she guessed they did a brisk business.

Instead of outdoor singing, as she'd hoped, the crowd began counting down. Thayne made his way over to her, and she noticed Thayne had one of Joshua's ears pressed against his chest and a hand firmly over Joshua's other ear.

"Five, four, three—"

"Look up, Emma," Thayne said.

"Two, one!" The people roared, and a deafening blast shook the ground as bright lights erupted from the tree. Emma clung to Thayne's sleeve.

Though they were far back in the crowd, a wave of heat washed over them. Joshua cried, and beneath his stocking cap, his eyes peeked out, wide with fright. He leaned over, reaching for Emma. She took him in her arms.

"What's happening?" she asked.

"They've blown the tree is all," Marcus said.

"Blown it? What do you mean?"

"That's Christmas, Deadwood style," Thayne explained. "Every Christmas Eve the town gathers to explode the largest fir tree they can find." He looked as if he'd enjoyed it about as much as she had.

Around them, the miners were starting to push and shove their way from the square back to the saloons.

"*That* is what we came here for? That's considered a celebration of Christmas?"

"Yep. Had enough?" Thayne asked.

She nodded and held Joshua close as they were jostled about by the men surging past.

"You sure you don't want to go over and see the tree burn?" Thayne's eyes twinkled with mischief.

"Absolutely not," Emma declared. "This is the most absurd—"

"Watch it," Thayne growled at a man who bumped her so hard she pitched forward. "Come on." Wrapping his arm around her, they began walking along with the crowd.

"If I never see Deadwood again, it shall be too soon," Emma exclaimed. Her nose wrinkled as a particularly drunk prospector leaned close to her face.

"Good." Thayne smiled for the first time since they'd climbed in the sleigh that evening. "I'm glad to see we're of the same opinion. Let's get out of here and go home."

* * *

"You sure you can't stay the night?" Marcus asked as he climbed from the sleigh.

Thayne shook his head. "I've got the animals to get home to, and Emma and Joshua are already asleep. I've got the lanterns, and I'd just as soon go now. It's easier while Josh is sleeping."

"Come inside for just a minute, then," Marcus said. "Samuel will watch out for them."

"I will, Mr. Kendrich," Samuel said, stepping over to the sleigh.

"Only for a minute," Thayne said, casting a glance back at Emma and Joshua. There'd be no resting easy until they were far from Deadwood, safe at home again. He followed Marcus into the cabin.

Marcus went to the mantel, took a jar down, and pulled a scroll of papers from it. He handed it to Thayne. "This is for you. Open it."

Expecting the latest documents regarding the mine, Thayne untied the twine holding the sheaf of papers together. He unrolled the top page and scanned the title: *Application for Writ of Divorcement*.

He raised his eyes to Marcus. "What's this?"

"Just returning the favor," Marcus said, a huge grin spread across his face. "You helped me find Pearl—gave me back my wife and my *life*. Now I'm giving you back yours by helping you get *rid* of your wife."

Thayne rolled the papers back up. "I appreciate it, Marcus, but I don't even know where Christina is, so it isn't likely the state would grant—"

"You ever looked into it?" Marcus prodded.

Thayne shook his head. "I had no reason to."

"Till you met that fine woman outside."

Thayne didn't respond.

"Well, I looked into it for you," Marcus said. "And you know what I found out? South Dakota has such lax divorce laws, other folks come here to get one. In fact, they call Sioux Falls the divorce mill."

"Sioux Falls is a long ways off," Thayne said.

"Good thing you don't have to go there," Marcus replied. "All you got to do is fill out them papers, take a little bit of money, and go see a judge in Rapid City. Miss Christina will have a certain amount of time to show up and agree to or argue against your petition. If she don't show up in the time allowed, you get your divorce straightaway."

"And if she does show up?"

"She has to answer to the accusations you're bringing against her. Take a look at the next page," Marcus urged.

Thayne did his best to flatten the papers and found the second page. "Adultery—"

"We all know she was back working at the saloon after you married. Shouldn't be too hard to prove that one."

"Extreme cruelty."

"To her son, no less," Marcus said.

"Willful desertion, willful neglect, *habitual intemperance*." He looked at Marcus. "Well, you've about covered it all. That list sums up my entire marriage."

Marcus's lips twisted in a wry smile. "I know, and I'm sorry. Good man like you deserves better. That's why I'm helping you get it."

Thayne brought a hand to the back of his neck. "I'm not sure this is the way."

"What's there not to be sure of?" Marcus asked. "Tell me you ain't still pining for Christina."

"No," Thayne said. "No worries there."

"No worries anywhere," Marcus said, walking him to the door. "You go get yourself your freedom, and then you get yourself Miss Emma for a wife."

Thayne stepped out into the night air, his breath visible in thin wisps before him. "I'll think on it. Thank you, Marcus."

"Merry Christmas, Thayne."

CHAPTER 36

EMMA PULLED THE CHAIR IN her room over to the window and reread the letter from her father for the third time. It was good to hear the news from home—her older sister and her family were well, Father was planning a trip overseas, and Wilford was practically engaged to one of her friends.

Emma could not have been more pleased.

Thayne's Christmas present to her had been contacting her father— via a telegram Marcus sent—and providing him a return address, a post office box in Deadwood. Now she could get letters from home as often as Marcus and Pearl came to visit. It was a cheering thought.

Not so cheerful was the coming of the new year and the possibility that some time during it, she would be leaving Thayne and Joshua.

Sighing, Emma refolded the letter and placed it in the bottom of her trunk, along with the silver she'd brought from home, her jewelry, and the dresses that were too fine for crawling around the floor with a little boy.

A year ago tonight she'd been at a ball, Wilford lingering annoyingly near as the clock approached midnight. Looking at the moon tonight, Emma knew it must be nearing the same hour, and Thayne had yet to come in from the barn. She wished he would, wished he would take her in his arms and kiss her for luck as the year changed. In her heart, she knew he wouldn't, though—any more than he had cornered her under the mistletoe placed conspicuously under every eave in Marcus and Pearl's cabin.

Before closing the trunk, Emma reached in and pulled out her mother's portrait. Once Thayne had told her she looked just like the photo, but Emma could not see the similarities. Her mother had been beautiful, *striking* even, capturing her father's heart and settling into marriage at the age of seventeen.

"I'm not like you at all," Emma said, regret in her voice. "I don't care for parties or fancy dresses. I'm not beautiful." She laid the portrait on top of her gowns. "I'll be twenty-three this year, and I've no prospects for marriage. I'll never capture someone's heart as you did. I can't even garner a little interest from the man I've spent the past five months with."

Emma closed the trunk, set the candle atop it, and blew it out. Rising, she went to the window and looked out again. The snow-covered hills painted a magnificent backdrop for the evergreens topping them. Moonlight illuminated the farmyard and silent fields. Peace emanated through the small valley. It was a beauty that made her heart ache because she knew it was not hers to keep.

Taking the heavy shawl Pearl had crocheted for her, Emma crept down the stairs, rationalizing that if Thayne could leave them alone at the house so long, she could certainly sit for a spell on the porch. She opened the front door, stepped outside, and jumped, surprised to see him sitting in one of the rockers.

"Goodness, Thayne." Emma brought a hand to her chest. "You scared me. I thought you were still in the barn."

"I've been here awhile. Care to join me?"

"I'd love to." *I really must stop using that word.* She sat in the vacant chair and started rocking, her chair moving in the opposite direction as his.

She went forward. He rocked back. The rhythmic sound was soothing, the silence between them comfortable.

"You remember that first day we got home?" Thayne asked.

"I do. I'd been worried you lived in a tent, and instead you had this fine home tucked away in this beautiful valley. I was enchanted the moment I saw it."

"I didn't know that." Thayne glanced at her, an appreciative smile on his face. "I was rather enchanted myself that day."

"Oh? Had the cows grown bigger than you'd hoped in your absence?"

He chuckled. "Actually, they had, though fat cows aren't what I'd consider *enchanting*." His chair stopped rocking. "I remember coming back from the barn, and you were sitting here in that rocker, Joshua snuggled on your lap. It was the most perfect thing I'd ever seen."

Emma's heart seemed to skip a beat. "It was?"

He nodded. "You completed the picture of this place, filling in what we'd been missing. I didn't want to go inside. I just wanted to stand there, watching the two of you."

Slowly, Emma let out the breath she'd been holding. *What is he trying to say? Don't read too much into it,* she warned herself.

Thayne leaned back in his chair, legs sprawled out in front of him. Emma looked down and caught a glimpse of fraying blue yarn poking up above his right boot.

"Oh, dear."

"What's wrong?" Thayne followed her gaze.

"Those socks I made are just awful." She reached down to tuck the stray yarn back inside. "I don't know why you're wearing them."

"'Cause Pearl said she'd turn me upside down over her knee if I didn't," Thayne confessed.

Emma laughed. "And I'll do the same if you wear them anymore after this."

"Is that a promise?"

"Of course not." She blushed and turned away. "I guess I can't get away with saying things like Pearl does."

"No, you can't," Thayne agreed. "That's not who you are."

Who am *I then?* Emma wanted to ask. *I'm not Wilford's fiancé anymore. My father is still displeased with me—I can read between the lines of his letters. I'm not really your cousin . . .*

"Do you remember when we made a toast that first day we got home?" Thayne asked suddenly, pulling Emma from her thoughts.

"I do. Though I don't know if it really qualified since we weren't having anything to drink—or using glasses for that matter."

"It qualified," Thayne assured her. "And it's worked fine. We've kept up the ruse that you're my cousin all these months."

"Since the dance, there hasn't been anyone to come around and question it," she reminded him.

"That doesn't matter. What does is that I'm proposing a new toast, seeing how it is New Year's Eve."

"Do we have something to drink and real glasses this time?" Emma asked, looking around the porch.

"Nope. Don't need them." Thayne turned to her and reached for her hand. "I propose a toast to a happy new year—one filled with the truth."

His fingers were warm over her chilled ones. Emma was taken aback, uncertain what he'd intended with such bold words. Did she dare hope another time?

He lifted her hand close to his mouth and blew on it, trying to warm her. She closed her eyes; his simple touch filled her with yearning.

Inside, the parlor clock struck twelve.

"Happy new year, Thayne."

He kissed the back of her hand. "Here's to a *very* happy new year, Emma."

CHAPTER 37

THAYNE TOSSED UNCOMFORTABLY ON THE settee and wished he were out in the barn. *Least the hay out there is softer than this thing.* But it was storming outside, and Emma had asked if he would stay close tonight.

Should've chopped this thing up for firewood long ago, he thought, punching his pillow as he rolled to his back. Outside, wind whipped the bare tree limbs, and driving rain beat against the windowpanes. It was only the beginning of March—early to be having rain instead of snow— but this was the Dakotas, where the only thing certain about the weather was that it was varied and unpredictable.

Thunder echoed from the sky just after a flash of lightning lit the yard. Thayne hoped the animals weren't too spooked out in the barn. He considered going to check on them but decided against it. Just now he had too many other things on his mind.

Yesterday, Marcus and Pearl had come by on the premise of delivering a letter to Emma. But while she and Pearl visited in the kitchen, Marcus had sought Thayne out in the barn, presenting him with the real reason for their unexpected call.

Such a little thing, Thayne had thought as he looked at the envelope from Rapid City, *to hold so much of my future.* Thayne ripped open the seal, scanned the documents, and saw the date printed at the top right.

April. Another month to wait. But then, it seemed, he'd be a free man.

"Free to go and get yourself hitched again," Marcus said, chuckling.

"If I had it my way, we'd go the same day," Thayne said.

"You'd best not have it your way," Marcus warned. "You'd best do things right by Miss Emma. You need to tell her the truth and do it soon."

Tell her the truth and do it soon.

Another particularly loud clap of thunder shook the house, and Thayne sat up, deciding to check on the animals after all. He swung his legs over the side of the settee just as Emma appeared in the doorway.

Lightning framed a quick portrait of her, feet bare beneath the long flannel nightgown Pearl had made for her. Emma clutched Joshua close, and tears streaked her face.

"What's wrong?" Thayne stood and came to her quickly, placing his hand over Joshua's brow as soon as he'd reached them. *Cool.* "He's not ill?"

She shook her head. "No. Sorry to have worried you."

He took her elbow, guiding her across the room. "Are *you* ill?"

"No—yes. The storm." She shuddered suddenly, and Thayne remembered her irrational fear during the storm they'd encountered last September.

Taking Joshua from her, Thayne bent over, placing his sleeping son in the middle of the settee. Emma wrapped her arms around herself as if cold, and Thayne stood again and pulled her close. She turned her head to the side, her damp cheek pressing against his chest. He rested his chin on her head and rocked slowly back and forth, waiting for her to calm.

Though she was obviously upset, Thayne couldn't help but enjoy the minutes as they ticked past on the clock behind them. The last time he'd held Emma this close she was trying to escape from him. Now her arms wrapped around his waist, and she clung to him as if her very life depended on it.

He wanted her to feel that way—protected and cared for. He wanted her to come to him anytime she needed assistance or comfort. He wanted to be the one she depended upon. He'd yet to tell her any of that.

"Thank you." At last, she stepped back, wiping the moisture from her face with her hand.

"You want to tell me why storms upset you so much?" Thayne asked, wondering why he hadn't bothered to find out months ago. *Because I didn't want to get too close to her. I didn't want to risk knowing any more than I had to.*

She hesitated, fingers pressed to her lips as if trying to decide whether or not to trust him with her fear.

Why should she trust me with anything when I've lied to her from the very first day?

"Yes," Emma finally said. "I would like to tell you. Maybe it will help."

"Maybe I'll be the one scared, then." Thayne's attempt at a joke elicited only a brief smile.

"I don't think so." She turned around, eyeing the uncomfortable parlor chairs. "Perhaps it should wait until morning."

"You'll change your mind by then," Thayne said. "Just a minute. I'll be back." He ran up the stairs, taking them two at a time, and pulled the feather tick from her bed to haul it down to the parlor. "Hold Joshua, please," he said when he returned.

Emma did as she was asked then watched as Thayne wrestled the feather mattress on top of the settee.

"You take my bed," he said, indicating she lie down.

Emma bit her lip and made no move to comply.

"Here," Thayne said. He took Joshua from her and placed him on the center of the mattress. "You stay with Joshua. I'll be on the floor." He pushed the table aside and moved his bedding to the rug. It'll be just like last summer—all those nights we slept under the stars."

"I miss that sometimes," she said quietly, refusing to look at him as she spoke.

"I miss it all the time," he confessed.

Emma swallowed, then stepped out of his reach. Holding her nightgown carefully, she crawled to the far side of the bed. Thayne lay on the floor. As he rolled to face Emma, thunder boomed directly overhead. She flinched.

"Have storms always frightened you?" he asked.

"I don't think so. As a little girl, I liked the rain."

"I've always liked it too," Thayne said. "Unless, of course, I'm stuck out in a downpour, rounding up a stubborn cow. What changed your mind about storms?"

Emma pulled the blanket up higher and rested her arm on top of it. "When I was ten, my mother and I went on an outing. It was supposed to be a special day, just the two of us. I remember she bought me hair ribbons—much like those you purchased for me in Sidney." Emma looked over at him, smiling in that way of hers that made his heart go crazy.

"That day at the hot spring . . . those ribbons, they unearthed a memory, made me recall things I thought I'd forgotten."

"Was that a good thing?" Thayne asked warily.

"That day, yes. But later—"

Between them, Joshua stirred. Their eyes went to him, watching until he had settled once more.

This is how life's meant to be, Thayne thought. A *man, his wife, their child.* "Later, when?" he prompted.

She inhaled deeply, as if shoring up her courage. "When we ran into that storm on the way here, I couldn't help but think of my mother . . . of the day she died."

"Go on," Thayne encouraged when several seconds passed and Emma had not spoken.

She looked up at the ceiling, her fingers fidgeting. "I'm afraid to tell you, afraid of what you'll think of me."

"What I'll think of *you*?" he asked, stunned by her unexpected admission. "Do you have any idea of the things *I've* done in my lifetime?"

"Yes. And they're all good." Emma sat up suddenly, turning to face him. "You help *everyone*. The Lakota, Marcus and Pearl—you gave up a fortune with your mine."

"Anyone can give money away, Emma. That's not so hard."

"But it's so much more than that," she said. "You're kind, thoughtful, generous—the best man I've ever met, ever had the privilege of knowing."

If she only knew the truth about me. Thayne swallowed an uncomfortable lump forming in his throat. "Emma, there are things you don't know. Things that might change your mind."

She shook her head in adamant denial. "I very much doubt that. But . . ." Her voice lowered to a whisper. "I fear you'll see me different when you know what I've done."

"You don't know that," Thayne said, unable to imagine anything that could alter his feelings for her at this point. The initial attraction he'd felt for her all those months ago had turned into something much more—a deep and abiding respect and gratitude for the fine woman she was. And love, heaven help him—feelings of affection so deep that at times it literally hurt to be around her. He'd never thought he could trust a woman that way again, but he did. She held his heart in her hands and didn't even know it.

She stared at him now with such vulnerable pleading that Thayne could almost believe she understood his pain.

"Tell me," he coaxed, hoping he could put at least one of them out of their misery.

"It was *my* fault she died," Emma said softly. She turned away from him, staring out the window to her past. "I went out to play in the rain. Mother came looking for me. She couldn't hear the thunder to know how close the lightning was. She went to my favorite tree, but I'd already run farther away." Emma's words tumbled out one after the other like a stream rushing over rapids. "Then the whole world lit up, and . . . I saw her fall."

"Lightning?" Thayne asked, doing his best to make sense of what she'd just told him.

Emma nodded, then looked up at him, her face filled with anguish. "She was hit because she was out looking for *me*."

"As any mother would have done." Thayne ran his fingers through his hair as he searched for appropriate words of comfort. "You can't blame yourself for something that happened when you were a child. And it was an accident, an act of nature."

"You don't understand," Emma said, her voice choked. "I should have been in the house with her. I should have come inside when it started to rain. I should have taken more care."

"You were *ten*," Thayne reminded her.

"And my mother was deaf."

Deaf. Thayne let out a long, slow breath. *Deaf—like Joshua.* Once more, the miracle of Emma's presence in his life hit him.

"A downright miracle," Thayne said. "That's what you are—what this is."

"Wha—at?" Emma looked at him, some of the sorrow on her face replaced by confusion. "I've just told you how my mother died, how it was my fault, and you call me a—"

"A miracle," Thayne reiterated. "What would have happened if your mother hadn't come looking for you? Would you have run off, or would it have been *you* beneath that tree when lightning struck?" He didn't wait for her to answer. "It's like I've been telling you all along. Just like *my* mother always taught me. There's a bigger hand at work in this life than our own. Sometimes it reaches down and takes away. Other times it gives. Mostly though, it just knows—knows us and our sorrows and our needs."

"For an outlaw, you're sounding rather pious, Mr. Kendrich." Her words were accusatory, but Thayne read hope in her eyes—hope for redemption from the burdens of guilt and fear she carried.

"For a believer, you're being awful stubborn, Miss Madsen." He imagined her as a frightened ten-year-old girl, alone in a storm, kneeling beside her dead mother. Compassion swelled in his heart. "It must have been awful to see her killed like that."

Emma nodded, lips pressed together as she swallowed.

"I'm sorry," Thayne said inadequately. What words were there for such a tragedy? He hurried on before the tears he saw in her eyes could fall. "But I've no doubt your mother would have chosen her death over yours. I'm not saying that's how these things work. No girl should be without her mother." He was the one rushing to get words out now, wanting her to understand what was suddenly so clear to him. "Just like no son should be without his father. And because you *lived*, because you're *here*, Joshua and I are together again. And more than that, you've given him the gift of speech—something you learned from your own mother."

"Yes," Emma whispered. The hope in her eyes grew.

A corner of Thayne's mouth lifted. "Can you imagine a girl from Boston—who knows *sign language*—ending up in the backwoods of South Dakota with a little boy who doesn't hear so well and needs to be taught to speak?"

Emma shrugged. "Possible—if an outlaw boards her train."

"Exactly," Thayne said. "Come on." He stood and reached for her, pulling her off the end of the settee toward the doorway.

"Where are we going?" Emma asked.

"Outside." Thayne stopped in the entry, took her shawl from its peg, and threw it around her shoulders. "You've helped Joshua and me heal. It's time I do the same for you."

"What do you mean—Thayne, it's still raining." Emma tried to pull back as he opened the front door. "You're *insane*," she hollered above the steady patter on the porch roof.

"Yep." *About you, that is.* "You've got to overcome your fear of storms." He tugged her to him then reached down, scooping her in his arms.

She shrieked with laughter—not fear—as the first drop hit her face.

"You're gonna have to learn to like the rain again," Thayne said seriously. "Storms, too. They're a part of life in the Hills, and if you're gonna spend the rest of your life here . . ." He stopped, looking down into her startled, questioning eyes. "We have to get rid of your fear once and for all."

"What are you saying, Thayne? Don't make me hope—"

"I'm saying we need you, Emmalyne Madsen," he shouted, trying to be heard above the thunder. "See? That's the Lord agreeing with me."

She wrapped her arms around his neck tightly.

"*I* need you," he said, quieter this time, holding her close to his heart while the rain continued to fall around them.

CHAPTER 38

EMMA STOOD AT THE STOVE, stirring the porridge, when she heard Thayne come in. Unconsciously, her hand went to the ribbon tied in her hair, and she felt her face heat to crimson as she thought about their conversation last night.

She'd been grateful to find Thayne already out to do the chores when she awoke this morning, but now she had to face him. Behind her, she heard his boots drop, one at a time, followed by the rustle of his coat as he hung it on the peg. His footsteps were nearly silent as he came into the kitchen and walked toward her.

A second later, his hands were gentle on her shoulders. The spoon slipped from her fingers, and Thayne turned her around to face him. Thinking again of the impropriety of the previous night—*dancing in the rain in my nightgown*—she kept her gaze level with his shirt.

He would have none of that. "Look at me, Emma."

She found she was powerless to disobey. Lifting her chin, she bravely met his gaze.

"About last night," he said.

"Oh, Thayne. I'm sorry. I shouldn't have come down, I shouldn't have told you—"

He pressed a finger to her lips. "I decided some things. And the first one is—" He took a deep breath. "I'm breaking my promise to stay away from you. For months I've wanted to kiss you every day, and now I'm going to."

Taking her face in his hands, he bent to kiss her. Emma pulled back, though it nearly killed her to do so. *How long have I wanted him like this? And he's felt the same for months?* That knowledge both elated and infuriated her. So she wasn't the only one who'd been feeling the attraction between them. *But why keep that from me this whole time?* And now what did Thayne expect? *Does he think he can just kiss me every day and—and . . . Perhaps it is time he knows* my *expectations.*

"I'll let you break your old promise, but only if you'll make a new one."

"Name it," Thayne said, his lips still dangerously close to hers.

Emma plunged ahead. "I want to talk about marriage. I don't want to live here as your cousin or friend. I don't want to worry about ever leaving Joshua. I want to be his mother—and your wife."

Thayne broke into a grin, then pulled her close, brushing his lips across the top of her nose. "Such demands," he teased. A thoughtful look crossed his face. "I believe I've just been proposed to."

Emma looked down at her toes, but she couldn't conceal her smile.

Thayne took both her hands in his. He pulled her over to the table and held out a chair. When she was seated, he knelt down in front of her. The teasing had left his eyes.

"We will talk about marriage, Emma. Be certain, I want us to be a family. But first—" He held her gaze. "I've got to tell you about the past."

"It won't change things." She wanted to offer him the same gift he'd given her last night, the same relief from a burden long carried.

He nodded. "That's what I'm hoping, though I reckon you might feel different anyhow." He squeezed her hands and gave a resolute sigh. "We have to talk about my—wife."

"Your late wife?" Emma asked, not at all certain she really wanted to know about the woman he had loved before her.

Thayne swallowed, and the lines of his face creased with worry. Anguish filled his eyes as he met her gaze. "No, Emma. My wife. I'm married."

* * *

The door opened on creaky hinges, and Thayne beckoned Emma to go inside ahead of him. Hesitant, she stepped into the room, though she really wanted to be running in the opposite direction, as far away as possible.

Walking along the edge of the floor, Thayne crossed to the window and pulled the curtain aside. Dust filled the air, illuminated in the shaft of sunlight struggling to come through the dirty window. Emma's eyes widened as she took in the empty room—the charred walls, the bare, blackened floor.

"Careful where you step," Thayne warned. "Since the fire, I don't trust the integrity of those center boards. I'll have to get in here and repair everything. This can be Joshua's room. We will take the other."

We will? How can he say that with such confidence? A few minutes ago, she'd practically proposed. But that was before Thayne had told her he was *still* married, that his wife was *still* alive. Emma had assumed Christina had died at least a year ago and that Thayne *legally* could be hers. It had been a good thing she'd been sitting down.

She wanted to cry or scream or kick something—possibly him—but she hadn't recovered enough from the shock of his words to do more than stand there, feeling limp and tragic.

Emma wasn't even certain how she'd been able to follow him up the stairs. Her feet felt leaden; there was a physical ache where her heart was. She wished she had the strength to run to her room, bolt the door, and throw herself across the bed where she could cry out the anguish she already felt. She didn't want to know more, didn't want to try to understand. Thayne was married. What else mattered?

The entire time I've known him . . .

"I can see your thoughts racing a mile a minute," he said. He captured her hand and pulled her to a spot where the floor wasn't as badly burned. He spread out the blanket he'd grabbed from the parlor and beckoned for Emma to sit down.

She did, making sure she was as far away from him as the blanket would allow.

Thayne joined her, keeping his distance. "I think it's best I tell you these things in here. I've got my own ghosts that need banishing."

She nodded. *Hear him out. Hear what he has to say. And then—run.*

"What is her name?"

"Christina," Thayne said. "I met her in '75. She was one of the first girls that came up to Deadwood to work in the saloons. I was full of myself, and my pockets were full pretty soon after that. We hit it off well."

"You married a *saloon girl*?" Emma asked, incredulous. She rallied enough to glare at him.

"Yep. Guess I shoulda known better, huh? But I didn't, and I felt bad for Christina. Her boss wasn't content with her working the barroom. Several of his clients wanted favors upstairs, and she was expected to meet those demands."

Emma wrapped her arms around her middle, sickened by what Thayne was telling her.

"I envisioned myself the hero, taking her away from a hard life. So we got married and lived in a little shanty in Deadwood those first few months. I was busy mining and getting rich; Christina was busy spending my money and earning more of hers."

"You don't mean . . ." Emma began.

Thayne nodded. "I didn't know at the time, but it wasn't my house she was tending while I was at the mine all day."

"That is—that's awful," Emma blurted. "How could she—"

"Don't know. Don't particularly care to think about it, either," Thayne said. "'Bout this time, Christina got pregnant, and she was vicious and ornery. I'd go out and work my claim for days at a time, just to get some peace. It was during one of those spells that I came across the injured Lakota boy and his brother."

Emma nodded. It was a story she'd never forget.

"As I've told you, I came back from that experience a changed man. Unfortunately, while I was gone, Christina had *really* changed. In my absence, she'd taken up with her old boss, and I was none the wiser. Needless to say, she wasn't happy when I closed down the mine and moved us out here.

"The next four months we hardly spoke to each other. Joshua came early and was sickly. His care fell largely to me, as Christina said she still didn't feel back to normal. I believed her and hoped things would get better between us if she recovered. I even drove her into Deadwood several times on the premise of seeing the doctor there. Had the wool pulled over my eyes a few more months."

Emma looked down at her lap, unable to stop the swell of pity she felt for Thayne. *That's what he hopes I'll feel. Be careful.*

"I finally figured out what was going on," he continued. "And after that, I kept her here, wouldn't let her go to town anymore. It was miserable for all of us. It seemed Joshua cried day and night—we *had* seen the doctor in Deadwood about that. He told us Joshua's ears were infected, but the things he suggested doing to help weren't things I'd allow."

"Like *what?*" Emma asked. Her gaze flew across the hall to her bedroom where Joshua was still sleeping. Her heart twisted as she imagined him sick or in pain.

"Like puncturing his eardrum to let the fluid out," Thayne said, his voice grim. "I wouldn't allow the doc to do it, so Christina did it herself."

Emma gasped. Though her stomach was empty, she felt like she might be sick. *How could—his own mother?*

"I'd be out working, and if Joshua cried too long, Christina would shake him, hit him—or worse. After a while, young as he was, he didn't cry anymore."

Tears slid down Emma's face, and it was all she could do to keep from running into the other room to pick up Joshua. For the first time, she understood why Thayne had brought his son to the Lakota camp for protection, why Joshua had been so reluctant to communicate.

Oh, Josh. You sweet little boy. She felt her anger slipping away, replaced by grief and an overwhelming desire to protect him.

"I didn't know until the end." Thayne's voice was gruff. "And then it was almost too late. We had a fight, and she ran upstairs." He closed his eyes, pain evident in his features as he relived the moment.

Emma waited, suddenly wanting to comfort Thayne nearly as much as she wanted to go to Joshua.

A silent minute passed before Thayne composed himself, looked at her again, and continued.

"Christina brought Joshua to the top of the stairs. He'd been sleeping—" Thayne's words were choked. "And she dropped him."

"On purpose?"

Thayne nodded, his Adam's apple bobbing in his throat as he tried again to speak. "I ran to get to him, tried to stop his fall, but I wasn't fast enough. When he landed, legs and neck all twisted, bone sticking out, I thought for sure he was dead. While I knelt over him, Christina went and got a gun she had hidden upstairs. I saw her coming and pulled my own gun out and shot her. Then I took Joshua and left to get help."

"But you didn't kill her."

"No."

I wish you had. Emma clapped a hand over her mouth as if she'd just spoken the terrible thought. *I just wished Thayne had committed murder.*

"I didn't aim to kill," Thayne said quietly, almost as if he'd read her mind. "If I had, I'd be in jail—or dead. And then what would have—"

"What would have become of Joshua?" she finished in an equally quiet voice. Thayne's actions in what must have been his most anguished moment—when hate and anger and revenge all had to have been coursing through him—told her much about his character. *Much I already knew.* Somehow he had managed to push all else aside and think only of his son, his boy who might have already been dead.

Her eyes clouded with fresh tears. *Thayne is no outlaw. He's about as far from one as possible.*

"Joshua was all that mattered," Thayne said. "Until I met you."

And what of me? Emma wondered with her next breath. If Thayne *had* killed his wife, Emma realized she never would have met him. *This very moment I'd be teaching school in Sterling, none the wiser.* She felt a sharp pain in her chest as she imagined—for a brief moment—what her life would be like if outlaws hadn't boarded her train, if Thayne had not been among them and chosen her as the one who could help his son. *And who will help* Thayne *if I don't?*

Thayne continued, seemingly anxious to finish the telling. "When I finally came back, Christina was gone, and what belongings she hadn't taken, I set fire to right here in this room. I burned up the bed, the dresser— would've burned down the whole darn house if Marcus hadn't stopped me. He hauled me outta here, threatened to knock some sense into me, kicked me out of my own house, and cleaned things up." Thayne paused. "Since then, I haven't been in here, and I haven't spoken about it to anyone."

"*She* is the one who should be in jail," Emma said angrily. "She tried to kill her own son."

"I know what she did." Thayne reached across the blanket and took Emma's hand. "I know what I did. Now you know it too. And I hope never to speak of it again."

Emma's lips pressed into a thin line, but she nodded.

"Only one thing more I need to find out about now. And that's if you'll still marry me when my divorce is final next month." His eyes sought hers.

Divorce. He is in the process of getting a divorce. An ugly word, she thought. *For an ugly situation. Marriage is supposed to be for life—isn't it? But was what Thayne had a real marriage?*

Emma turned away, her mouth quivering as she tried desperately to get her own emotions in check. Anguish, confusion, pity, and sorrow all battled for the most prominent position in her mind. For the moment, *love* was banished to the back. She couldn't think of her feelings for Thayne when . . .

No, that is all *I need to contemplate.*

Had Thayne not pushed all else aside and acted purely out of love for his son? *Can I not do the same?* The earlier hurt she'd felt at being deceived for so long had not completely dissolved, though she thought she understood, now, why Thayne had not told her of his—wife—sooner. *And even if I don't understand*—she would never understand why he married a saloon girl—*what does it really matter?*

I love him.

A fierce, overpowering need to share that love with him and Joshua, to somehow make up for all they'd endured, swept over her. She turned, seeking Thayne's gaze, but he was already rising from the floor.

"I see." His voice was brusque.

"What?" Emma lifted her tearstained face. "Thayne, I—"

"I'll go to town first thing tomorrow and find out about getting you a ticket. Stage comes about once a—"

"I don't want to go home." She scrambled to her feet as he turned to leave the room. "Thayne, please." She caught his sleeve, panicked that he'd misunderstood her so terribly. Slowly, he turned around. His jaw was set in a hard line, but there was uncertainty on his face and hurt—deep and terrible hurt—reflected in his eyes. Realizing her supposed rejection had put it there, Emma felt the final piece of her heart break. She took a step forward and flung her arms around him, holding him with all the passion, protectiveness, and love coursing through her.

Thayne stood stiffly for a moment, and then his arms circled her waist and he pulled her to him, returning her love with equal ardor.

"Oh, Emma," he breathed when at last they parted.

"I don't want to go home," she repeated, then looked up at him and smiled through her tears. "I *am* home."

CHAPTER 39

EMMA PACED THE OVAL CARPET before the parlor window. Every fifth round, she stopped, leaning forward to pull the lace curtain back and check once more for any sign of Marcus. It was nearing noon, and he had yet to arrive. Worry nagged at her heart, and instinct told her something was wrong.

Very wrong.

She tried not to think of him, cold and alone, out in the storm. It was difficult not to, and only her other worry—for the animals in the barn who were overdue for milking and feeding—was able to pull her mind from Marcus for a few brief moments. She paced some more, watching as Joshua played on the floor with the blocks Thayne had carved for him at Christmas.

"All right," Emma said at last, hands on hips as she marched resolutely toward the pegs by the door. "Joshua, we're going out for a few minutes."

Joshua did not look up until her skirt swished past, brushing his leg. Emma pulled his coat from the hook and knelt down at his level. "Out," she said slow and loud.

His face lit up, and he scooted toward her. She wiggled his arms into the sleeves and fastened the buttons, taking no notice, for once, of the pleasure that task usually brought. Thinking again of Marcus, Emma tied the hat that Pearl had crocheted for Joshua on his head. What would happen to her dear friend if her husband were hurt—or worse? Emma slipped the heavy woolen mittens over Joshua's little hands, then stood. She held her finger up, motioning that they would go in one minute. She took her cloak from its peg, pulled the hood up, and tied the string, dismayed to find her hands unsteady.

Bending down, she lifted Joshua to her hip. For a second, she was tempted to leave him in the warm house. She wasn't certain how she'd keep him out of the muck and mud in the barn, and it would certainly make the chores go faster if she didn't have to watch out for him. But Thayne's warning rang in her head. There were too many dangers. The stove could catch fire; he could pull something over on himself—any number of things. She would just have to find a pile of straw to set him in and hope the work went quickly.

Bracing herself against the biting cold, she opened the front door, slamming it shut behind her as she hurried down the porch steps. Holding to the railing, she followed it to the edge of the porch, then found the rope Thayne had knotted there for use during the heavy snowstorms. Clinging to the rope with one hand and holding Joshua tight with the other, she began the laborious walk against the pouring rain. After only a few steps, her nose stung from the cold, and her hair was plastered to her head. *At least we'll have plenty of water for the crops,* she tried to tell herself.

Joshua turned his face into her chest, and Emma let go of the rope long enough to wrap her cloak around him. She hurried as fast as her legs would go, eyes stinging as the wind hit them. She prayed Marcus had found shelter somewhere, and she prayed that Thayne had made it safely to Rapid City before the storm hit.

Early this morning she'd bid him good-bye, part of her wishing she were going. She knew at least a part of him wanted her to come too. They might have married there at the courthouse as soon as his divorce was final, and even now she might have been at a hotel, enjoying her honeymoon supper instead of looking forward to spending time with a bunch of smelly cows. But Thayne had not thought it advisable for her and Joshua to come.

She recalled their conversation a few days past.

"I won't do that to you," he'd insisted. "Fine woman like you deserves a wedding with all the trimmings—pretty dress, flowers, and your father to give you away. Doubt he'd be too happy to do that if he had to listen to the judge pronounce my divorce final first."

"I don't care what my father thinks," Emma had protested. "Once he gets to know you, he'll see what a fine man you are."

"Let's hope you're right." Thayne had smiled as he took her hands. "Truth is, it's more than that. I'm selfish enough to marry you just about anywhere and under any circumstances, but I'm worried."

"About what?" Emma's brow wrinkled. "I'm not going to change my mind."

"I'm not planning to let you." Thayne chuckled, then his face grew serious once more. "It has been over a month since Christina was located and served her papers. She won't want this divorce. It will mean the end of any possibility she might have had to get her hands on my money, my old mine."

"You think she's going to try something?" Emma asked, feeling her own inkling of worry.

"I do," Thayne said solemnly. "But I think she'll be clever about it—won't resort to violence unless she's forced to."

"What do you—"

"I think she's going to appeal to the judge to give her Joshua."

Emma's intake of breath was sharp. "She can't. She nearly killed him."

"But the judge has no evidence of that. It will be my word against hers. Who do you think he'll believe?"

"You," Emma said. "You've cared for him this entire time while his mother's been off being—a saloon girl."

"It doesn't matter a whit what she's been off doing. All she's got to do is convince the judge to rule in her favor. And Christina's very talented at getting men to do exactly what she wants. She'll be banking on that and on the fact that I'd give her anything to keep Joshua safe." Thayne released Emma's hands and ran his fingers through his hair. "It comes down to this. We can't have Joshua there, and we need to be prepared to run if the judge gives her any kind of custody. I *will* become an outlaw if that's what it takes to protect my son."

So Emma had stayed behind. Thayne had told her he'd be back in a few days. In the meantime, Marcus was coming to stay with them to take care of the chores.

Except, he hadn't.

And now she was worried and alone out here for the first time.

At last, Emma reached the barn. She stumbled inside, sat Joshua on the floor between her legs, and reached for the lantern hanging near the door. Her hands trembled as she lit the wick and it flickered to life. Holding the lantern high in one hand, she reached down, scooping Joshua up with the other.

"Let's go feed the horses and get you some milk." She took two steps toward the stalls, then stopped, suddenly realizing how quiet it was.

"Gm," Joshua said, pointing to the stall of his favorite horse.

Emma held the light higher and looked to the right and left. Though numb with cold, her feet hurried down the row of stalls, and she looked in each one.

"Gm," Joshua repeated.

Emma's grip on him tightened even as her hand holding the lantern began to shake. She turned and ran toward the door, blowing out the light and hanging it back on its hook as she moved.

"Gm," Joshua said with the same urgency she felt.

"Yes," Emma acknowledged as she pulled his head close to her heart. "The animals are all gone."

CHAPTER 40

THE TRIP BACK TO THE house seemed to take twice as long as getting to the barn had. Emma's fingers slid along the rope, her mitten hitting snags every few feet. Each time she pulled her hand free, she looked around, peering through the blinding rain and hail for any sign or sound of a cow or horse. The animals couldn't have all just vanished. Someone had to have taken them, and that someone could not have gone far in the storm.

How she wished they'd stayed in the locked house—even wished she had Thayne's pistol. She had no doubt she could use it now if need be. She'd do anything to protect Joshua. Still fresh in her mind was Thayne's tale of the terrors Josh had suffered at Christina's hands. She clutched the little boy closer, for the first time knowing a mother's fear. She loved Joshua as if he were her own.

The panic gripping Emma's heart turned partly to relief when her hand hit the railing. The rope had brought them safely through the blinding rain. No one had cut it in her absence. They were safe.

She clamored up the porch steps, threw open the door, stepped inside, and immediately shut the door behind her, throwing the bolt with a heavy finality. *They were alone, but so long as they stayed in the house,* she told herself, *they were safe.* At all costs, she had to protect Joshua.

Again, she thought of Marcus and wondered what had become of him. She prayed he'd seen some of their livestock loose and was busy tracking them down. But somehow, in her heart, she knew that wasn't the case. She feared that whoever had gotten to the animals in the barn had also intercepted Marcus on his way here.

Dropping to her knees, Emma began removing Joshua's coat. *Please let Marcus be all right. Let Thayne be all right. Keep us safe until the storm stops and the men can come home. Watch over the animals.* There were too many things to pray about.

Leaving their wet things on the floor, Emma carried Joshua to the kitchen. *Keep things as normal as possible. Stoke the fire. Fix supper.*

Instead of the usual smells—the burning pine, simmering soup—the strong aroma of perfume tickled her nose as she entered the kitchen. She held Joshua closer. Everything appeared the same—untouched.

She turned slowly in the doorway, her eyes drawn to the half-open parlor door. With a will of their own, her feet crossed the entryway. Her trembling fingers pushed open the door.

The room was empty.

Relief made her sag against the frame. *It was only my imagination.*

"Hello, Joshua."

Emma whipped her head around toward the stairs. A woman, the bronzed silk of her elegant dress swishing, descended slowly.

Her eyes narrowed as she looked at Emma. "The girl in the portrait. How sweet."

Portrait? She means Mother. How dare she—For a split second, anger overtook Emma's fear.

"I'm Christina." The woman held her hand out. "And you are?"

Keeping her arms firmly wrapped around Joshua, Emma took a step backward toward the door.

A wicked smile curved Christina's lips. "I wouldn't do that if I were you. Alexander is just outside, and I've given him orders to shoot anyone who crosses that porch."

Paralyzed, Emma stared at her.

"Oh, I know what you're thinking," Christina said. "*Why* am I here when I should be in Rapid City getting a divorce?"

Joshua whimpered. *Does he recognize her voice?* Emma placed her hand against his head, hoping to soothe him.

"It's all right," she whispered.

"Yes, quite all right," Christina said. "There isn't going to be any divorce, though perhaps an untimely death or two. And, best of all—" She pulled a small pouch from the pocket of her gown.

Emma recognized it at once.

Christina held it up near her face. She shook the pouch gaily. "It seems my husband has found gold again."

"Thayne doesn't mine anymore," Emma said firmly.

"No. He doesn't." Christina surprised her by agreeing. "And he refused to keep any of the gold from our mine near Deadwood—which makes it all the more curious where this came from." She dangled the pouch from her fingers. "I'm certain that with a little persuasion, he'll be happy to tell me."

* * *

Emma sat stiffly on one of the uncomfortable parlor chairs. *This room makes sense now,* she realized. *It was Christina who chose the furniture, decorated it to be something it's not.* Emma remembered how she and Thayne had held the crystal candlestick holders and toasted. Now she wished she could hurl them to the ground. *If we get out of this*—when *we do*—*every last thing in this room will burn.* Thayne's misuse of the bedroom upstairs now seemed perfectly justified.

Joshua squirmed in her arms, and Emma looked down at him and the book in his lap. Pointing to the picture, she whispered the story close to his ear.

Near the fireplace, Christina paced, much as Emma had earlier today. *If only I'd never gone out to the barn. If only I'd gone with Thayne. It doesn't matter. This would have happened anyway. "If only's" don't matter. Take what has happened, and do something good with it.*

Joshua batted the book away, arched his back, and rubbed his eyes.

Not now, sweetheart. Please be good. If he wasn't . . . Christina had already told Emma that the only reason she and Joshua were still alive was to lure Thayne back home.

"En route to Rapid City," Christina had said. "He's going to get a message that will likely persuade him to turn around." The wicked smile reached her eyes. "Until then, keep the brat quiet." She looked repulsed as she pointed to Joshua. "Or I might decide we don't need to use him after all."

Emma turned Joshua around to face her and tried playing pat-a-cake with him. He wanted nothing to do with that and fussed again.

"Shh," Emma whispered. "I know you're hungry and tired and—" The backside of his pants was suddenly warm and wet. Little wonder; it had been hours since she'd changed him.

"What's wrong with him?" Christina demanded.

"He needs to use the outhouse," Emma said as an idea seized her. She wasn't certain what had prompted her to say such a thing or if Christina would believe it. Joshua still wore nappies. Until he could get around on his own, there was no point in trying to teach him about the privy.

"I could take him," Emma suggested. "You can see it right from the kitchen window."

"I *know* where it is," Christina snapped. "Godforsaken place," she mumbled, pulling the curtain back to look outside. "*Where* is he?"

Joshua started to cry.

Christina advanced toward them, and Emma placed a hand over Joshua's mouth, certain the woman was about to use the gun dangling from her fingers.

"Get out!" Christina screamed. "Take him out. Take care of him. Shut him up. Alexander," she yelled at the man in the other room. "Watch them from the window. They're allowed to go to the outhouse, and that's it."

CHAPTER 41

EMMA SLAMMED THE PRIVY DOOR shut, never so grateful in all her life to be in the damp, smelly building. Joshua was cold, wet, and crying. Christina had not allowed them to get their coats.

Cringing, Emma set Joshua on the floor and leaned over the seat, running her fingers over the splintery boards along the back of the outhouse. *Please let him not have fixed it. Please.* The center board swung forward, and a wide swath of light filled the space. Emma looked down at Joshua's tearstained face.

"It's all right," she said, almost giddy. "We're going to be all right."

Lifting him carefully over the hole, she lowered him to the ground outside the back of the outhouse. He fit easily between the boards. Emma bit her lip, uncertain she would be so lucky.

Climbing up on the seat, she lowered one leg, planting her foot on the wet ground beside Joshua. He clung to her leg, screaming. For once, she felt grateful for the howling wind and rain. Even if Christina had opened the window, no one at the house would have been able to hear anything. Nor would they see anything, either, as the privy faced the kitchen.

With her weight on the leg already outside, Emma wedged her body through the opening. The top of her dress snagged on a nail as she went. Heedless of the tear, Emma ripped the fabric free, then dropped the torn cloth down the hole. Her shoulders cleared the board, then her head, and she was free.

Emma pressed the loose board back into place and left Joshua for a second to grab a good-sized rock. This she placed at the base of the board so it would not come loose as easily.

Scooping up Joshua, she ran toward the mountain, looking down so she wouldn't fall. The forest floor of pine needles and decomposing leaves hid her steps.

Reaching the wall of granite, Emma ducked behind the stand of aspens Thayne had painstakingly transplanted last fall. Though the branches were still bare, the trees hid the two-foot-high entrance to the mine. Setting Joshua down once more, Emma knelt and began tossing rocks to the side. Within a few minutes, she had cleared an opening.

Placing Joshua in first, she quickly followed, then reached out to pull the rocks and debris back over the entrance. When she'd done that as best as she could, she picked up Joshua and scooted to the back of the cool cave. Once there, she set him down and removed her wool petticoat; all the while he held her leg and cried. She picked him up again, then sat on the ground, doing her best to remove his wet things as fast as possible in the dark. When she'd finished, she wrapped him in her discarded layers, bundling him tight and holding him close. She began to rock him, praying he would stop crying and fall asleep, praying they wouldn't be found.

* * *

It was dark when Emma awoke. The sliver of light that had shone through the tunnel entrance was gone, and the cave storeroom was still and quiet. It was also cold—oh, so cold. Carefully, Emma shifted Joshua to a different position and felt his forehead. Cool. She reached into the bundle and touched his hands and feet and was relieved to find them warm. Hers felt like blocks of ice.

A new danger. We'll freeze to death if we stay here much longer. She closed her eyes, remembering the terror of the afternoon. Her choices weren't good. If they returned to the house, they'd be killed, but she didn't know how long they could last out here.

As if he knew she was thinking about him, Joshua whimpered in his sleep. She started her rocking again, soothing him with a whispered lullaby.

Go outside.

The thought came to her mind, much as the idea to escape through the outhouse had. *Just as the idea to come west led me here.* Following nothing more than instinct—God-given instinct, Thayne had taught her—Emma placed Joshua gently on the ground, then stood. Running her hands along the wall, she made her way to the entrance. She glanced back, her heart torn at the thought of leaving Joshua alone in the dark.

Thayne needs you.

But he is a grown man. Joshua is little more than an infant.

Go!

Unable to ignore the urgent thought, Emma pushed at the rocks until some fell away. A few more minutes and she had a hole big enough to crawl through. Holding her breath, she poked her head out and looked around as best she could in the dark. A light rain drizzled down. The sky was cloudy. No moon or stars were visible to light her path.

Perhaps that's a blessing. Uncertain what she was to do, Emma stumbled from the cellar and began walking blindly toward the house. She reached the privy and crouched behind it. Wrapping her arms around herself, she sank to the ground and waited. Thoughts and images wandered in and out of her mind. *Thayne. Joshua. Marcus. Pearl. Her father. Her mother.*

Distant lightning flashed in the sky, and thunder rolled over the hills. *Oh no. Don't let the storm start up again.* She stood, peeking around the outhouse, looking longingly at the lights of the kitchen—*her* kitchen. She'd learned to cook there. She'd read to Joshua there, proposed marriage there.

Oh, Thayne. Please, God, let everything be all right so I can marry him. She thought back to that afternoon on the train and the prayer she'd uttered there. *And thank you, God, for letting him choose me.*

Hoofbeats sounded in the distance. Emma crept to the other side of the privy and strained to see down the drive. She listened carefully and was certain it was *two* horses she heard. *Not Thayne, then?* She told herself it was good he wasn't here. So long as he didn't come home, he was safe.

A streak of lightning tore across the sky, illuminating the path to the house. In a split second, Emma saw Thayne jumping from his horse. He reached up to the man slumped over on the second animal. *Marcus.*

Another flash of lightning lit the sky. Emma counted the seconds. At three, angry thunder shook the skies.

The front door opened. Christina stepped outside. "Hello, darling."

Thayne turned toward the voice, his hand instinctively going to the holster at his hip.

From her vantage point behind the outhouse, Emma saw what Thayne could not—Alexander crouched and waiting, his gun drawn as he hid off to the side of the porch.

No! Emma dropped to the ground, her frozen fingers searching for the rock she'd placed behind the loose board earlier. Her hand brushed against something rough, and she grabbed it, holding it close as she began making her way toward the house and Alexander.

Thayne glanced back at Marcus, then pulled out his gun and took a step toward the porch. "What are you doing here? Where are Josh and Emma?"

"Oh, put that away," Christina said, a trill of false laughter accompanying her order. "Do you really think, after the last time, that I'd challenge you again? You're the faster draw." Her voice turned cold. "I almost died learning that lesson."

Keeping his pistol trained on her, Thayne took another step. Emma swung her gaze over to Alexander and saw him take aim. She cringed as lightning flashed in the sky, closer this time. She waited only a second, then ran forward when the thunder echoed around the canyon. She lifted her arms above her head and brought the rock crashing down on Alexander's head. As she struck, his gun went off.

"Thayne!" Emma's eyes strained through the dark as she ran past Alexander in the direction of the horses. Lightning struck again, hitting the tall pine near the front of the house. A terrible sound split the air as Emma felt fire burn up her arm. She pitched forward to the ground, her face landing in cool mud.

Christina screamed, and men were yelling. Alexander staggered to his feet and took off toward the woods. Marcus ran past, following. Christina fled the porch. Another shot fired, perilously close to where Emma lay.

"Emma." Thayne knelt beside her, rolling her gently to her back. "Are you hurt?"

She gasped, shocked at the pain the simple movement had caused. "Thayne." Relief flooded her. "There's a man with—"

"Marcus got him."

"Christina?" Emma asked.

"She's gone. Don't worry about her. Where's Joshua?" There was urgency in his voice.

"Safe. The mine. Cold." She meant to tell him Joshua was cold, but it was her teeth that had begun to chatter.

Thayne picked her up and began running toward the mountain, shouting to Marcus as he went. Over his shoulder, Emma saw the east side of the house engulfed in flames. "Your house."

"You're sure Joshua's not in there?" Thayne demanded.

"I left him in the mine." It was all she had the energy to say. The cold was worse now, and it was making her sleepy. Everything but her arm felt numb. Her arm felt like fire. She thought of the lightning. "Was I hit?"

"Yes. But I don't think it's too bad. Looks like a clean shot." Thayne's words were as brief as her own. His breathing was labored as he ran, carrying her in his arms.

"I was shot?" *How extraordinary.* She turned her head, trying to see the wound.

"Hold still, Emma." They'd reached the entrance to the hidden mine. She could hear Joshua crying.

"Thank you," Thayne breathed a prayer of relief. He stood Emma on the ground beside him. "Lean against the mountain." He started digging through the rocks and pushing aside the branches near the entrance.

Emma touched the arm that burned. Her finger found the hole in her sleeve, then felt the blood oozing from the wound. With a gasp of dismay, her eyes rolled back in her head, and she slumped over, falling through the opening Thayne had just cleared.

CHAPTER 42

"Thayne?" Emma reached up, touching his face.

"Mmm-hmm."

"I understand why you nearly swore that day on the trail when I asked how your shoulder was. This really does hurt like—"

"Ahem." Marcus cleared his throat loudly, then chuckled. He glanced at Joshua, asleep again after a fitful night. "Got your little one here, and he sure does like to imitate whatever you say, Miss Emma. And I say—" Marcus cast a doleful glance in Thayne's direction. "You been hanging out with this fellow too long without the company of other ladies."

"I know your arm hurts, and I'm sorry." Thayne's voice was tense as he worked over her. Daylight was beginning to stream through the mine entrance, and he could finally see well enough to attend to her wound. He needed to get Emma and Marcus some real medical attention and Joshua warm clothing and food, but even those necessities paled compared to his concern over where Christina might be. *Waiting outside to ambush us? Returning with reinforcements?*

"Thayne?"

"Yes?"

"I forgive you for being married before. For loving someone before you loved me."

He made a peculiar noise in the back of his throat. *I didn't—not really. Not like I love you.*

"Thayne?"

"What Emma?"

"I forgive you for not telling me sooner. For kissing me when you were still a married man. For trying to take me from the train, for making me walk across the prairie without food or water, for letting me think I was going to have to live with Indians, for—"

"Emma?"

"What?"

"Be quiet."

Marcus laughed louder. "You two gonna have a fine life together. I can tell already."

"She was a better patient when she was unconscious," Thayne grumbled, but his eyes were tender as he looked down at Emma, teeth still chattering, pain etched in her features as she tried bravely to endure his doctoring. He hated that he was going to have to leave her here, but he'd already given Christina too much of a head start to delay any longer.

"Rest now," he urged, placing a gentle kiss on Emma's forehead. "I'll be back as soon as I can."

"Where are you going?" Alarm filled her voice, and instead of doing as Thayne had suggested, she struggled to sit up.

"I've got to get a wagon, get some help. Marcus can't walk, and you're not likely to make it far, either, Brownie." *I've got to find Christina, got to put a stop to this once and for all. We won't be safe until I do.*

"You're going after her, aren't you? Don't Thayne. It doesn't matter. I'll pretend to be your cousin again." She put a hand on his arm. "I'll go—"

Thayne stared at her a long moment, then took her hand and pressed his lips to it, his eyes still locked on Emma's.

"Ain't never seen no cousins look at each other like that," Marcus said after several long seconds.

"Exactly." Thayne pulled back, pleased that the yearning on Emma's face matched the way he felt. "That's the way a man looks at the woman he loves—his wife. And I intend to make you mine as soon as possible." He got to his feet, bending low beneath the sloped ceiling. "I'll send help back. Someone will be here by tonight. Take care of each other until then."

* * *

Marcus shifted his weight, trying to get comfortable on the hard dirt floor. "How you doing over there, Miss Emma?"

"Better now that Joshua is calm." She glanced down at the little boy nestled in the crook of her good arm. For the moment, he was content, sucking happily on a stick of candy. "Bless you for having that peppermint in your pocket, Marcus."

"A little treat from the missus," Marcus said. "She picked that up special for him last time we were in town. Glad I remembered, and glad it wasn't crushed. I'm just sorry I don't have something for you."

"I'm perfectly fine," Emma said, hoping the strain wasn't too evident in her voice. Truthfully, she couldn't remember feeling worse in her life—even after her ordeal of crossing the prairie with Thayne—but she didn't want Marcus to know that. "Besides, you gave me something already. Thayne told me you saved my life last night."

Marcus shrugged, but Emma caught the corner of his lip turning up. "Thayne gave my life back a time or two; I wasn't about to let him lose the woman who'll mend his."

"Well, I thank you," Emma said. "When I saw you bent over that horse, I admit, I feared the worst."

"That's what Thayne wanted anyone who saw us to believe. It woulda been the truth too, if we hadn't crossed paths early yesterday morning."

"What do you mean?" Emma peered into the dim light, trying to read Marcus's expression.

"I was on my way down to your place—met up with Thayne halfway."

"But wasn't that *out* of his way?"

"Yep." Marcus nodded. "But he decided last minute to change his route. 'Had a feeling,' he said. "

"Thayne and his instincts," Emma murmured.

"And a good thing too," Marcus said. "He found trouble afore it could find me."

"What trouble?" she asked, worrying her lip as she awaited his answer, which was slow in coming.

"Couple of Miss Christina's thugs. Planning to fill me full of lead and leave me on the road to Rapid City as a message for Thayne."

Emma suppressed a shiver.

"No worries," Marcus said. "Thayne took care of them."

"He *killed* them?"

"Now don't be concerning yourself over his soul," Marcus assured her. "It was a bit of a nasty fight, and one *was* unconscious when we left, but he'll be all right. And I reckon someone'll find them in a day or two. They won't be tied up there forever."

"Up where?" Emma asked, leaning her head against the cool wall, trying to ignore the throbbing in her arm.

"The shortcut between here and Thayne's old mine near Deadwood. Not too many know about that road. Mostly, Thayne and Christina used it when—" The rest of the sentence died in Marcus's throat. He looked over at Emma. "Don't guess you want to hear about those times."

"I suppose not," Emma replied. Something about what he'd just said was bothering her—something other than thinking of the time period when Thayne was married to Christina—though she couldn't put her finger on it. "So the two of them met on that road, before you met Christina's men?"

"That was the way of it."

"Do you think that's where Christina fled last night? Back that way, I mean?" Emma asked.

"It's right possible," Marcus said. "For a lady—though it'd be a stretch to call her that—she knows these Hills well. Better'n half the men in these parts, I'd reckon. I've no doubt she could navigate that path in the dark, bewitched as she is," he added under his breath.

"But that means she and those men could be waiting for Thayne. And that's where he's gone, hasn't he?" she asked.

"Now don't go borrowing trouble. Thayne will have thought of that. He'll travel the main road to town."

"No, he won't." Emma shifted Joshua away from her side. "He said he'd have help for us by tonight, but he never said *he* would be back tonight." She looked into Marcus's eyes, daring him to deny the dread that had settled over them both in the last minute.

"I know what you're thinking, and Thayne'd skin me alive if I left you two." Marcus held out his leg, a strip of Thayne's shirt bound tightly around his bloodied ankle, sprained—or worse—in last night's unsuccessful chase through the dark and the storm. "Even if I could walk, I'd dare not leave you two here alone."

"I'm not asking you to," Emma said. She rose to her knees, then, holding on to the wall, she stood.

"What're you thinking? What're you *doing*?" Marcus held his arm out as if to block her from passing.

"I'm doing what Thayne taught me to do," she said, stepping over him on her way to the cave entrance. "Acting on my God-given instinct."

CHAPTER 43

THAYNE FOUND CHRISTINA RESTING IN the clearing just past the thugs he'd taken care of the previous morning. He'd been surprised to find both still there, tied as they had been when he'd left them. He checked their bindings to make sure it wasn't some kind of trick. Christina had either come a different way or ignored them as she passed, displeased as she was with their service. He guessed it was the latter. It had always been like that with her. Men were for using, one way or another.

Drawing his gun, he walked toward her. "Get up. You're not done walking yet."

"Good morning, Thayne." She took her time stretching before she stood, the bag with the gold nuggets in it dangling from her fingers. "I'll walk, but it won't be to Rapid City. You want your divorce, then show me where your new mine is."

He laughed. Keeping his pistol aimed at his wife's heart, he took a step closer. "You think I *just* want a divorce now—after you tried to kill Joshua and Emma?"

"I didn't try to kill anyone," Christina said. "Your servant is the one who did the killing last night."

"Marcus isn't a servant."

Christina shrugged and turned away from the gun, unconcerned. "The fact remains that my friend is dead, and a colored man shot him. It won't go well for your man in court, you know."

"I know that you're a vile woman who deserves to die for the things you've done."

"But you won't be the one who kills me," Christina taunted, turning to face him again. She moved closer, still out of his reach but easily within range of his gun. "You loved me once. Part of you still does."

"Not anymore." Thayne took another step. *If I could just reach her.*

"I gave you a son. You'll always love me for that."

"My son can't hear because of you. He can't *walk*." Thayne lunged at her, but she darted out of the way.

"This is kind of fun—just like old times." Christina flashed him a brilliant smile. It hardened his heart more.

"Except in the old times, there was always another man waiting in the wings. That smile was never for me."

"It still isn't, darling. You should know by now. There will always be another man waiting in the wings."

Thayne turned around too late.

* * *

"I really don't care to get involved in matters such as these." Orville crossed his arms, scratching furiously on either side as he stared down at Emma, who was blocking his way in the middle of the road. "Look what happened at the barn raising. If your—cousin—finds us together now, who knows what he'll do."

"He'll thank you, that's what." Emma cradled her injured arm and gritted her teeth against the pain. "*Please*, Orville. What happened to Citizens for Law in the Hills?"

"Too many citizens and too little law, that's what."

"If you won't help, then lend me your wagon," Emma demanded. Coming around to the side, she reached up with her good hand, somehow managing to haul herself into the seat next to him.

"You're hurt," he gasped, staring at her limp, bloody arm.

"I told you that five minutes ago," she said, exasperated. "Haven't you heard a word I've said?" She grabbed for the reins.

Orville held them out of her reach. "You can't drive with that arm."

"Then drive for me," Emma pled. "Thayne's life may depend upon it."

"You were serious with all the gibberish about his wife and the fire and—"

Emma nodded vigorously. "Dead serious. Please, Orville. The shortcut is that way." She pointed to an opening in the woods up ahead.

"Oh—all right." Orville snapped the reins. "What'll we do if we find them there? If there really is trouble?"

"One thing at a time," Emma said. "Sometimes you don't know how everything is going to work out. You just know where you're supposed to go."

CHAPTER 44

ORVILLE SLOWED THE WAGON. REMOVING his hat, he nodded to the woman walking along the road and spoke in a surprisingly even voice. "Excuse me, ma'am. I'm new to these parts and am trying to find a claim up near Deadwood. Might you tell me if I'm headed in the right direction?"

"You might be. Depends on which claim you're headed to."

"A Mr. M. Jones has sold me his claim."

From her hiding place beneath the canvas wagon cover, Emma heard Christina's laugh.

"You'd best turn around and go back home. The Jones mine has never yielded anything but dirt."

"There's an actual mine there?" Orville asked excitedly.

He's playing his part well. Just don't overdo it. Emma lifted her head the tiniest bit, peering through a hole in the canvas. There was no sign of Thayne anywhere that she could see.

"Listen, greenie." Christina looked up at Orville. "There's no way to break this gentle to you, but you've been had. Whatever you paid for the Joneses' place was too much. Make it easy on yourself and give up now. Go home before you lose years of your life along with the money you've already wasted."

"But—but I haven't wasted anything," Orville said. "I've already found a gold nugget. On my way here. Want to see?" He hopped down from the wagon.

Emma gripped the handle of the rifle, bracing herself for the moment the canvas lifted. Her knees pressed into the splintery wood, and the balls of her feet tensed. She heard the rustle of Christina's dress, and a second later the flashy fabric came into view. With all her strength, Emma pushed forward, ramming the tip of the rifle into Christina's chest, knocking her to the ground.

Orville fell across her like a pancake. "In the name of the Citizens for Law in the Hills, you are under arrest."

Emma jumped down from the wagon and held the rifle against her body, using her good arm and hand to point it at Christina. "Where is he? Where is Thayne?"

Christina was in obvious pain and spoke with a wheezing, gasping breath. "You're too late."

"She's lying." Thayne burst through the bushes on the side of the road. He had a nasty gash on the side of his face, and he looked as if he'd been rolling around in the mud.

He rushed to her. "Emma, are you all right? Where's Joshua?"

"With Marcus. Oh, Thayne." She let him take the rifle from her hands, then leaned into him, relishing the security of his arms around her.

"Help Orville tie her up," Thayne said to the man emerging from the brush behind him. Emma looked up and saw that it was Marcus's son, Samuel.

Thayne followed her gaze. "It was lucky for me Samuel came to replace his dad doing the chores at our place this morning. He had my back when we met up with Christina later. She almost fooled me, but I didn't want to take a chance at facing her alone, as she's never *been* alone. She ran off earlier, after leaving me in the care of one of her many admirers."

Samuel pulled Christina to her feet, marched her over to the wagon, and held her there while Orville got rope from beneath the wagon seat. Thayne guided Emma down the road, away from the others.

Emma buried her face in Thayne's chest and allowed herself to feel the fear she'd kept at bay the past hours. He stroked her hair, trying to soothe her trembling.

"I'm sorry," he said sincerely. "For all this and more." His fingers gently brushed her injured arm. "If I hadn't brought you here, none of this would have happened. You'd be whole and hearty and happy at your school in Sterling."

"You've disrupted my life," Emma agreed. She tilted her face to look up at him. "And given me the adventure I sought, the meaning I was looking for, the love I didn't know I was missing."

A corner of Thayne's mouth lifted. "In that case, Miss Madsen, I'd say perhaps we're about even."

EPILOGUE

Black Hills, Summer 1880

MARCUS PULLED THE GOLD CHAIN from his pocket, checking his watch just as the shrill whistle of a train pierced the forest.

"Right on time," he said, a slow grin of anticipation on his face. The steady click of the wheels along the steel track reached his ears, and he set the brake on the wagon and climbed down. He sauntered toward the platform, eagerly awaiting his first view of the Burlington Northern Line and the occupants it carried who were dear to his heart.

The sounds grew louder, then changed to a grinding squeal as the train prepared to stop. The whistle blew again as the locomotive rounded a bend and headed toward them.

"She's a beaut, ain't she?" the man standing next to him said.

Marcus nodded in agreement, though he still worried that the presence of a railroad in the Hills might destroy the real beauty nature had created. The engine chugged past them, then two more cars rolled by before the train finally came to a halt.

Marcus walked forward, nearer the passenger cars. It had been a long three months, and he could hardly wait to see Thayne, Emma, and Joshua again—not to mention the new addition to their family.

Emma was the first one to spot him. She paused in the doorway, one hand shielding her face as she searched the crowd. "Marcus," she cried, then ran down the steps and into his arms. "It's so wonderful to see you. We're home!" she exclaimed. She didn't allow him a chance to return the welcome. "Where's Pearl?"

He laughed and stepped back from her embrace. "I left her back at your place. She wanted to be sure and have a fine meal all ready for you."

He looked up at Thayne, descending the train with more care than his wife had, a pink bundle in his arms.

"Pearl and I been so anxious to see you and especially that new little one," Marcus said. He pulled his hat from his head and began twirling it nervously.

Thayne made his way toward them. "Marcus," he called. "Good to see you. Thanks for coming for us." He stepped forward, clapping the older man on the back.

"I didn't come all this way to view your ugly face," Marcus said good-naturedly. "I want a peek at this daughter of yours."

"Well, here she is." Thayne pulled the blanket back as he tipped his arm up, revealing their two-month-old. "Marcus Whitford, meet Jennifer Lynn Kendrich. We call her Jenny."

"Looks like a doll," Marcus whispered reverently as he leaned forward for a better look.

Thayne chuckled. "She's no doll about nine o'clock every night, believe me."

As if to prove her point, Jenny's mouth opened in a yawn, which quickly escalated into a cry as she opened her eyes and took in the stranger a few inches from her face.

"Let me take her," Emma said. Thayne placed Jenny into her arms. "There, there," Emma soothed.

"Where's Joshua?" Marcus asked suddenly, worry in his voice.

"Here," the little boy said, and Emma and Thayne stepped aside so he could come forward.

"Who said that?" Marcus asked, partly serious.

"Me," Joshua said, looking up at him. "My—legs—got—better," he said, moving forward on his own with the help of a walker. "This—is—Grandpa."

Marcus's eyes traveled from the lad to the gentleman standing next to him.

"Marcus, this is my father, Daniel Madsen," Emma said. "Papa, meet Marcus Whitford. He and Pearl are two of our dearest friends."

"Their *only* friends," Marcus teased.

"That too," Emma agreed, laughing. "But they more than make up for the lack of other families in the area." She tipped her head back, looking past her father at the tall pines towering over them. "Isn't it exactly as I described? Take a deep breath and smell the fresh forest air." She closed her eyes, doing just as she had instructed him. "It's so beautiful here." A serene smile lit her face, and she opened her eyes again. "Let's get going. I don't think I can stand waiting another minute. I want nothing more than to walk up the path to our home and go inside and sit at our own table."

"And sleep in our own bed," Thayne muttered under his breath.

Marcus shot him a sideways glance. "The wagon's just over there. Let's get your trunks."

"Emma, why don't you and your father take the children and get settled in the wagon," Thayne suggested. "Marcus and I will be over with our things in a minute."

"Thank you, dear." She went up on tiptoes and gave Thayne a kiss on the cheek. "It's so wonderful to be home. We won't ever leave again," she promised. "The next baby will be born right here."

"*Next* baby," her father said sharply.

Emma said nothing but smiled coyly at Thayne. He gave her a slow wink in return before heading back toward the train. Emma, her father, and Joshua disappeared in the crowd.

"Nothin's changed, I see," Marcus said. "Married a year and a half and parents of two children, and you two still carrying on like a couple of love-struck kids—can't keep your eyes off each other."

"Can you blame me?" Thayne asked. Recognizing their trunks sitting on the platform, he took the larger one and left the smaller one for Marcus to carry.

"Well," Marcus said as he hefted it onto his shoulder. "Everything is done as you'd hoped. The sleigh bed arrived last week. It's a perfect match to the crib, and Pearl finished up both quilts real nice."

"I owe you, friend," Thayne said. He smiled with happiness as he anticipated the changes in the upstairs room. From here on out, it would be for their children a place of only happy memories. They walked toward the wagon, and Thayne noted with satisfaction that Emma was seated in front, holding Jenny.

They were home in these hills he loved. It was his ranch . . .

Emma turned to him just then. She'd taken off her bonnet and was pulling the pins from her hair, letting it fall freely down her back. She caught his eye and smiled. Thayne's heart constricted. Gone was the Boston Emma. His Emma was back.

"Mine," he mouthed silently.

She nodded.

Emma's mine, he thought. *Forever. All mine.*

ABOUT THE AUTHOR

Michele Holmes spent her childhood and youth in Arizona and northern California—often with her head in a book instead of out enjoying the sunshine. She has been married to her high school sweetheart for more than twenty years, and they live in Utah, having traded the beach for the mountains.

Michele graduated from Brigham Young University with a degree in elementary education—something that has come in handy with her five children, all of whom require food, transportation, or help with their homework the moment she sits down at her computer.

In spite of all the interruptions, Michele is busy writing, with more story ideas in her head than she will likely ever have time to write. Michele's first published novel, *Counting Stars*, won the 2007 Whitney Award for best romance. The companion novel, a romantic suspense titled *All the Stars in Heaven*, was a 2009 Whitney finalist. *Captive Heart* is her first historical romance and has a character tied to *All the Stars in Heaven*.

To learn more about Michele's writing, please visit her website at michelepaigeholmes.com, or at the Writers in Heels blog. You may also contact her via Covenant e-mail at info@covenant-lds.com or through snail mail at Covenant Communications, Inc. P.O. Box 416 American Fork, UT 84003-0416.